Cities became ovens. Grasslands became seas of flame. As the touch of dawn swept westward across the spinning planet Earth, its fiery finger killed everything in its path. Glaciers in Switzerland began to melt, floodwaters poured down on the burning, smoking villages dotting the Alpine meadows. Paris became a torch, then London. North of the Arctic Circle, Lapplanders in their summer furs burst into flame as their reindeer collapsed and roasted on the smoking tundra.

The line of dawn raced westward across the Atlantic Ocean, but as it did the brightness diminished. The sun dimmed as quickly as it had brightened.

The Americas escaped the Sun's wrath. Almost.

"A hard, dark book, the story of mankind after the fall...compulsive reading...the battle to rebuild Earth after its almost total destruction by a gigantic solar flare."

Harry Harrison

Tor Books by Ben Bova

AS ON A DARKLING PLAIN
ASSURED SURVIVAL
THE ASTRAL MIRROR
ESCAPE PLUS
GREMLINS GO HOME (with Gordon R. Dickson)
ORION
OUT OF THE SUN
PRIVATEERS
PROMETHEANS
TEST OF FIRE
VOYAGERS II: THE ALIEN WITHIN

A Tom Doherty Associates Book

This is a work of fiction. All the characters and events portrayed in this book are fictional, and any resemblance to real people or incidents its purely coincidental.

TEST OF FIRE

First printing: October 1982
Second printing: January 1983
Third printing: October 1985

A TOR Book

Published by Tom Doherty Associates
49 West 24 Street
New York, N.Y. 10010

Cover art by Howard Chaykin

ISBN: 0-812-53208-2
CAN. ED.: 0-812-53209-0

Printed in the United States

0 9 8 7 6 5 4

Fire is the test of gold; adversity, of strong men.

—Seneca

To Jay Kay Klein, gentleman songster. And to Frank and Bev Herbert, who know some good songs, too.

PROLOGUE

It was a fine moonless night. A light summer breeze rustled through the forest, making the trees murmur in the darkness. High up on the mountaintop, far from the noise and lights of cities, the sky was deep and wondrous, sparkling with thousands of stars.

Pipe clamped tightly in his teeth, Dr. Robert J. Lord leaned against the parapet surrounding the observatory dome. He could just make out the lovely features of the student beside him in the shadows.

"This is what your life will be like," he said to her, his voice a calculatedly soft whisper. "If you go ahead and take your degree in optical astronomy, you'll be here night after night, working 'til dawn."

Jenny Robertson tried not to show how cold she felt. It was mid-August, but up here on the mountain the New England night was almost wintry. I won't let him see that I'm freezing, she told herself. Physical discomfort is something that astronomers have to face. And besides, one shiver and he'll try to put his arm around me.

"All night long," Lord repeated wistfully. "It gets pretty lonely."

Jenny knew about his reputation. Dr. Lord was in fairly good shape for a man of fifty, she thought, even though that age seemed ancient to her. Every female student in the department knew his statistics: married twice, divorced twice, and you could get an A from him the same way Hester Prynne got hers.

"But doesn't the computer handle the telescope once you've programmed in the coordinates for the night's observations?" she asked, clasping her arms to herself and wishing she had worn a heavier sweater. "I mean, like, you don't *really* have to stay up here all night, do you?"

Lord took the pipe from his mouth and fiddled with it while he arranged a reply in his mind. He wanted to impress this pert-faced, ample-bosomed graduate student with his dedication to astronomy.

"Oh, sure, you can let the computer and the image enhancers and the cameras do your work for you," he said lightly, almost carelessly. "But some of us prefer to stay on duty right here and make certain everything is going right. I'm probably old-fashioned about it, I guess."

"Oh no," she said quickly. "I think you're very . . . well, like, dedicated." And she told herself silently that the trick is to get a good grade out of him without letting him get his hands on her.

Lord shrugged modestly. "You see, there's always the chance that something unexpected might happen. Equipment glitch, maybe, or maybe something pops up there in the sky and you want to get onto it right away."

"Have you ever come across a totally unexpected phenomenon?" Jenny asked. "Something that nobody's ever seen before?"

"Well, no," he admitted. "Not yet, but . . ."

He stopped. It suddenly struck him that he could see her face clearly. Turning, he looked up at the eastern sky. It was milky white. He glanced at his wristwatch. It was bright enough to see the hands easily.

"Two-twelve," he muttered. "Dawn isn't for another five hours."

A breath of warm breeze gusted past them. Jenny felt herself relax; her goosebumps disappeared. But Lord was staring open-mouthed at the brightening sky.

"It can't be," he said. "It can't be."

The wind rose sharply and became warmer, hot as midsummer noon. The vast forest surrounding the mountain sighed and groaned under the wind. The sky turned molten copper, the stars faded from sight. Birds began chirping in the trees below.

And still Lord stared at the glowing sky. "Oh my god," he whispered. "Oh my god . . ."

* * *

In Rome the sun had been up for more than an hour and the city was alive with honking, beeping automobiles driven by impatient, excitable Romans who banged on their horns and leaned out of their car windows to hurl imprecations at each other.

Without warning the air suddenly became unbearably bright and hot, as if giant floodlamps had been turned on everywhere. Traffic crawled to a halt, people stared in fright, drivers clawed their way out of jampacked cars, sweating, staggering, and still the light became brighter and hotter, intolerably white-hot like a vast burning iron pressed down everywhere. Women screamed and fainted. Men collapsed onto bubbling asphalt streets. Trees began to smolder along the sidewalks as people ran shrieking indoors. Awnings burst into flame. The Vatican gardens blossomed into a firestorm. Fountains turned to steam. The entire city began to smoke and flame under the burning sky.

All of Italy, all of Europe, Africa, Asia burst into flame. Wherever the sunlight touched, flame and death blossomed. By the millions, by the hundreds of millions, people died in their tracks. Whole forests of equatorial Africa blazed as animals panicked blindly, racing for shelter where there was no shelter. Human animals panicked too: pygmy hunters deep in the burning forests and western-dressed businessmen in modern cities, they all died, their clothing bursting into fire where the sun touched them, or suffocating in the firestorms that swept whole continents as they tried to hide from the sun inside their white-hot buildings.

Cities became ovens. Grasslands became seas of flame. As the touch of dawn swept westward across the spinning planet Earth, its fiery finger killed everything in its path. Glaciers in Switzerland began to melt, floodwaters poured down on the burning, smoking villages dotting the Alpine meadows. Paris became a torch, then London. North of the Arctic Circle, Lapplanders in their summer furs burst into flame as their reindeer collapsed and roasted on the smoking tundra.

The line of dawn raced westward across the Atlantic Ocean, but as it did the brightness diminished. The Sun dimmed as quickly as it had brightened. The flare was over. It had lasted less than an hour, and on the scale of the Sun's seething furnace of energy it had been little more than a minor disturbance. But it left half the planet Earth a pyre. Smoke covered Asia from Tokyo to the Urals, all of Europe and Africa and Australia.

The Americas escaped the Sun's wrath. Almost.

* * *

Deep underground, beneath the solid granite of the Ural Mountains, Vasily Brudnoy stared at his communications screen in horror.

His was the biggest screen in the missile control center, a full fifteen meters across. It showed the entire Soviet Union, with white lights for each major city, red lights for military centers, and clusters of orange lights for the missile silos that held the ICBMs.

Vasily, a captain after ten years of service in the Red Army, could feel General Kubacheff's gasping breath on his neck.

"Try Moscow again," the general commanded.

Vasily touched the proper buttons on his keyboard console. He pressed his free hand against the earphone clamped to the left side of his head, leaning forward intently as if he could make Moscow reply by sheer force of his will.

Nothing. Only the hum of the carrier wave.

"They don't reply, sir."

General Kubacheff put a brown Turkish cigaret to his lips. "Leningrad," he snapped. And when Vasily told him again that there was no answer, the general puffed out a cloud of gray smoke. "Rostov. Gorki. Someone must answer!"

Vasily tried. In vain. He kept his eyes focused on his screen, wanting to see nothing of the men and women behind his back. But he could not escape the phantom images of their reflections against the screen's glass. Already they look like ghosts, he thought. He heard their whispers, their frightened murmurings. He felt the cold, clammy fear that gripped the underground command center.

"Vorkuta doesn't answer either?" the general asked, his harsh voice almost pleading.

"No sir."

"Bratsk?"

"No."

Vasily heard a woman sob. General Kubacheff laid a weary hand on the captain's shoulder. Shakily, he said, "There's no one left. It's up to us. Send out the strike order. Keep sending it until every missile is launched. Every last one of them!"

"My mother," someone was saying, in a dazed voice. "She lived in Rostov."

Lived. Already they were thinking in the past

tense. Vasily Petrovich Brudnoy unlatched the safety cover over the red button, his teeth clenched together so hard that he could feel the pain in his jaws. He leaned his thumb on the red button and looked up at his screen. If the Americans have knocked out our silos, he told himself, we have lost everything. But almost immediately the clusters of orange lights began to change to green.

General Kubacheff grunted behind him. "At least the automatic controls still work. Not even direct hits could knock them out, we buried them so deep." Vasily smelled, almost tasted, the general's final puff on his cigaret. "Well, that's the end of it all. At least the American bastards won't live to enjoy their victory."

* * *

Human life also existed precariously on the Moon, buried under the sheltering rock of the huge crater Alphonsus. Airless, almost waterless, the Moon was a harsh habitat for the few hundred engineers and technicians who lived and worked there.

Douglas Morgan was also sitting at a console, watching a monitoring screen, deep beneath the 80-mile-wide crater. On the screen he saw three people in stark white hardsuits working up on the surface. The instruments flanking his screen on either side told him every detail of information about his three charges: their heartbeats, breathing rates, internal temperatures, blood pressures, more. Other digital readouts told him the temperature of the Sun-scorched lunar rocks, the levels of radiation out on the surface, the number of days to go until sunset.

Morgan was a big man, with broad shoulders and a thick chest, heavy strong arms and a shock of sandy hair that he kept brushing back from his Nordic blue eyes. He chafed at being confined to the monitoring task. He was happier up on the surface, out in the open, even if it meant being sealed into a cumbersome hardsuit.

The screen seemed to brighten all of a sudden, and he blinked at the unexpected increase in light. Automatically he reached for the brightness control knob, but as he did three separate alarm buzzers came to life. His thick-fingered hands froze in mid-air.

"Lisa, Fred, Martin . . . get inside the airlock!" he shouted into the microphone set into the console. "Now! Move it!"

The three figures in the screen hesitated, looked up, as if someone had tapped them on their shoulders. Behind the heavily-mirrored curve of their visors, their faces could not be seen. No one could tell what expressions of surprise, or annoyance, or terror crossed their features.

But Douglas Morgan was no longer watching the monitor screen. With a single sweeping punch at the general alarm button, he bolted from his chair and raced from the monitoring room toward the powerlift that went up to the airlock on the surface.

The three figures on the screen brightened, the suddenly intense sunlight glinting off their hardsuits with wild ferocity. Harsh claxons sounded throughout the underground community, startling everyone, as Douglas Morgan loped in long, low-gravity strides through the corridors that led to the airlock.

By the time he got to the airlock and pulled on an emergency pressure suit, two of the hardsuited figures were already stumbling through the inner airlock hatch. He could not tell who they were.

"Lisa?" he called his wife's name. "Lisa?"

"I'm here, Doug." Her voice sounded frightened

in his helmet earphones. But she was safe, inside, alive, sheltered from the fierce radiation of the flaring Sun.

"Fred's still out there," said Martin Kobol, the second of the hardsuited figures. "I saw him go down as we ran for the airlock."

Lisa pushed her visor up into the top of her helmet, revealing an aristocrat's fine-boned face. But her dark eyes were wide with terror.

"We've got to get him!" she said, her voice low and urgent. "Doug . . . do something!"

But Douglas was staring at the radiation dosimeter on the chest of her suit. It had gone entirely black. Turning, he saw that Martin Kobol's badge was black too.

"It's too late," he said, the realization of it making his insides flutter. "You barely made it back in time. He's dead by now."

"No!" Lisa snapped. "Get him! Save him!"

She started to pull the visor down again. Douglas grabbed at her but she twisted free. It took the two men to hold her back from the airlock hatch.

"It's no use, Lisa!" Douglas bellowed at his wife. "The radiation! He's fried by now."

"No! Let me go! Let me go to him!" she screamed.

Others were racing up toward the airlock hatch now. Douglas and Kobol held Lisa grimly while she kicked and struggled in their arms. Slowly they backed her away from the hatch, while two technicians swung the heavy steel door shut manually and a third hovered helplessly, his head pivoting from the hatch to the two men struggling with Lisa Morgan.

BOOK ONE

CHAPTER 1

One man died on the Moon when the Sun emitted its superflare. Billions died on Earth. The Sun returned to normal, shining as steadily and peacefully as if nothing unusual had happened. It had spewed out such flares before, in the distant past, before human civilization had covered the Earth with villages and farms and cities. In another hundred thousand years or so it might emit such a flare again.

The entire Old World was a scorched ruin, burned to a smoldering black wasteland. From Iceland to the easternmost tip of Siberia there was nothing but silent, smoking devastation. All the proud cities of human history were pyres, choked with the dead. The Eiffel Tower stood watch over a charred Paris. The cliff of the Acropolis was surrounded by a scorched Athens; the stench of rotting bodies rose past the shattered remains of the Parthenon, which had finally collapsed in the unbearable heat from the flare.

Moscow, Delhi, Peking, Sydney were no more. For a thousand unbroken miles the tundra of high Asia was blackened, and the only animals that had survived were those who had been burrowed deep enough underground to escape the heat and the suffocating firestorms that followed the flare.

The whole of Africa was a vast funereal silence. Men, elephants, forests, insects, veldts were nothing more than brittle blackened corpses, slowly turning to dust in the gentle summer breezes. The ancient Pyramids stood undamaged by the scorching flare, but the Western Desert beyond them had been turned into hundreds of miles of glittering glass.

The Americas had escaped the Sun's momentary outburst, but not the rage of terrified men. Nuclear-tipped missiles had pounded North America. Almost every city had been blown into oblivion under a mushroom cloud, and the radioactive fallout smothered the continent from sea to sea, from the frozen muskeg of Canada to the jungles of Yucatan. Alaska received its share of nuclear devastation; even Hawaii was bombed and sprayed with deadly radiation.

Latin America survived almost untouched, but cut off from the rest of the world by oceans and the radioactive wasteland that blocked migration northward. The great cities of Rio de Janiero, Sao Paolo, Buenos Aires, Lima, soon began to disintegrate as their swollen populations drifted back to the subsistance farming that would feed them—some of them. Even in the lucky South, without the commerce of a worldwide civilization, the cities died. The old ways of life reaffirmed themselves: dawn-to-dusk toil with hand-made implements were necessary to raise enough food to survive. The veneer of civilization cracked and peeled away quickly.

The few hundred men and women living on the Moon watched with growing horror as their mother world died. They were safely underground, buried protectively against even the normal glare of the powerful Sun. In their telescopes they saw the Old World disappear under continent-wide clouds of smoke and steam. From their radio receivers they heard the cries of the dying. Then came the pinpoint bursts of light that marked the nuclear deaths of the cities of North America.

They watched, they listened, in silence. Numbly. And their horror began to turn into guilt. Everyone on Earth was dying. The human race was being flensed from the surface of its mother world. But they were here on the Moon, inside its protective rocky shell. They were safe. They lived while their mothers, brothers, friends, lovers died.

After three days of numb horror and mounting guilt they looked at each other and began to wonder: How long can we keep ourselves alive without Earth to supply us with food, equipment, medicine?

The guilt was there, in each man and woman's mind. The horror went beyond words; none of them could voice what they truly felt. The nights were filled with nightmare screams. But surmounting it all was the drive to live. Deep within each of them was the burning secret: *I'm alive and I'm glad of it. No matter what happened to all the others, I'm glad it wasn't me.*

Not every man and woman in the lunar community could face the secret. Some retreated into catatonic shock. A handful committed suicide. Others tried suicide, but in ways that easily caught the attention of their friends. Stopped in their attempts at self-destruction, convinced by the psychologists among them that they had no need to expiate their sins, they returned to the ranks of the overtly healthy. Two of them tried to sabotage the life support systems of the underground settlement, attempting to kill themselves and everyone else. Both of them were stopped in time. Both of them died in hospital beds: one received an improper dose of medication, the other had a totally unexpected heart attack. The physician who was in charge of both patients shrugged his shoulders about them and the next morning was found dead of a huge overdose of barbituates.

Douglas Morgan sat on the edge of the hospital bed, gazing at the sleeping face of his wife. The lunar settlement's hospital was only six beds and a pair of surgery rooms, carved out of the solid basalt of the lunar crust. Before the Sun's flare the most serious medical problems facing the community's four doctors had been broken bones among the miners and depression among those who had difficulty adjusting to an underground life.

The beds were empty now, except for Lisa's. All mining work had stopped since the flare. The depressions that afflicted everyone were being treated without hospitalization. The last patient to occupy one of the other beds had been the would-be saboteur who had died of a heart attack.

Lisa's exquisitely sensitive face was pale and drawn. With her eyes closed she seemed almost a mask of death. But if death is so beautiful, Douglas thought, no man should fear it. Her dark, short-cropped hair framed her delicate face and looked more lustrous for the contrast against the white pillowcase and sheets of the hospital bed.

Douglas looked down and saw that his left hand, pressing against the bed's surface, rested next to Lisa's hand. The contrast between the two fascinated him. Her hand was so tiny, delicate, almost fragile beside his heavy, thick-fingered paw. Her hand was made for a ballerina, a painter, a musician. His was built to carve rock from lunar caves, to punch equations into a computer, to point and command men. But he knew the strength that her china-boned hands were capable of; he had felt those fingers clawing at him even through the thickness of a pressure suit.

With a reluctant sigh he pushed himself up from the bed and, standing, stretched his tensed back muscles. Tendons popped as his fingers scraped the ceiling.

Lisa's eyes opened. She was looking straight at him. Her dark smoldering eyes betrayed the delicacy of her features. She was strong. Despite the seeming fragility of her body, she was as strong as a thin blade of steel.

"You're awake," Douglas said, instantly feeling inane.

"You're leaving," she countered.

"Yes." He glanced at his digital wristwatch. "The ship leaves in two hours. I've got to get my gear ready and . . ."

"Why you?"

He blinked at the question. It had never occurred to him that he would not lead the mission.

"Why take on this expedition at all?" Lisa went on. "It's all nonsense. None of you will get back alive."

"I don't think that's true," he said.

Lisa's eyes roamed around the bleak little chamber, the rock walls that had been laser-fused into smoothness and then painted pastel green, the five empty beds sitting stiffly starched and white around them. Finally she looked back at her husband.

"It's foolishness," she said. "Male foolishness. You're just trying to prove that you're brave."

He almost smiled. The terrible events of the past few days had not destroyed Lisa's spirit.

Sitting on the edge of her bed again, he answered carefully, "We are a community of five hundred and seventy-three men and women. Most of us are mining engineers and technicians. We have three physicians, five psychologists . . ."

"Four physicians," Lisa corrected.

"Three. Haley OD'd last night."

She took the news with no discernable reaction.

Douglas resumed, "As things stand now, we can't survive on our own. And there'll be no further help from Earth—unless we go Earthside and take what we need."

"If you go to Earth you will be killed."

"Maybe," he conceded, shrugging. "Maybe you're right and we're all subconsciously trying to kill ourselves in one grand final gesture, instead of waiting around up here in this underground tomb."

Lisa sighed, a mixture of weariness and impatience. "You're always so logical. The Earth has been destroyed, billions of people have died, and you're as cool and logical as one of your computers."

"We're not dead. Not yet, anyway." His voice was tight, grim. "And I want to live. I want *you* to live, Lisa. That's why I have to lead this mission Earthside. We'll only go as far as the space station, for sure. We won't go down to the surface unless . . ."

"I don't want you to kill yourself," Lisa said. Her voice was flat, devoid of emotion.

"Why not?"

"Because we need you here. *I* need you here. You're a natural leader. I need you here to hold this community together."

He thought for a few moments before replying softly, "What you mean is, you want me here so that you can run the community through me."

Her gaze never wavered from him, but she did not answer. The silence between them stretched achingly.

Finally Douglas said, "I don't mind, Lisa. You want the power. I don't."

"You're a fool," she said, unsmiling.

"Yeah. I know." He got up slowly to his feet. Looking down at her, "The baby . . . it was Fred's, not mine, wasn't it?"

The barest flicker of surprise crossed her face. Then she said, "What difference does it make now? Fred's dead and I've lost the baby."

"It makes an enormous difference to me."

She turned away from him.

Suddenly his hand flashed out, grasped her slim jaw and wrenched her head around to face him.

"Why?" he demanded. "Why did you do it? I love you."

She stared at him, eyes blazing, until he released his grip on her. Then she said, "Go to Earth and kill yourself. Just as you killed him. Just as you killed my baby. You deserve to die."

CHAPTER 2

"We can make it," Martin Kobol said, his long face somber. "We can survive—I think."

Six of them had crowded into the tiny bedroom. Like the rest of the underground settlement, it had been carved out of the lunar rock, designed originally as a standard dormitory room for a mining technician or a scientist. Its furniture consisted of a single bed, a wall unit that combined closet, desk, bureau drawers and bookshelf, and the same type of shower stall and toilet system that had been developed for the space station.

William Demain shared the room with his wife, Catherine. Now it was being used as a meeting place for the Demains, Kobol, and three other men. The Demains and one of the men sat on the narrow bed. Kobol had the room's only chair. The other two men had hunkered down on the thinly-carpeted floor.

"Each of us is in charge of a key section of the settlement," Kobol said, pointing to each individual in turn. "Hydroponics, communications, life support, medicine, mining." He jabbed a thumb at his own narrow chest and added, "Electrical power."

"You forgot administration."

They turned, startled, to the accordian-fold door to the corridor outside. Lisa stood there, gripping the door jamb as if she would collapse if she didn't have something to hold onto. Her face was white. She wore a jet black jumpsuit, so that it was difficult to see how frail she had become.

"You shouldn't be out of the hospital!" Kobol was at her side in a single bound. Catherine

Demain pulled herself up from the bed and also went to Lisa. Together, they moved her to the chair.

"I'm all right," Lisa protested. "Just a little weak from being in bed so long."

"You walked here from the hospital?" Catherine Demain asked. At Lisa's nod she said, "That's enough exercise for one day. You still have a lot of recuperating to do."

Kobol glanced at her with a curious grin. "How did you know we were meeting here? I mean, we didn't broadcast . . ."

Fixing her dark eyes on his long, hound-sad face, Lisa answered, "The day that you—any of you—can get together like this without me knowing about it, that will be the day I resign as head of administration."

LaStrande, the other man sitting on the bed, said gravely, "We're happy to see you up and around."

The rest of them murmured agreement.

"Thank you," said Lisa. "Martin, you made a slight misstatement a moment ago. You are not in charge of electrical power; Douglas is."

Kobol nodded unhappily. "That's right, Douglas is . . . when he's here." His voice was nasal, reedy, and had a tendency toward screeching when he got upset. "But it's been nearly two weeks since he went Earthside. We haven't heard a report from him for three days now."

"He'll be back," Lisa said.

"Of course. And when he's back he'll be in charge of electrical power. But until he comes back, I'm in charge."

Lisa smiled at him. "Naturally."

Kobol was tall, almost as tall as Douglas, but bone-thin. Cadaverous, Lisa thought. He looks like those mummies the archeologists dig up in Egypt. For a briefest moment a hot pang of remorse shot through her as she realized that the temples, the museums, the archeological digs, the people of Egypt and England and everywhere else were all gone, dead, burned, melted by the fury of the Sun and the even hotter fireballs of human retaliation.

She forced the thought down, just as she forced away the pain that surged through her abdomen. Instead she concentrated on the other people in the room, the self-proclaimed leaders of the isolated little colony.

Demain sat on the bed, his back pressed against the stone wall, his legs pulled up against his chest fetally. His bulging, balding dome gave him an infant's look, but his eyes were crafty. The eyes of a peasant, a farmer. And that's exactly what he is, Lisa thought, even if his farms are complicated hydroponics facilities that use chemicals and electrical energy and sunlight filtered down from the surface through fiber optics pipes.

His wife was in charge of the hospital. White haired but still radiantly lovely, her skin unwrinkled, her life truly dedicated to caring for others, Catherine had given up a brilliant medical career Earthside to be with her husband on the Moon.

LaStrande was a little gnome of a man, already half-blind despite the laser surgery performed on his failing eyes. But he was a powerhouse of a personality, argumentative yet never offensive, a genius at maintaining and even enlarging the settlement's vital life support equipment on a shoestring of personnel and materials.

Blair was dying of cancer. They all knew it, despite the fact that he looked pinkly healthy and went about his work at the communications center with unfailing good cheer. Marrett was a burly, loud-voiced diamond in the rough who had retired from a career in meteorology to spend his final days on the Moon and somehow—restless, talented, a born leader—had become chief of the tough, no-nonsense miners.

And Kobol. She looked up at him as he stood next to her chair, automatically taking charge of the meeting, reaching for the power to rule them all the way an eager little boy reaches for a jar of cookies.

What would they think, Lisa wondered, if they knew that Kobol had fathered the baby I've lost, and not Fred Simpson? What would Douglas do, if I ever told him? She closed her eyes for a moment. Catherine Demain noticed and thought that Lisa must be in pain. But Lisa was merely holding tight the anger she felt at Douglas, her husband, the man she had chosen five years ago to mold into a leader, a giant, a commander who could take charge of this pathetic little community on the Moon and use it as a base for political power on Earth.

She shook her head, trying to dismiss the thoughts from her mind. The Earth was gone now. There was nothing left. Not that Douglas would have followed her lead anyway; he had turned out to be far too stubborn and self-centered to be influenced by anyone else. What a mistake I made! Lisa told herself. To think that I believed I could mold that domineering, simple-minded bull into a world leader.

But he's gone too, she realized. He'll never come back. He's probably dead by now. Strangely, the thought saddened her.

". . . and if the hydroponics output can be increased fifteen percent," Kobol was saying, in his reedy twang, "we ought to be able to get along without importing food from Earthside indefinitely."

If the population stays level, Lisa thought.

Demain was bobbing his head up and down, over his drawn-up knees. "I can do it," his soft voice was barely audible, "if you can get me more room, more acreage. And more energy. It takes energy."

"We'll carve out the acreage for you," Marrett assured him.

LaStrande waggled a hand in the air. "Listen, I know how we can get a leg up on the energy problem. The safety margins we've enforced on the life support systems are ridiculously large. Typical Earthside overengineering. I can run the air and heating systems on half the energy we now allocate . . ."

"Half?" Kobol snapped. "You're sure?"

LaStrande peered at him myopically. "If I say I can, I can. The recyclers don't need all that standby power. There's no reason we can't shunt it off to hydroponics."

Kobol rubbed his chin in thought.

Lisa smiled inwardly at him. He's not easy to mold, either, she told herself. But at least he *wants* power. He has the ambition that Douglas lacks. But he's insidious. Like a snake. He'd never challenge Douglas face-to-face. But he didn't mind slipping into my bed when I invited him. And now he's trying to take charge of the community.

With a weary sigh of regret, Lisa realized, this is all the world we have now. Martin can be made into its ruler. And I will rule him.

"It's settled, then," Kobol was concluding. "The standby power goes to hydroponics. Marrett, your miners will start enlarging the hydroponics bay immediately. Jim . . ."

But Blair and the others were looking past Kobol, to the doorway. Lisa turned in her chair and saw a youngster standing there in a drab coverall. She wore the shoulder patch of the communications group.

"Yes?" Blair said to her. "What is it?"

Her youthful face seemed flushed with excitement. She stepped into the tiny, crowded bedroom, maneuvered past Kobol and Lisa's chair, and handed Blair a flimsy sheet of ultrathin plastic—the lunar settlement's reusable substitute for paper.

Blair read the message, his face lighting up.

"It's from Douglas," he said, his eyes still scanning the typed words, as if he could not believe what they said. "He's on his way back. He'll arrive in forty-five hours."

They all gasped with surprise. Lisa felt an irrational pang of joy spring up inside her. Idiot! she raged at herself. He'll spoil everything. Everything.

Yet she could not control the surge of happiness that coursed through her.

Kobol's face was as gray as a corpse's. His mouth pressed shut into a thin, bloodless line.

"That's not all," Blair told them, waving the flimsy sheet in his hand. "Douglas says he's bringing twenty-five people back with him. He says most of them are in very bad physical condition and will need hospitalization immediately."

CHAPTER 3

The biggest chamber in the underground community was a combination warehouse, depot, and garage just inside the big double metal hatch of the main airlock leading out to the surface. Vehicles were parked next to the airlock's gleaming, vault-like doors, assembled in precise rows along colored lines painted on the smooth floor: electric forklift trucks, springy-wheeled lunar surface rovers, bicycles for pedalling along the underground corridors.

Supplies were stacked in equally precise ranks and files, each box or crate carefully labelled and arranged in sections according to what was inside it. Machinery, foodstuffs, medicines, clothing—all the things that the lunar settlement did not make for itself were stacked there, row upon row, piled up almost as high as the rugged stone ceiling of the cave.

They are a reminder, thought Lisa as she entered the big chamber, a reminder of how much we depended on Earth. Can we survive without Earth? Kobol says we can, but is he right? Can we survive?

Kobol stood beside her, and at her other side was Catherine Demain. They waited before the airlock hatch, at the end of the wide aisle separating the stacks of supplies from the rows of parked vehicles. Behind them stood a specially-picked team of volunteers, ready to help the survivors from Earth to beds and medical care.

Kobol studied his wristwatch. "Another few minutes, at most."

"The radar plot is still good?" Lisa asked.

He shrugged his bony shoulders. "I could check

with Blair," he said, gesturing toward the phone set into the wall next to the hatch.

"No. Don't bother. If anything goes wrong he'll put it on the public address system."

She heard the sounds of shoes scuffing on the plastic floor of the cavern, sensed the presence of other people. Turning, Lisa saw that dozens of people were stepping off the powerlift, milling around the cavern expectantly.

Kobol turned too, and his long face sank into a scowl. "Why aren't these people at their jobs? Nobody's been given permission to come up here except those . . ."

Lisa laid a land on his arm, silencing him. She saw that still more people were coming up on the powerlift, chatting, grinning to each other, pressing forward to make room for even more. They were dressed in their work fatigues, almost all of them, but the air was like a holiday excitement back on Earth.

"There must be at least a hundred of them," Catherine Demain said, smiling happily.

"And more coming."

"ATTENTION," the loudspeakers in the ceiling blared, echoes reverberating along the rock walls. "THE TRANSFER SHIP HAS TOUCHED DOWN AT THE LANDING PAD . . ."

The growing crowd cheered, drowning out part of Blair's message. Lisa held her hands to her ears; the noise of the crowd was painful as it rang through the cavern.

" . . . SHOULD BE AT THE AIRLOCK IN APPROXIMATELY FIVE MINUTES. MEDICAL TEAMS SHOULD BE AT THE AIRLOCK IN APPROXIMATELY FIVE MINUTES."

The crowd was laughing and talking and surging forward now. Lisa felt herself pushed closer to the metal hatch; not that anyone touched her, but the emotional energy of the crowd had a vital force to it.

"Who the hell gave anyone permission to leave their jobs?" Kobol snarled, his voice rising. "We can't have people meandering around like this!"

Catherine Demain laughed at him. "What are you going to do about it? They're excited about Douglas bringing back survivors, I guess."

Lisa watched the crowd. Almost every one of the settlement's five hundred and some people seemed to have suddenly jammed into the cavern, filling up the big central aisle, spilling over into the narrower passages between stacks of crates. Even the children had come, to clamber over the lunar buggies that they were never allowed to touch.

They were happy. They were excited. They kept a respectful distance from the medical volunteers and the trio of leaders next to the hatch, but they had come to see Douglas' return, to witness his rescue of a handful of people from Earth.

They want to see that Earth isn't totally dead, Lisa realized. They've come to see survivors of the holocaust with their own eyes.

The crowd surged forward again, kids standing on tiptoes atop buggies and forklifts, an expectant crackle of excitement running through the cavern. Lisa suddenly felt cold, shiveringly cold. She turned and saw the airlock indicator light had turned from red to amber.

Everyone seemed to hold their breath. The big cavern went absolutely silent. The light finally flashed green and the massive metal door began to swing slowly open. Kobol stood as tense as a steel cable just before it snaps. Catherine Demain took an unconscious half-step toward the slowly opening hatch.

"Help them," Lisa commanded. Two of the medical volunteers dropped the stretcher they were carrying and rushed to the hatch. They leaned their weight on it, swinging it fully open.

The first man out was one of the pilots, grinning

broadly as he stepped through, searching the crowd with his eyes until a tiny blonde woman raced through the people standing in front and threw herself into his arms. A murmur ran through the cavern.

A younger man stepped out next. Lisa recognized him as one of the communications technicians. His coverall was stained with mud, his face was grimy. But he too had an enormous grin on his face, a smile of satisfaction, of relief, of accomplishment.

The crowd watched, hushed, as the survivors from Earth came out one by one, most of them supported by members of Douglas' crew. The medical volunteers helped them onto stretchers and carried them toward the powerlift to the makeshift infirmary that had been prepared for them. The crowd melted back to make room for them.

They were awed into silence as the survivors were carried past. The people from Earthside were mostly men. They seemed weak, they looked thin, as though starved. There were no obvious burns or wounds on their raggedly-clothed bodies.

When the last of the survivors came out, Catherine Demain hurried after his stretcher. Lisa stood where she was. The crowd began to murmur again, to talk excitedly. The rest of the crew who had gone Earthside stepped through the airlock hatch, each of them wearing that same grin of victory. As each of them came into sight, the crowd cheered and applauded. The noise was growing, building, reverberating off the rock walls and ceiling. One by one, the men who had participated in the mission came out and were quickly surrounded by friends, family, lovers.

And then, last of all, came Douglas Morgan. His smile was not as broad as the others'. There was less of joy and relief in it, more of irony and doubt. But only Lisa saw this. The others simply roared their approval once they saw him, rushed to him cheering wildly and raised Douglas to their shoulders.

He looked genuinely surprised. Lisa saw that his eyes were tired, sleepless. His coverall was grimy and stained with what might have been blood along one sleeve.

But the crowd noticed none of this. All they knew was that Douglas had led the expedition to Earth, had brought back living survivors of the holocaust, had proved that they were not totally cut off from their mother world, had shown that the Earth was not entirely dead.

They paraded with him on their shoulders and cheered themselves hoarse. Their noise was absolutely head-splitting. But Lisa stayed where she was, her hands at her sides no matter how much she wanted to press them to her ears.

Almost as an afterthought, a pair of wildly laughing men grabbed her and hoisted her up onto their shoulders, then fought their way through the circling, howling, triumphant mob to march side-by-side with their pair holding Douglas aloft. He looked at her and grinned boyishly, almost guiltily. He shouted some words at her but Lisa could not hear them over the ceaseless animal roar of the mob.

Douglas laughed and shrugged his broad shoulders. Lisa knew, in an utterly unmistakable flash of insight, that her husband could lead these people wherever he chose to take them. They worshipped him. And she knew with equal certainty that he would throw it all away, that he did not want to be their leader, that he thought it all an absurd cosmic joke.

Then she looked back over her shoulder at Kobol, standing alone now back by the open airlock hatch, his face twisted with anger and envy, halfway between weeping and murder.

* * *

Dr. Robert Lord sat staring at the open refrigerator. There were only four lumps of what had once beer food in it, but now they were green, slimy, shapeless blobs that dripped between the rungs of the refrigerator shelves. The stench made his stomach heave. The emergency power generator had run out of fuel four days earlier, and the food had quickly rotted.

Fungus, Lord thought. At least the simple life forms are still working.

His stomach pangs were so insistent that his hand started to reach out for the festering mess.

"No!" he said aloud. The sound startled him. He pulled his hand away, then grabbed the edge of the refrigerator door and slammed it shut. Slowly, weak with hunger and the fever that was sapping his strength, he made his way out of the observatory's basement kitchen, up the spiral iron stairs that clanged as hollow as his stomach, and entered the big dome.

The telescope stood patiently, a massive monument to a dead civilization. With each step across the cement floor Lord's boots echoed eerily through the vast, sepulchral dome. He had always thought of the astronomical observatory as a sacred place. Now it was truly a tomb. He was the only one left alive in it. Two days after the sky had burned, a wild, frenzied mob from the town had sacked the observatory, killing everyone they could find in their madness and hatred for scientists.

"It's their fault!" the mob screamed as they attacked the handful of men and women in the observatory.

Lord had fled to the film vault and locked himself in without waiting to see if any of the others could reach its safety after him. The vault was almost soundproof, but some of the tortured shrieks of his colleagues and students seeped through, burning themselves into his mind. He waited two days before he dared to come out, weak from hunger, filthy from his own excrement. They were all dead. The pert little Robertson girl had made it almost to the door of the vault before they found her, stripped her, and raped her to death.

Lord knew he should have buried them, but he did not have the strength. Now, as he tottered across the observatory's main dome, smudged here and there by fires that the mob had started, there was no one to talk to, to confess to, except himself.

"It was a solar disturbance," he said to the empty, silent dome. His voice quavered and echoed in the accusing shadows. "Maybe a mild nova. My paper on the fluctuations of the intrinsic solar magnetic field . . . it'll never be published now. There's nobody left to read it."

He sank to his knees, buried his face in his hands, and cried until he collapsed exhausted on the cold cement floor.

For weeks he had patiently sat at the observatory's solar-powered radio, calling to other astronomical observatories around the world. When none answered, he swept the frequency dial from one end to another, searching for sounds of life.

He heard voices. There were people out there. But the tales they told made his blood freeze. Cities blasted into radioactive pits. Disease ravaging the countryside. Maddened bands of looters prowling the land, worse than animals, killing for the insane joy of it, raping and torturing and enslaving anyone they found.

Lord shuddered, remembering their voices, pleading, angry, bitter, sick, frightened. He still heard them sometimes, and not always in his dreams.

One woman, a psychology professor at Utah State, actually engaged him in a pleasant conversation over several days, reporting clinically on the devastation of Salt Lake City, the enormous levels of radiation that blanketed the state thanks to the heavy megatonnage that had been targeted for the mobile missile sites along the Nevada border. The wrath of the Lord, she had called it, not knowing his name.

On her last day she told him with mounting excitement in her voice as she watched a group of young men nosing around the wrecked campus. Her excitement turned to disgust as they set buildings on fire and finally broke into the room she was in. She left the radio on as the marauders kicked down her door and poured into the room. Lord could still her screams whenever he tried to sleep.

Her screams awoke him.

He was lying on the cold cement floor of the observatory, exhausted and stiff. And starving. He could not tell how much of his weakness was due to the fever that raged through him, how much the fever was due to his hunger. Every muscle in his frail body ached hideously. It was dark now inside the dome. Night had fallen.

Slowly, painfully, he pulled himself to his feet and tottered outside to the balcony ringing the observatory dome. In the shadows of night, the forest was as dark and mysteriously alive as ever. The warm breeze rustled the leafy boughs the way it always did. Insects buzzed and chirped. Frogs sang their peeping song.

"It's only the men who have disappeared," Lord whispered to himself. "Life goes on without us."

He wondered idly, almost calmly, if he were the last man alive on Earth. Why wonder? he asked himself. Why prolong it? The world will be better, safer, without us. With eyes that glittered of fever and the beginnings of madness he stared down from the parapet ringing the balcony into the inky darkness that fell away to the forest floor a hundred feet below.

"Life goes on without us," he repeated, and cast

his head up for one last glimpse of the stars.

The stars!

Lord gaped at the sight. He had hoped for a glimpse of them, but the clouds had broken at last, after weeks of virtually uninterrupted overcast, and the stars were blazing at him in all their old glory, ordered in the same eternal patterns across the sky. Ursa Major, Polaris, the long graceful sweep of Cygnus, Altair, Vega—they were all there, beckoning to him. Lord almost fainted at the splendor of it.

The Moon rode high in the sky, a slim crescent with a strange unwinking star set just on the dark side of its terminator.

"It can't be . . ." he muttered to himself. But even as he said it, he stumbled through the shadows to one of the low-powered binoculars set into steel swivel stands along the balustrade. They had been put in place for visitors, a sop to keep them from pestering the staff to look through the big telescope. They were ideal for gazing at the Moon.

Hands trembling, Lord focused the binoculars on that point of light. It resolved itself into several rings of lights: the surface domes of the lunar colony.

"They're alive up there," he whispered to himself, almost afraid that if he said it too loudly the lights would wink out. "Of course . . . they live underground all the time. The flare wouldn't have affected them, only their instruments on the surface."

He stood erect and stared naked-eyed at the Moon. "They're alive!" he shouted. The lights did not disappear.

Babbling with nearly hysterical laughter, Lord staggered to the stone stairs that led down to the observatory's parking lot. A dozen cars were there, surely at least one of them would have enough fuel in its tank to take him as far as . . . where?

He stopped halfway down the winding stairs, panting and trembling on wobbly legs. Where? Most of the cities were radioactive rubble. Barbarian gangs roamed the countryside. But somewhere there must be a scientific outpost that still survives. With a radio powerful enough to reach the lunar colony.

"Greenbelt, Maryland!" Lord exclaimed. "The NASA Goddard Center. They're far enough away from Washington to have escaped the blast. Radiation may have been heavy, but most of it should have dissipated by now."

Nodding eagerly, he resumed his descent of the stairs. "Greenbelt," he muttered over and over again, convincing himself that it was true. "I can call them from Greenbelt. They'll have rocket shuttles up there. They'll come to pick up survivors. I'll call them from Greenbelt."

CHAPTER 4

Once they were alone in their one-room quarters, Lisa turned to her husband and said, "So now you're a hero."

Douglas almost laughed. The wild joy of his reception at the airlock had been completely unexpected. For more than two weeks he had shouldered the responsibilities of the leader of an expedition into hell. He had seen more of death than any man wanted to see, had forced himself to accept it, to deal with it. He had even steeled himself to killing a few of the wild marauders who had attacked his men almost as soon as their shuttle had touched down on the long airstrip in Florida.

Then came the long return back to the Moon, with the sick and starving survivors they had picked up. And the memories of the others they had been forced to leave behind, too weak to make the trip, too old to be useful once they got back home, too sick to be saved by the lunar settlement's limited medical staff.

Douglas felt he had aged ten years in less than a month. His nostrils still smelled the stench of decaying corpses; the smell seemed to cling to his clothing, his skin.

And then the outburst of welcome, the hero's return, the tumultuous enthusiasm of his friends and colleagues, carrying him on their shoulders, praising him, laughing, cheering, blessing him. For what? Douglas had wondered. For adding two dozen casualties to their already-strained facilities? Or for giving them hope that they might eturn to Mother Earth some day?

Now Lisa faced him, lithe and deadly in her severe black jumpsuit, her expression unreadable. He had never understood her, he realized. He loved her, but he could not for the life of him fathom her moods. Or maybe, said a mocking voice within him, maybe you love not her, not the real Lisa Ducharme Morgan, but your own idea of what she should be. That would be just like you, Douglas: in love with the theory and trying to force reality to fit your flight of fancy.

"How does it feel?" Lisa asked. "Being a hero, I mean. Having men hoist you up on their shoulders."

All the excitement of the reception drained out of him. He replied defensively, "But they put you up on their shoulders, too."

Her dark eyes glittered coldly. "Yes, didn't they? But they didn't kiss my hand. They didn't fall to their knees and worship me as their savior."

"Nobody did that."

"Not quite," she said, turning toward the desk unit, putting her back to him. "Almost, but not quite."

Their room was a duplicate of all the other living quarters in the underground settlement. Spartan utility, nothing more.

Lisa pulled out the chair, looked down at it for an uncertain moment, then let it go and sat instead on the edge of the bed. Her back was ramrod straight, her hands clenched with tension. Douglas stood just inside the door, knowing that if he went to sit beside her she would move away from him.

"We have a lot to talk about," he said.

"I don't feel like talking."

"Sooner or later . . ."

She looked up at him. "What would you have done if Fred hadn't died out there? Would you have killed him?"

Douglas searched his mind for an answer.

"Well?"

"There's been enough of death," he said, seeing the blood-soaked remains of the towns around Cape Canaveral. The radiation level had quickly tapered off, but the towns had self-destructed in orgies of terror and greed. There was no place to dig in Florida, no place to hide from the fallout. But even in the blast-hardened blockhouses of the space center human beings had clawed each other to death over scraps of food or a safer corner to huddle in.

"Is your honor satisfied?" Lisa asked scornfully. "He's dead, and so is the baby."

"What does honor have to do with it?" he snapped. "When did you become interested in honor? Did you do it in this bed, right here? Or over in his quarters?"

A bitter smile turned the corners of her lips. "What makes you think we did it in either place? Or that we did it only once. It's only in melodramas that a single copulation gets the maiden pregnant."

He snorted with disgust. "Maiden. Who else have you been doing it with?"

"Before I met you or since?"

He took an involuntary step toward her, his fists clenched.

"Would you like me to evaluate them for you? On a scale of one to ten, you come pretty close to zero, you know."

He swung without realizing it and only at the last instant did he open his hand. The slap rang through the tiny room, knocking Lisa over backward across the narrow bed, halfway over its far side.

She pulled herself up slowly, the side of her face burning with the red imprint of his fingers.

"Thank you," she said slowly. "That's precisely what I expected from you."

He turned and stamped out of the room.

* * *

For hours Douglas strode the underground corridors, walking blindly through the rough-hewn tunnels that laced the various parts of the settlement together. Past the long, pipe-fed vats of the hydroponics farms he strode, looking neither right nor left, seeing nothing and no one except his wife's shocked face with the imprint of his angry hand on it.

I could have killed her, Douglas told himself. How can I come so close to murdering her if I love her?

He stopped briefly at the rock processing facility, soaking up the clamoring noise and bone-jarring vibration of the big grinding machines. It blotted other thoughts from his mind. The heavy machinery was fully automated: lunar rock went into one end of the massive crushers and grinders, out the other end came pulverized separated powders of aluminum, silicon, titanium, oxygen, and other ores. Some of them were channeled to the metal refineries. Others were fed through conveyor belts into the copper-clad electrolyzers of the water factory.

Douglas felt a tap on his shoulder. Turning, he saw one of the younger technicians. The kid held out a pair of earphones with one hand as he shouted over the rumbling roar of the grinders:

"Regulations, sir. No one allowed this close without protection."

Douglas looked up at the wide window panel of the control room, set into the raw rock wall above. Larry LaStrade stood at the window, peering through a pair of binoculars at him. With a shrug and a wave, Douglas turned and left the big, noise-filled cave, leaving the youngster standing there with the earphones in his hand.

Finally, inevitably, he went up to the surface. He spent nearly an hour worming himself into a hard-suit, checking out all the seals, the breathing system, the radio and heater and circulation fans. He allowed the thousand details of dressing for vacuum to occupy his mind, blanking everything else from his thoughts.

After going through the checklist with the safety team on duty at the control office, he clumped into the airlock and swung its heavy door shut behind him. In a few minutes the metal womb of the lock was emptied of air, and the indicator light on the wall beside the outer hatch turned green. He nudged the toggle with a gloved hand and the hatch slid open.

It was a strange and barren land out there, almost colorless, the raw pockmarked ground a study of grays on more grays. Behind him rose the terraced wall of Alphonsus' rim, massive, rugged, silent. Through the tinted visor of his helmet, Douglas' eyes traced out the rimwall's edge against the eternally black sky until it disappeared below the brutally close horizon. The crater's row of central peaks sat out there, worn by eons of meteoric bombardment, eroded to tired, slumped, gray lumps of stone.

A dead world, Douglas thought. Frozen stone dead. No air. The only water available is what we squeeze out of the rocks. The only life here is our own, barely hanging on.

His glance took in the glittering swath of solar panels that covered hundreds of acres of the roiled, pocked floor of the giant crater. With a resigned sigh, Douglas headed toward them. Might as well check on the meteor damage, he thought, and see if the flare did any long-term harm.

As he walked with dreamlike lunar slowness, kicking up tiny puffs of moondust with each booted step, he glanced up at the sky. The Earth hung above him, huge, gibbous, blue and white and gleaming where the sunlight touched it. You're still alive, he said to the beckoning home world. Despite everything, you're still alive.

He forced his gaze back to the dead bare rock of the Moon.

"How weary, stale, flat and unprofitable seem to me all the uses of this world," Douglas murmured, inside his helmet.

Inevitably his eyes turned Earthward again. But now he saw not the gleaming blue and white globe a quarter-million miles distant, but the world that had greeted him when he had landed there nearly three weeks earlier.

Despite all the devestation that the traitorous Sun and nuclear-armed men could wreak on the Earth, it was still a green, living world. Palms and cypresses still graced the Florida shores. Wild birds crossed the soft blue skies. The wind sang its ancient harmony. And people were still alive, too, even though they were sick from radiation, starving, injured.

Winter will be on them soon, Douglas knew. Those who lived in the warmer climates might be able to get through, but what about those further north? What would they do when the snows came, with no fuel except the wood they could hack down with their own hands, no electricity, no food or medicines?

"I can't save them all," he told himself, his voice strangely muffled, muted, inside the hardsuit helmet. "I can't even begin to save one percent of them."

But even as he said it he knew he had to try. Without the knowledge and skills represented by the tiny handful of people here on the Moon, all of human civilization on Earth would soon expire. Some people would live, as their ancestors had lived five thousand years ago. But knowledge, art, freedom, the great works of the human mind and heart that had been built up so painfully over so many millennia—that would all perish. Civilization would die. And soon.

"Unless we do something about it," Douglas said to himself. And immediately an inner voice answered. Not we. You. Unless *you* do something about it, they will all die.

He nodded his head inside the bulbous helmet of the lunar hardsuit. He admitted his responsibility.

"I've got to save them. No matter what it costs, I've got to try."

CHAPTER 5

"You're sure Douglas won't . . ." Kobol left the thought dangling.

Lisa shook her head. "I checked with the comm center; he's up on the surface, walking by himself."

Kobol sat on the edge of her bed. He wore the usual worksuit of the underground community, a faded gray coverall. On the left shoulder was sewn an equally faded circular patch of blue, slashed by a yellow lightning bolt: the symbol of the electrical power division.

Still in her black jumpsuit, Lisa pulled her legs up and rested her chin on her knees.

"That's a nice little bruise you've got on your cheek," Kobol observed.

"I can cover it with makeup."

"Sure." He glanced around the cramped little room. "And what will you do when the makeup runs out? Send him back to Earth to raid a drugstore?"

"That's not funny."

"It's not meant to be. There's nothing funny about any of this."

"You never expected him to come back, did you?"

Kobol did not answer.

"Martin, look at me!" she snapped.

He turned slowly on the edge of the bed, but made no move to come closer toward her.

"Douglas doesn't know it was you," she told him. "You don't have to worry about that."

His long somber face betrayed no emotion whatsoever. "I've been thinking about that. About us.

About him. You saw the way the people flocked to him. He's a natural hero. They want to worship him."

"Yes," Lisa admitted. "But he's not a natural *leader*. There's a difference."

Kobol made an impatient snorting noise.

"No. Listen to me. I know." Lisa sat up straighter, pressed her spine against the wall behind her. "He doesn't know how to be a leader. Not really. He knows how to charge off and do what he thinks has to be done. But he assumes that everyone else sees things the way he does, and that they'll follow along with him. He doesn't even realize that he has to convince people, to cajole them or force them to fall into step behind him."

With a slow, reluctant smile, Kobol agreed. "You're right. That's him. Charging off into the enemy guns without even glancing back over his shoulder to see if his troops are following behind him."

"We must form a real government," she said, more firmly. "These little meetings of the department heads must be turned into a board of governors or a council of some sort, with regular meetings . . ."

"And elections?"

"Yes. Elections. Of course. Not right away, naturally. But next year, after things have settled down a bit."

"They'll elect Douglas our maximum leader," he said, that sardonic smile touching his lips again.

"Perhaps."

"You think they won't?"

"I'm not certain that it matters," Lisa said, her voice hard and cold as the rock that supported her. "Let the fools vote him any title they choose. In the council he'll have to deal with *us*. And he won't know how to handle that. Three or four of us acting together can run rings around him."

Kobol's lean, bony hand stroked his jaw. "You'd do that to him?"

"Why not? It would be for the good of the community, wouldn't it? He'll want to fly back to Earth and drag as many survivors as he can find back here. We can't handle them, you know that."

"But you'd deliberately . . . knife him?"

Lisa fixed her dark, unblinking eyes on Kobol. "Don't make it sound so dramatic, Martin. I married the wrong man. We may have to share this room, even this bed, but that doesn't mean that I love him or I'll follow him like a blind little slave."

"I don't know," he said slowly. "I was watching you when he came through that airlock. You looked . . ." He hesitated.

"Well?"

"You looked happy to see him. *Very* happy. Almost like a schoolgirl with her first crush of puppy love."

Her face went red. "Don't be absurd."

"That's what it looked like to me."

"Nonsense." But she turned away from Kobol, turned her gaze to the polished metal mirror hung on the opposite wall, over the drawer unit.

"About you and me . . ." Kobol started to say.

"Nothing's changed," Lisa said. "He doesn't know a thing."

But Kobol shook his head ruefully. "Something *has* changed, Lisa. I have. I'm not going to live in his shadow. I want you to leave him."

She looked genuinely shocked. "I can't do that! Not now. Not yet, anyway."

"Why not?"

"How can I, with the whole world turned inside out? Don't you see what's happening, Martin? Don't you understand? The life of this entire settlement is hanging by a thread. The Earth is dead, and we're on our own. It's dangerous enough, just as it is, without adding our personal problems to the mix."

He pointed a long unwavering finger at the growing blue bruise on her cheek. "Don't you think your personal problems are already out in the open?"

"No," Lisa said firmly. "I'm putting that behind me. For the time being. I'm going to be his wife, and he's going to be the head of the new government."

"You mean *you're* going to be the head of the new government and I'm going to be out in the cold."

She reached out to touch his hand. "Martin, please. You've got to understand. We can still be . . . together. The way we have been."

Kobol pulled his hand away. "No, Lisa. *You've* got to understand something. I want to be the head of whatever government we put together. I want to have it all for myself. Including you. Especially you."

"You will," she said soothingly. "You will. But it will take time, Martin. You must be patient."

"You'll leave him for me?"

"In time."

"You'll work to make me chief of the council?"

She hesitated. "I'm not sure that they would elect you chief, Martin. They'll elect Douglas. He's their hero. We'll have to work through him."

Kobol broke into a bitter, barking laughter. "What you mean is, *you'll* run the council through him. You intend to be boss, one way or the other."

Lisa pressed back against the stone again, feeling its strength along her spine. "Is that what you think?"

Kobol's laughter choked off. "No matter who wins, you want to come out on top. You want to be queen bee."

"And what do you want, Martin?" she asked icily. "Isn't your interest in me based at least partially on jealousy of Douglas? Don't you want to be the top man, to have everything for yourself?"

Kobol's laughter choked off. His face went grim. "Christ, Lisa, we're two of a kind. If we don't tear each other to pieces we can make one hell of a great team."

"I'll keep my claws sheathed, Martin, as long as you don't get in my way."

"And you're staying with him."

"For the time being."

"Do you think he'll have you?"

Lisa smiled. "Oh yes. Douglas has one glaring weakness. He wants to do the right thing. He wants to be good."

"Not like us."

Lisa's smile faded. She swung her legs off the bed, got to her feet. "We'll have to start making arrangements for a permanent council—a schedule of meetings, official titles, things like that."

Kobol nodded agreement.

The intercom phone by the bed buzzed. Lisa picked it up, listened briefly, then thanked the caller and hung up. Turning to Kobol, she said:

"He's come back to the airlock. He'll probably be here soon. Time for you to be on your way, Martin."

CHAPTER 6

Living space was at a premium in the lunar community. The original airlock and storage chamber had been a natural cave eroded into the terraced side of Alphonsus' ringwall. The living and working quarters below had been blasted and carved out of the lunar rock by the miners, down at a depth that would assure full protection against radiation and the wild swings of temperature during the 648-hour-long lunar day/night cycle.

The staff psychologists and mining crew foremen had agreed, though, that the living quarters needed more than just dormitory rooms. So despite the cost and labor, they had carved out a few social rooms as well. Before the Sun had devastated Earth, the lunar community boasted a recreation room, complete with a billiard table and extra-sized (for lunar gravity) ping-pong table; a library stocked with real books and video viewers that could access the tapes in most of the libraries on Earth, and a small conference room with a real wood table.

The self-appointed governing council chose the conference room as their meeting place. Nine department heads arranged themselves around the walnut table. Douglas unconsciously took the chair at the head of the table. Lisa sat at his right. Kobol slouched in a chair halfway down the table.

Their first order of business was to elect a chairman pro-tem. Douglas was unanimously chosen.

Standing at the head of the group, smiling at them boyishly, he said, "Thank you. I appreciate the confidence you've shown in me, and I respect the responsibilities of the job. Now I think we've got to work out an agenda for this committee . . ."

"Council," corrected James Blair, down at the far end of the table. "This is a governing council, not a committee."

Douglas shrugged. "Council. We need to agree on an agenda for action. As I see it, the most important thing is to ensure the survival of our community. The next thing, and it's closely coupled to the first, is to re-establish our links with Earth. The two . . ."

"Our links with Earth?" William Demain asked, his high-domed babyish face wrinkled into a puzzled frown. "What Earth? Earth's gone."

"Not entirely," Douglas said. "Not by a long shot."

"As head of life support systems," LaStrande interrupted, his voice as strong as an operatic baritone's despite his frail frame, "I think that the most important issue before us—the only issue that really matters—is the one you mentioned first, Doug. We've got to make ab-so-lutely certain that we can support ourselves. Food, air, water, electrical power, medicine . . . all the things that we need for survival. We've got to make certain that we can provide these things for ourselves. *Without* any connections Earthside. We can't depend on Earth for anything! To do that is absolute nonsense."

A murmur of agreement went around the table.

"Now wait a minute," Douglas said. "I've been Earthside. The planet isn't dead."

"No, just half dead," LaStrande stage-whispered.

"There are people on Earth who need our help," Douglas insisted. "And there are supplies on Earth that we need: medicines, replacement parts, equipment . . ."

"We can't bring more people up here!" Catherine Demain blurted, her voice pleading. "We just can't! We don't have the room, the medical facilities, the supplies for them. It wouldn't be fair to the people who live here."

They argued back and forth for nearly an hour as Douglas stood helplessly at the head of the table, looking confused and frustrated. Kobol said nothing. Lisa said nothing. They carefully avoided each others' eyes as the debate dragged on.

"We have got to be able to take care of ourselves," LaStrande kept insisting, clipping each word for emphasis. "We cannot depend on Earth for *anything!*"

"But we can't just turn our backs on the people Earthside," Douglas countered. "They need our help, and we need the things they can provide for us."

"No! Never! The Earth is gone! Write it off."

"That's inhuman!"

When the digital clock set into the wall next to the room's only door showed that the argument had raged for fifty-five minutes, Kobol finally unfolded his lanky frame and got to his feet.

"You're both right," he said, looking first at LaStrande and then at Douglas Morgan. "We've got to be able to support ourselves. We can't depend on supplies from Earth anymore. But there are supplies that we lack, and Earth has. To become fully self-sufficient, we've got to send teams to Earth to get those supplies."

Douglas, who had been on his feet for the whole debate, sank into his chair. LaStrande peered through his thick glasses, eyeing Kobol owlishly.

"We should organize an expedition," Kobol went on. "More than one, if necessary. Go Earthside, take what we need, and bring it here."

"What about the *people* Earthside?" Douglas asked.

With a forlorn shake of his head, Kobol replied, "Catherine is right. We just can't take on more people. We haven't got the room, the facilities, or the food or medicine. Most of the Earthers you brought up, Doug, are too sick to work. Half of them are going to die of radiation poisoning. Bringing them here was a waste of time and energy."

Douglas stared at him, his face showing more hurt than anger. But he said nothing. Kobol looked around the table, abruptly sat down.

Lisa broke the lengthening silence. "We'll need a list of requirements from each department. Catherine, you'll have to go through the medical stores and tell us what you need from Earthside. Prioritize the list; put the things you need most at the top."

Catherine Demain nodded and murmured, "A pharmaceutical factory would be nice."

Lisa leaned forward, arms on the polished surface of the conference table. "Each of you . . . I'll need a prioritized list of needs from each of you."

"I've been thinking," LaStrande said, his voice softer now that he was no longer arguing, "that we could ease the strain on the air systems if we simply grew more grass and other greeneries throughout the settlement. Can't we peel off the flooring in the corridors and plant grass along them?"

"It'd be trampled down, wouldn't it?" Blair asked.

"There were resistant strains developed Earthside," LaStrande said. "For lawns where kids would play . . ." He blinked behind his owlish glasses and took a long, deep breath, as if fighting back tears. "Anyhow—if we could find the right seeds, or even strips of sod . . ."

"Put it on your list," Lisa said.

Douglas slumped back in his chair, saying nothing, his eyes focused a quarter-million miles away. Lisa glanced at him and knew that he had not accepted defeat; he was merely planning the next round of the battle.

"Who's going to head this expedition?" asked Blair. "Any volunteers?"

Inadvertantly, even against their conscious wishes, everyone turned to Douglas.

He nodded. "Sure, I'll do it."

"No," Lisa said.

The single syllable filled the conference room with ice. Everyone froze where they were, unable to move or speak.

Finally Douglas blinked and asked, "What do you mean?"

Her beautiful face, framed by her black hair, took on the look of a saint facing martyrdom. "Douglas has already led one mission Earthside. My husband has taken enough risks for the time being. I won't chance losing him again. It's not fair to ask him to go again."

Douglas started to reply, but held his silence. The others turned to one another, muttering.

Kobol said languidly, "I'll volunteer for it. It's my idea, basically, so I guess I ought to put my money where my mouth is."

"You mean, put your ass on the line," Marrett joked.

A ripple of relieved laughter went around the table.

"We should take turns on this," LaStrande suggested, "if we're going to send more than one expedition. No one of us ought to be out under the pressure more than anyone else."

"Take turns, yes. That's fair."

"That's the democratic way."

Douglas shook his head. "Running a quasi-military expedition isn't a democratic chore."

"Come on now, Doug," Catherine Demain chided. "You can't be the hero every time. Give somebody else a chance."

Walking down the curving corridor that led toward their quarters, Douglas scuffed a boot against the worn plastic flooring.

"Can you imagine grass growing along these tunnels?" he asked.

Lisa, walking beside him, looked up at the raw rock of the arched tunnel roof. "We'll need special lights for it. Infrared, I think. Or is it ultraviolet?"

"Near-infrared," he answered. He mused aloud, "We can get inert gases for fluorescent lamps easily enough. And there's plenty of glass in the rocks."

"All we need is the grass seed."

"And fertilizer."

"Sylvia Dortman, in the bio labs, she might be able to engineer nitrogen-fixing microbes for the grass. It was done on Earth before . . . before . . ." Lisa's voice suddenly choked up.

They walked in silence for a few moments, then Douglas asked, "Why did you object to my leading the next expedition Earthside?"

She glanced up at him, then pulled her gaze away and looked rigidly straight ahead. "I don't know. The words just blurted out of me."

Douglas watched her carefully as they walked slowly side by side. This was the Lisa he had known long ago, back on Earth, the vulnerable warm beauty he had fallen in love with. Not the ice-hard statue she had become. Has the ice melted? he asked himself. Has all that's happened over the past few weeks brought her back to me?

He started to speak to her, but the words caught in his throat. Like a damned schoolboy! he thought. He coughed, swallowed.

"Lisa," he managed at last, "you . . . in there, in the meeting, you said you didn't want to risk losing me again."

"Yes. I know." Her voice was so low he could hardly hear it.

"Did you mean that? Did you really . . ."

She stumbled on a loose bit of floor tile and he put out his hand to steady her. She gripped his arm tightly and he swept her to him, wrapped both his arms around her slim body and kissed her hungrily. Lisa felt warm and vibrant in his arms; he wanted to hold her and protect her and love her forever.

She clung to him fiercely. "Oh, Doug, don't ever leave me again. Please, please, please. Let's forget the past. Let's hold onto each other from now on."

"Yes, yes, of course," he said. "I'll never leave you, Lisa. I love you. I've always loved you, every minute of every day."

He was blinking tears away. She was completely dry-eyed. But he never noticed that.

Hours later, in the darkness of their room, the musky odor and body heat of passion slowly dissipating into the shadows, Douglas sat up in their rumpled bed.

"What is it?" Lisa asked drowsily.

"Fissionables."

"What?"

"Uranium, thorium—fissionables for the nuclear generators. We can't run the rock machines or the water factory without them."

"But I thought we had enough for years and years."

"About five years," he said.

"Oh, by that time we'll have found more right here on the Moon."

He shook his head in the darkness. "Not likely. Nothing heavier than iron's ever been found here. Not in any quantity above microscopic. We'll have to go to Earth for fissionables."

"They can convert the factories to solar energy."

With a sigh, he answered, "Wish we could, but that would require conversion equipment that we just don't have. And we don't have the facilities for making it, either."

"Then we'll send a team down for the fissionables," Lisa said.

"We'll have to."

"In five years. Now lie down and go to sleep."

"Yeah. In five years. Maybe sooner."

They both knew that he would lead the expedition back to Earth to obtain the fission fuels. Or he would try to.

CHAPTER 7

Five years passed. The lunar community grew both in numbers and living area. Miners quarried rock ceaselessly, expanding the settlement as rapidly as possible. The rocks they carved and lasered and exploded out of the underground spaces became the raw material for the factories. Out of that dead rock came aluminum and glass, silicon for solar panels, oxygen for life support, trace elements for fertilizers and vitamins. From the bulldozed surface soil came meteoric iron, carbon, and hydrogen embedded in the soil from the infalling solar wind: hydrogen to be mixed with oxygen to yield water, the most expensive and precious material on the Moon.

Expeditions went to Earth. At first they went every few months. Then twice a year. Finally, one per year. They modified the Earth-built transfer rockets to burn powdered aluminum and oxygen, then rode the spidery little spacecraft to the giant wheeled station still orbiting a few hundred miles above Earth's blue-and-white surface.

Everyone at the station had been killed by the superflare, and most of the station's electronics had to be rebuilt because of the radiation damage. But there were four space shuttles in the station's docks when the flare had erupted. Four winged reusable ships that could land on Earth and return to the station, time and again.

The first trips to Earth brought medicines, seeds, electronics parts, fertilizers and tank after tank of nitrogen to the lunar settlement. And people. A few men and women, starving, ragged, sick, who were able to convince the armed visitors from the Moon that they had technical skills that would be valuable in the lunar community.

It was the sixth expedition that met organized resistance for the first time. Twelve men were killed or left behind; four wounded were brought back to the Moon. Kobol led that trip and came back with a gunshot wound in the hip that left him with a slight but permanent limp.

After that the expeditions became rarer. The landing sites were changed each time. Florida was too obvious. Marauding bands congregated at the old Kennedy Space Center, waiting to ambush the shuttles as they glided down to land at the three-mile-long airstrip there.

But picking the landing sites was no easy task. Most of the major airfields were close enough to nuclear-devastated cities so that the dangers of radiation still persisted.

Four months passed before the next expedition landed at the remains of Dulles International Airport, more than ten miles from the edge of the dully-glowing crater that had been Washington, D.C. The landing team ransacked a nearby Army base for weapons and ammunition, always keeping one careful eye out for marauding gangs, and another on the radiation dosimeter badges they each wore pinned to their shirts.

That expedition picked up one Earthside survivor; a skinny, raving, white-haired man who insisted he was an astronomer who could tell when the next flare would erupt on the Sun. On the way back to the Moon, once safely past the space station and irrevocably bound for the safety of the underground community, Dr. Robert Lord admitted that he had been lying, there was no foolproof way to predict a solar flare—yet. But he promised to spend the rest of his life studying the Sun to find a way.

As the lunar community felt safer, and as the

armed resistance to their landings grew stronger, the time between expeditions stretched. Six months. Then ten. By the time the fifth anniversary of the flare arrived, it had been almost exactly a full year since the previous expedition.

"Why go Earthside?" people said. "There's nothing there but maniacs and death. We're doing all right here. We don't need Earth."

Douglas tried to convince them that they owed the world of their birth a debt. "We should be helping them to rebuild. We should establish a permanent base on Earth, a base where people can come to and be safe, a foothold where the rebuilding of civilization can begin."

They smiled at Douglas and congratulated him on his ideals. But they outvoted him at council meetings.

Midway through the sixth year they sent a small expedition down to what had once been Connecticut. Three nuclear powerplants nestled among the rolling hills in the western part of the state, untouched by the bombs that had wiped out New York and Boston. The team met little opposition, but found little nuclear fuel. Only enough uranium to run the lunar factories for a few years was brought back. And two of the team members who handled the fuel rods fell ill almost immediately of radiation sickness. They both eventually died, after long cancerous agonies.

"I've got to take a team down there myself," Douglas told his wife.

There were wisps of gray at his temples now, although Lisa's midnight-black mane was as lustrous as ever. She could feel her whole body stiffen; the moment of challenge, the moment she had known would inevitably arise, had come at last.

"No, Doug," she said softly. "I won't let you go. You're too important to me here."

They were sitting facing each other across the

tiny dining table of their new, enlarged, three-room suite. As chairman of the council, Douglas had been forced to accept the first of the bigger apartments. It included a sitting room where five or six people could be squeezed in for informal meetings, a dining area with its own cooking unit, and an indecently large bedroom.

He reached across the tiny stone table and grasped her slim hand in his. "Lisa, there's no way around it. I've got to go. No one else can handle the job. It's my responsibility."

"You have responsibilities here," she said.

"None of them mean a damned thing if the nuclear generators run out of fuel."

"There are others who can lead a team Earth-side."

With a dogged shake of his head, "It's my responsibility, Lisa. I've got to do it."

She looked into his ice-blue eyes for long moments and saw that there was no way to talk him out of his resolve. Except one. Lisa knew she had one final card to play, one unbeatable trump that would bend him to her will.

"Doug . . . it's not just for me," she said, her voice light, almost girlish. "I . . . well, I'm with child, as they say."

"You're pregnant?"

She nodded slowly, and let a happy smile spread across her lips.

He grinned back at her. "Really?"

"I had a checkup with Catherine this morning."

"A son," he said, gripping her hand tighter than ever. "Do you think it'll be a boy?"

She laughed. "I hope so."

"A son." He was beaming. "Even if it's a girl, that'll be okay. I won't mind."

Not much, she said to herself. How transparent you are, Douglas. How malleable.

Lisa had feared that just the mention of pregnancy might trigger memories of nearly six years ago and the moment they had come so close to tearing each other apart. Her cheek still stung from his hand every time she thought about it. But she had spent the years being faithful to him, being the model wife for the leader of the community, never allowing the slightest hint of a rumor to spring up in this hothouse settlement where gossip flew along the corridors faster than a pistol shot. For nearly six years now she had done everything in her considerable power to keep him happy. And for nearly six years he had jumped through hoops for her in unsuspecting gratitude. Douglas Morgan was chairman of the council. Lisa Ducharme Morgan ran it.

"I . . . Doug," she stammered, "do you think . . . well, could you . . . postpone the expedition Earthside? Until after the baby is born?"

"Nine months?" The grin on his face slowly dissipated, replaced by an introspective frown. "Nine months," he repeated, almost to himself. "I'll have to check. That's slicing it very thin."

But she knew he would wait. And after the baby was born she would find other ways to keep him by her side. Especially if it was a son.

But she reckoned without Martin Kobol.

Five months passed without incident. Douglas chafed, but kept postponing the Earthside expedition. Kobol watched and waited as the nuclear generators' supply of fuel rods slowly dwindled.

"At this rate," he told Douglas, "we'll be eating into the emergency reserves before the year's out."

They were standing in the cubbyhole office just off the control room of the nuclear powerplant. Through the leaded window Douglas could see the broad sweep of the control board, with its array of dials and switches. Two bored, sleepy-looking technicians sat there. Beyond the massive lead-line doors across the chamber from them was the nuclear generator itself, silently converting the energy of splitting uranium atoms to electricity.

Douglas nodded unhappily. "I know. We've got to bring up more fissionables from Earthside."

"And we can't wait much longer," Kobol pointed out, tapping the computer screen that showed the fuel supply numbers.

"A few more months . . ." Douglas muttered.

Kobol sat on the edge of the desk to ease his aching hip. "We should have gone three months ago, in the spring. It's high summer now. In a few more months it'll be winter."

"I know the seasons!" Douglas snapped.

Kobol closed his eyes momentarily. He looked almost as if he were praying. "It's Lisa, isn't it? She's making you wait until the baby's born."

"I *want to* wait until he's born," Douglas corrected.

"While we run out of fuel."

"We won't run out, Martin. Don't try to pressure me."

"Doug, this is a serious matter. If you won't act, I'm going to have to bring it before the council."

"Do that," Douglas snapped. "Do anything you damned well please. Lead the expedition Earthside yourself. You tried that once and it didn't work out so goddamned well, did it?"

His voice had risen to a room-filling roar, he suddenly realized. Both the technicians on the other side of the thick window had turned in their chairs to stare at him.

Kobol said nothing.

With a self-exasperated sigh, Douglas went over to Kobol and grabbed his bony shoulders. "Marty, I'm sorry. You're right, we should have gone at least three months ago. It's just that . . . Lisa lost her first baby, and the radiation dose she got—

well, I just want to be here and make sure this one's okay."

Kobol pulled free of him and walked, one leg slightly stiff, toward the door. Without looking back at Douglas he said, "Why should this one be so special? She's aborted three or four others."

It was such a strange thing to say, such an incredible statement, that Douglas did not believe he had heard the man correctly.

"What did you say?" He heard a weird half-chuckle in his own voice.

Kobol put one hand on the doorknob, then half-turned toward Douglas. "She's keeping this baby to hold onto you. You're the puppet; the baby's the string."

Douglas could feel his blood turning to ice. "What did you say about three of four others?" His voice was deadly calm.

Shrugging, Kobol replied, "Nothing. I shouldn't have mentioned it. It's none of my business."

"But it's *my* business, Marty." Without being consciously aware of it, Douglas was advancing on Kobol, fists clenched.

"It's just . . . something I heard." Kobol's voice quavered. "Ask Catherine Demain about it. She knows."

He yanked the door open and rushed through it and out into the corridor, leaving Douglas standing there alone.

"It's true, isn't it?" Douglas said to his wife.

Lisa lay in their bed, a black robe pulled around her. To Douglas she looked more beautiful than ever, glowing from within. Her belly was just slightly rounded.

She said nothing, merely watched him with her dark enchantress's eyes.

"I checked with Catherine. She didn't want to admit it, but she finally did. Four abortions in the past five years. Four sons or daughters we could have had. *Why?* Why did you kill them?"

"I didn't want them," she said, her voice as flat and controlled as if she were reading off a list of numbers. "Other things were more important."

"And for five years I worried that the radiation you'd been exposed to in the flare . . . Jesus Christ, Lisa, why didn't you at least *ask* me?"

"It was none of your business. It was my decision to make."

He sank onto the end of the bed, head bowed, tears of frustration welling up in him. "Four children," he muttered. "Four children of mine . . . and you never even said a word to me about it."

"We had more important things to do than to argue about having babies," Lisa said.

He looked up at her. She was perfectly calm, totally in control of herself.

"They were mine, weren't they?" he heard himself snarl at her. "Not Demain's or Blair's or Marty's. Or maybe some of the miners? Do you know who the fathers were?"

Even that failed to crack her facade. "They were yours, Douglas. Only yours. But the decision to keep them or not was mine."

Nodding bitterly, he hauled himself to his feet. He swayed there at the end of the bed for a moment, as if drunk.

"Okay," he said. "You made your decisions. Now I'm making mine. I'm taking an expedition Earthside as soon as we can get it ready. You can lie there and swell up and burst, for all I care. I don't believe it's my kid. I'll never believe a word you say to me, never again!"

He stamped out of the bedroom. Lisa lay unmoving, listening to him rummaging around the other rooms for a few moments. Then she heard the corridor door slide open and slam shut.

He'll be back, she thought. He's angry now, but he'll cool down. He'll come back, feeling sheepish. And I'll ask him to forgive me. He will, and then

I'll forgive him. We're having a son. I'll tell him that all the tests indicate that. He'll stay to see his son born. He'll be back. Soon. He won't stay away long.

But he never returned to her.

It took three months to organize the Earthside expedition to Douglas' satisfaction: three months of frantic preparation, of meticulous detail work, of unceasing training for the men he hand-picked to go with him, of driving, flogging everyone—himself most of all.

Lisa watched the takeoff of his spidery transfer craft on the video screen in her bedroom. Every ship in the settlement was needed to lift the expedition members toward the Earth-orbiting space station. Douglas, she knew, was in the very last spacecraft. When its rocket engines ignited and it leaped off the Moon's dusty surface and out of view, she felt a sudden, searing pain in her abdomen.

Her son was about to be born, five weeks prematurely.

BOOK TWO

CHAPTER 8

Alec stood at the observation dome's main window and gazed across the tumbled, broken wingwall floor to the bleak horizon.

Hanging above the weary, slumped mountains of Alphonsus, floating softly in the blackness, shone the blue, beckoning crescent of Earth. It glowed, catching the light of the now-quiet Sun on bands of glistening white, casting vivid shadows across the pitted gray lunar floor.

From slightly behind him he heard a soft voice:

"All of beauty's there,
And all of truth.
Let me leave this land of mirthless men
And return to the home of my youth."

Turning, Alec saw Dr. Lord, the astronomer. The old man was smiling faintly; the Earthlight coming through the window caught the wispy remains of his dead-white hair and produced a halo for him against the darkness of the room's dim interior lighting.

"I didn't realize you were a poet," Alec said.

Dr. Lord's voice was the whisper of a dying man. "Oh, yes. Back before the sky burned, when there were still girls for me to impress, I spent hours memorizing poetry. Between the poetry and the observation work, I made out rather well. You know, working all night at the observatory . . . you asked a girl to keep you company." He chuckled faintly at his memories.

"Has the Council meeting started?" Alec asked.

"Yes, about ten minutes ago. Your mother said the vote won't come until after considerable debate, and it would be impolite for you to be present while they're trying to decide."

Alec nodded. "I wouldn't want to offend any of the Council members."

"No, that wouldn't do," Dr. Lord agreed.

Turning back to the window, Alec thought, All of beauty's there, and all of truth . . . and much, much more.

Dr. Lord moved up to stand beside him at the window, and Alec could see their faint reflections despite the deliberately low lighting of the observation dome. Lord was ancient, frail, his chalky skin stretched over the bones of his face like crumbling antique parchment. He breathed through his mouth, so that his lips were drawn back to reveal big, rodent-like teeth, surprisingly strong and healthy in his deathlike face.

Alec studied his own face and wondered what it would be like if he ever reached Dr. Lord's age. He was taller than the old man, but not by much. Not as big as his father or most of the men he knew. His features were too delicate, almost feminine, and his hair curled in golden ringlets no matter how short he cropped it. But he had his mother's dark, smoldering eyes. And he saw that there were tight, angry lines around his mouth. Tension lines. Hate lines.

"I was there when it happened," Dr. Lord muttered, more to himself than to Alec.

Alec said nothing and hoped that the old man wouldn't go through his entire litany. For a few moments the only sound in the dome was the faint electrical hum of the air fans.

"We had no idea . . ." Dr. Lord looked as if he was still dazed by it, even now, more than twenty-five years later. "Oh, I had proposed that perhaps the Sun emits a truly large flare every ten millennia or so . . . Tommy Gold had suggested it earlier, of course, and I was following his lead."

He paused, and Alec tensed himself to beg the old man's permission to leave. But, "When it happened, I was at the observatory in Maine . . . it was summer, but the nights were cool up on the mountaintop."

Alec had missed his chance, he knew, and he could not risk being called impolite. So while the old astronomer rambled away, Alec stared out at the luminous crescent of Earth, narrowing his thoughts to the debate going on in the Council. He knew that the choice was between Kobol and himself. Kobol had the advantages of age, experience, and no personal involvement. As a Council member, he was physically present at the debate. No risk of impoliteness for him. Alec's only advantages were his mother, and the urgings that burned inside his guts.

". . . the sky just lit up. For a moment we thought it was dawn, but it was too early. And too bright. The sky burned. It got so bright you couldn't look at it. The air became too hot to breathe. We ran down to the film vault, down in the basement, behind the safety doors where the airconditioning was always on. But they all died. Peterson, Harding, Sternbach . . . that lovely Robertson girl. They all died. All of them . . ."

Alec put a hand on the old man's frail, bony shoulder. "It's all right . . . you made it. You survived."

"Yes. I saw you here. I saw this dome." Lord's soft voice was agitated, shaking. "I think I must have gone a little mad, back then. You have no idea . . . no conception . . . everyone dying . . ."

"But we found you," Alec soothed. "You're all right now."

"It all burned. The sky burned. There was no place to turn to. Nowhere to go."

Very gently, Alec led the old man away from the window. "Come on, let's get you down to your quarters. You're tired."

Dr. Lord let Alec lead him to the powerlift. Usually it stayed unpowered and people clambered up and down using their own muscles. But for the old man, Alec touched the ON switch. A strong whiff of machine oil puffed up from the recess beside the ladder, and a motor whined to life, complainingly. The ladder rungs began creaking past them. Alec helped the aged astronomer onto one of the steps and hopped onto it beside him. Wordlessly they descended five levels, to the living quarters.

He left the old man at his door, then followed the rough-hewn corridor toward the settlement's central plaza, where the Council's meeting room was. The rock walls of the corridor were lined with pipes carrying water, electricity and heat: the settlement's three necessities. Light tubes shone overhead, not so much for the aid of the pedestrians as for the benefit of the grass that carpeted the corridor floor.

As he padded on slippered feet through the meager, oxygen-producing growth, Alec wondered what it would be like on Earth. To be outside without a suit. Would he be frightened? There were stories about men going crazy, out in the open with nothing to protect them. And the gravity . . .

With a shake of his head, he dismissed all fears and strode doggedly toward the central plaza and the Council meeting room.

CHAPTER 9

There was a crowd in the central plaza. Alec knew there would be, but still it shocked him to see so many people in one place, milling around, not working, almost touching each other at random. The big high-domed cavern was buzzing with a hundred muted conversations.

The elaborately carved doors of the Council chamber were still closed. No one was allowed in or out while the Council was in debate. The doors had been lovingly designed and produced by one of the original members of the Council, after he had retired from active duty. He had died not long ago, and willed his remains to the food reprocessors.

Alec drifted through the crowd aimlessly, careful not to touch or be touched by any stranger. He was too nervous to wait in his quarters for word of the Council's decision. But this crowd was making him even jumpier. He could see that everyone was reacting the same way: the more people who poured into the plaza, the more excited everyone became. The noise level was growing steadily.

"You look like a man in need of refreshment."

The voice startled Alec. He turned to see Bill Lawrence, one of the settlement's bright young engineers and one of his lifelong friends. Thick dark hair cropped short, beard neatly trimmed, Lawrence approached the world with a kind of stiff formality that melted into playfulness with his friends.

"Do I look that uptight?" Alec asked him, forcing a grin.

"Everybody's that uptight," Lawrence answered. "Why do you think they're clustering here?"

Lawrence took him by the arm—a privilege granted only to friends—and guided Alec through the shuffling, chattering crowd back toward the stone benches that circled the dwarf trees at the far end of the plaza. Several more of Alec's closest friends were there, sipping from plastic cups.

Alec sat in their midst, wishing that Lawrence's brittle bones hadn't ruled him out of the Earth mission.

Handing him a cup, Lawrence explained, "Deitz brewed this stuff in his chem lab, in between experiments on rat poison and rocket fuel. It's strictly illegal, but sells for twenty-five units a liter."

Alec took a cautious sip. The liquid burned his tongue and almost gagged him. "Yugh . . . who would buy a liter of *that?*"

"Nobody."

They all laughed.

Zeke, a roundish golden-haired young man who was called "the Bumblebee" because of his constant air of busy-ness, said, "We're going to turn Deitz in to the Council . . . as soon as we've finished drinking up the evidence."

Alec shook his head. "You'll be dead long before then." He placed his cup down on the bench beside him.

"It's sort of scary seeing everybody hovering around here," Joanna said in her throaty voice. She was tall, dark, leggy.

Alec nodded agreement. "Isn't anybody at work today?"

Lawrence, still standing, eyed the crowd. "Only those with really essential duties. Everyone else just walked off and came here."

"I don't understand it," Alec said. It *was* frightening.

"Kobol's people had a little parade just before

you arrived," said Zeke the Bumblebee. "All the miners and techs . . . they said it was a spontaneous demonstration."

"A parade! Without permission?"

Lawrence nodded grimly.

"First they leave their jobs and then they parade without the Council's permission." Alec's voice sounded shocked, even to himself.

"Kobol wants to head the Earth mission," Joanna said.

"It's not just the Earth mission," Lawrence corrected. "It's control of the Council. If Kobol can get his way, he'll head the mission and then return to take over the Council. Your mother's fighting for her Chairmanship in there."

"Kobol can't defeat her," Alec snapped.

"If he comes back from Earth with the fissionables," Lawrence said, "he'll demand an election and Lisa will be forced to step down."

"Which is why it's important that you head up the mission," Zeke took over. "I sure as hell don't want to see the miners and techs taking over. We'll be overpopulated and run into the ground inside of a few years. Kobol's followers never seem to understand that you can grow people a lot faster than you can carve out new farmlands."

"Kobol won't head the mission," Alec said tightly. "And he won't take over the Council."

"Says who?" a new voice shouted at him.

A man in his mid-thirties was standing between the bench on which Alec sat and the next one. He was big, shaggy-haired, and wore the fire-red coverall of a miner.

"It's impolite to break into a private conversation," Alec replied carefully, noticing that several other miners and techs stood behind the speaker.

"Oohhh." The miner pursed his lips. "Now we mustn't be impolite, must we? Wouldn't want to make the frail little scientists' darlings break into a rash."

Lawrence put a hand on Alec's shoulder. "Pay no attention to them."

Alec forced himself to turn back to his friends.

"Kobol's gonna set things straight around here," the miner continued loudly. "Put you brittle-boned sweethearts in your place. The settlement's gotta be ruled by the strong! You egg-shells push buttons all day while we break our asses for you. Gonna be a lot of changes."

Struggling to control himself, Alec got to his feet. "Let's get out of here," he said quietly to his friends. "There are limits even to politeness."

But the miner stepped lithely around the bench and planted himself squarely in front of Alec. Grinning, he rested his fists on his hips. He was a head taller than Alec, and bulged with strength and self-confidence.

"Hey, don't get upset. I didn't mean to make you cry!"

Alec stood glaring at him.

"In fact," the miner continued, laughing, "I really oughtta wish you good luck on your vote in the Council. You're gonna need it!"

He leaned his head back and guffawed; the miners and techs roared with him.

Alec could feel Lawrence's hand on his arm, tugging at him. "Come on, Alec; you're only embarrassing yourself by listening to him."

"Hey wait," the miner went on. "Listen, kid, I'd vote for you myself if I was on the Council."

Alec said nothing.

"Sure! I really would. Providing I got the same goodies that the rest of the Council*men* are getting!"

Alec could feel the heat of his anger giving way to something far colder than lunar ice. He pulled his arm free of Lawrence's grasp.

"What do you mean?" he asked in a voice so low that he could hardly hear it himself.

"Go ask your Momma, little boy." The miners and techs were all grinning hugely now. Most of the crowd in the plaza had swarmed up to surround them.

Alec took a step toward him.

"What's the matter, kid? She's already fucked half the Council for you, why not a couple of real men?"

Alec aimed for the throat. The miner put his hands up to protect himself and Alec slammed into him. They toppled over the stone bench together and landed on the grassy ground with a thudding grunt. Someone screamed, voices shouted, but that was all far away. Alec felt the solid strength of the miner's muscular arms grabbing at him.

The miner was big and catlike, hard-handed and strong. But he hadn't spent hours each day in the Earth-gravity centrifuge, as Alec had for months. Alec scrambled to his feet and turned, saw the miner still in a crouch, knees bent, one hand touching the ground like an ape's.

Looking up at him, the miner smiled. "I heard you got a temper, kid. Now you're gonna see what it costs you."

He got to his feet slowly. Alec stood still, realizing that they were standing between benches now, little room to maneuver. Every nerve in him, every muscle was screaming with rage and anticipation. But he held himself in check, waiting, waiting.

The miner towered over Alec, big as his father. He made a feinting move to his right. Alec ignored it. Another left, and again Alec did not respond. Then he launched a straightarm blow to Alec's head.

Alec slipped under it, kicked the man's knee out, chopped hard at his kidney and brought a cupped hand up into his face. It caught his nose. Blood spurted and he fell heavily against the stone bench.

He looked surprised now, with blood splashed over his face. The grin was gone. He got to all fours, tried to rise to his feet again, but the damaged knee would not support him. He went down again on his face.

Alec looked around at the circle of spectators. "Anyone else have something to say?"

Lawrence came to his side. "Come on, it's over. Let's get out of here."

Alec let his companions lead him through the hushed crowd while the miner's friends bent over him.

They made their way to Alec's quarters, which he shared with his mother. Gradually, one by one, his friends drifted away until only Joanna remained. They were drinking legitimate liquor now, part of the precious supply that was synthesized each year from the unusable waste products of the hydroponics farms.

Joanna was sitting on the padded sofa, feet tucked up beneath her. Alec sat beside her. The furniture was all made of lunar stone, their most plentiful material, and padded with foam cushions. The room was spacious by lunar standards, big enough for a large viewscreen on one wall, two chairs and a low stone table in front of the sofa. Paintings hung on the other walls, and the ceiling panels glowed with a soft fluorescence.

"You know," Joanna was saying, "I think Deitz's rat poison extract tastes better than this stuff."

Alec grunted. "How can you taste anything? It burns the taste buds off your tongue."

"It's strong, all right." Joanna stared down at her cup for a moment, then smiled up at Alec. "I had no idea you were so strong. You handled that miner as if he were a toy."

With a shrug, Alec answered, "Spend as many hours in the centrifuge as I do and you'll get strong, too."

"You really are dedicated," she said softly.

He didn't know what to answer to that one. Joanna was watching him, her large almond-shaped eyes almost as dark as his mother's.

"Doesn't anything interest you," she asked, a smile toying at her lips, "except the mission to Earth?"

"A lot of things interest me. But the mission comes first."

"Oh. I see."

"The life of the whole community depends on this mission," he said gravely. "If we don't get those fissionables, and soon, we'll be in irreversible trouble."

She nodded thoughtfully. "And that's why you've been so . . . inaccessible?"

The games they play, Alec thought to himself. Think of me before anyone or anything else. But he knew that he played the same game himself.

"I'm in training, Joanna. Facing a full Earth gravity is like carrying six times your normal weight. Half the people here can't stand it, their bones have become too brittle. And then there've been the classes in military tactics, logistics, all the planning . . ."

"You've been involved in those classes since we all were children," Joanna said.

"Yes," he said, "and it's paid off. Did you know that the Council's adopted my plan for the mission? I worked it out with old Colonel Dunn, all the details, the men and equipment, the timing—everything. They accepted it over Kobol's plan."

"No, I didn't know. That's wonderful." But her voice was flat, plainly uninterested.

"I've even studied the old tapes of Earth's weather . . . rainfall and temperature changes, things like that."

"But what about *you?*" Joanna asked. "What do you want out of all this?"

"Me?" Suddenly he was puzzled. "I want to lead the mission." There was more to it, of course, but he had no intention of discussing that with anyone.

"But why? What's the reason . . . your own personal reason?"

Alec did not answer. He couldn't.

Joanna made an impatient huffing sound. She turned squarely to him, kneeling, sitting on her heels. "Alec, what do you want? Why is the Earth mission so, so . . . all-encompassing for you? Is it because of your father, what he did? Or is it to keep your mother secure as Chairwoman of the Council, or what?"

He edged away from her. "It's not for my mother, and it's certainly not for my father. It's for me. I'm going because I want to go. It's my life."

"You enjoy risking your life."

"Don't get so personal," he said. "It's not polite."

Her mouth was a determined thin line. "Alec, don't give me any of that politeness crap. We've known each other since we were toddlers and I want to know why you're so anxious to throw your life away. It frightens me!"

"I'm the man best qualified for the job. Nobody in the community, from Kobol on down, has scored as high as I have in all the physical and mental tests. I enjoy doing what I've been trained to do . . ."

"And *she* trained you," Joanna said. "She's brainwashed you."

Alec jumped to his feet. "I think you'd better leave, Joanna. Either you don't understand or you don't want to."

"No, Alec. It's not either of those. I *do* understand . . . better than you do. I want to see you living your own life, not hers. Why should you throw yourself away for her career, her revenge?"

"Get *out!*" Alec shouted.

Defeated, Joanna got to her feet and went to the door. She opened it, turned her head toward Alec briefly and smiled sadly at him. "You poor fool."

He was almost asleep when his mother finally returned home. For hours he had lain on the air mattress in his own cubicle, the lights off, staring at the hand-woven tapestry that concealed the water tank and fuel cell, listening to the mattress sigh every time he moved, trying to turn off his mind, become a blank, a cipher, a nothing. But every time he shut his eyes, he saw that miner's leering face. It shifted and melted into the pictures of his father that he had seen. His father, who had left the Moon the day he had been born.

"You're sleeping?"

Alec's eyes snapped open. His mother was standing in the doorway, framed by the light from the main room.

"No." He reached up and flicked on the overhead lights. She looked very tired.

Watching her as she stepped into his cubicle and took the chair next to his bed, Alec could see why every man in the settlement desired her. Lisa Ducharme Morgan was an enchantress, a dark beautiful sorceress. Compared to her, Joanna and the other girls his own age were pale and insubstantial. But Lisa was a cool beauty, a distant Diana or Artemis, perfectly attuned to the task of governing this tiny hothouse of transplanted humanity.

"I heard about your roughnecking," she said quietly. "What were you trying to prove?"

"That you're not a whore," he answered, and immediately regretted it.

But she didn't even blink. "Oh, that again? Another little benefit we have to thank your father for."

"Has the Council voted?" he asked.

"No." She shook her head wearily. "The debate

drags on. Kobol's people are trying every trick they can play—even claiming that you're too emotionally unstable to lead the mission. I wouldn't be surprised if that fight wasn't arranged deliberately."

Alec thought it over briefly. "It could have been," he admitted.

She leaned toward him, suddenly blazing with intensity. "Then can't you understand how important it is for you to hold your temper? You broke every social rule we have today; how do you think the Council members will react to that? Save your anger for the real enemy, or you'll ruin everything for both of us!"

With an effort, Alec kept his voice level. "All I want to know is when the Council will vote, and whether or not I will win."

She stared at her son for a long moment. Alec looked back steadily into those endlessly deep, infinitely dark eyes. His own eyes.

"The vote will be tomorrow morning. I think we will win."

"Then I'm going to Earth."

"Yes. Just as your father did," she replied bitterly.

CHAPTER 10

Alec snapped awake the next morning like the sudden step from darkness into full sunlight up on the Moon's surface. He dry-bathed quickly and pulled a black jumpsuit over his trim frame. His mother was already dressed and waiting for him in the apartment's main room. She handed him a cup of hot soybrew.

"I've decided to bring you with me to the Council meeting," Lisa said.

He took a burning sip of the brew. "Kobol's going to be there?"

"Of course."

Alec watched her primp her thick, wavy hair in front of the room's only mirror. The blue-gray suit she wore was simple, even severe, from its high Chinese collar to the loose-fitting slacks that ended in foot slippers. Still, when she raised her hands over her head that way . . . when she walked and her hips swayed rhythmically . . . Alec heard all the whispered gossip again, all the taunting shouts from childhood. He could feel his face burning. He clamped his teeth tightly together.

Lisa turned to him. "You needn't look so grim. I told you that we'll win the vote, and we will. Now come along."

The Council chamber was purposely kept austere. The rock walls were unfinished, bare, as rough as the day the chamber had been blasted out of the virgin lunar stone. There were no decorations at all, nothing in the room except the big circular table and chairs, and a single viewscreen hung in the corner opposite the chamber's only door.

Most of the Council members were already seated around the circular table. Lisa swept in regally, extending her hand to the men nearest her chair, smiling her hello to the others. She allowed Alec to hold her chair for her, then directed him to a chair almost exactly across the table, which had been set up for him beforehand.

"I thank you for the courtesy of allowing me to invite Alec to join us this morning." Lisa smiled sweetly to the Council.

Alec kept his face blank as he took his chair. It was not polite to use your position for a point of personal privilege, but it would have been even more impolite for a Council member to object to Lisa's request. But how will this affect their voting? he wondered to himself.

Several Council members nodded to Alec. He knew them all, of course. Nine men, six women. But three of them were still missing: Kobol and his two closest allies.

"That's the chair your father used to sit in," said the fat old fool next to Alec. "We saved it for you. Perhaps in a few years you will grace the Council with your membership."

Alec nodded curtly. He did not trust himself to say anything.

Kobol arrived at last and all conversations stopped. Flanked by his two henchmen, he stood for a moment at the door and looked straight at Lisa. She returned his gaze without wavering. Then his eyes flicked away and he went to his chair.

Alec watched him, and knew that Kobol wanted the Council chairmanship, wanted to rule the lunar settlement, and especially wanted Lisa. And Alec felt a special brand of hate for Kobol. The man was his mother's age. Tall and spare, his bony face looked cadaverous to Alec. Deepset eyes that were almost impossible to see under their graying, shaggy brows. His teeth were large, too prominent, horsy. He had worn a bushy mustache as long as Alec had known him. At first, Alec had thought it was to show that he wasted no extra water or power on shaving. More recently, though, Alec had come to the conclusion that Kobol's mustache was there to divert attention from the fact that he was going bald.

As he sat at the Council table, at Lisa's right, he said in his reedy, nasal voice, "Sorry to keep you waiting. Let's get on with it."

Lisa allowed a slight smile to flicker across her lips. "We resume the adjourned session of yesterday," he said for the microphone link to the central computer file. "The question before the Council is, who will command the upcoming expedition to Earth. The nominees are Councilman Martin Kobol and Citizen Alexander Morgan. Arguments have been heard and a motion for a vote was tabled at the conclusion of yesterday's meeting."

She glanced around the table. "Are there any questions before we vote on the motion?"

"I have a question," said Councilman LaStrande. He looked like a wizened old gnome to Alec, diminutive, a scraggly beard sprouting from his chin, his eyes huge behind thick glasses.

Lisa acknowledged him with a nod.

LaStrande pushed his chair back and stood up. Jabbing a gnarled finger at Alec, he said, "Citizen Morgan is a very talented and capable young man. Everyone agrees on that. But he is *young*. Too young, I fear, to lead an expedition of such critical importance . . ."

"But the Benford expedition of . . ."

LaStrande cut him down with an imperious gesture. "Let's not waste our time by arguing about previous expeditions!" His voice filled the room. "Some have been successful, some have not. I might point out that Morgan's own father is responsible for the most disastrous expedition of them all, which is the direct cause of the crisis in which we now find ourselves."

Alec seethed in silent fury. So LaStrande has gone over to Kobol's side. Did my mother count this in her calculations about the vote?

Lisa fixed LaStrande with a cold gaze. "Surely you're not suggesting that my former husband's actions should bar my son from assuming his rightful duties as a citizen?" Her voice was razor-edged.

"Of course not," LaStrande replied smoothly, "but the Council must consider that every action has a cause. We are critically short of fissionable fuels. Why? Because twenty years ago Douglas Morgan led an expedition Earthside and refused to return here. *Refused!*"

"But he sent the nuclear fuels we needed," said the fat man next to Alec, his voice a placating whine.

LaStrande nodded. "Of course he did," he replied, dripping sarcasm. "And five years later, he was pleased to allow us to have a little more of the fissionables we need to remain alive. And then a third time, five years after *that*, he doled out a bit of nuclear fuel to us. But nothing since then. He has refused to send us any further shipments of fissionables, despite all our efforts and entreaties. For the past five years he has held us hostage to his renegade ego. And for the past five twitching years we have sat here politely discussing what we should do, while our fuel reserves dwindle toward zero."

The Council members mumbled to each other and shifted nervously in their seats.

"Morgan is still down there Earthside, turning himself into some sort of barbarian emperor and thumbing his nose at us!" LaStrande's powerful voice rang against the rock walls of the chamber. "He knows how desperately we need those fissionables. He knows we will all die without them. But does he care?"

"No!" several Councilmen shouted.

"And now we're expected to follow the lead of his wife, and send his whelp down there? To help us obtain the lifeblood we need? Or to help further Douglas Morgan's schemes for setting up an empire on Earth that will eventually kill us all?"

Several Council members pounded the table and roared their approval of LaStrande's attack. Kobol sat back, idly tugging at his ear, saying nothing and looking inscrutable behind his mustache and thick eyebrows.

Alec burned with anger. He clenched the arms of his chair, coiled inwardly and was ready to leap to his feet to shout them down. But then he looked at his mother.

She sat there silent and unmoving, an ice-queen, waiting for the fools to shout themselves out. Only her eyes were alive, and they blazed with cold fury.

The Councilors' shouting raggedly tapered off to a few scattered mumbles, then went dead. The chamber became absolutely silent.

Then, in a voice that Alec had to strain to hear, Lisa said, "Councilman LaStrande, your concern for our future and wellbeing has led you beyond the bounds of politeness and common sense. Surely you don't believe that the offenses of the father taint the son—and the wife, as well."

LaStrande blinked his watery frog's eyes at her. "I, eh . . . I merely wanted the Council to, em, to consider all the facts of this matter."

"Including," she countered, steel-hard, "the fact that I have lost a husband. Renounced him, years ago. Including the fact that my son, my only child, has been raised without a father, and feels all the taunts and sick little innuendos that you have so rashly brought into this debate. Including the fact that my son has volunteered to head this dangerous expedition so that he may prove to all the foul-mouthed and petty-minded fools in this community that he is his own man, not a duplicate of his traitorous father! Include those facts in your considerations, Councilors. Include them all!"

They all sank back in their chairs, as if pushed by the force of Lisa's words. LaStrande sat down and studied the table top before him. Kobol smiled wanly and crossed his legs.

"Madam Chairwoman," called white-haired Catherine Demain, sitting two seats to Lisa's left.

Lisa nodded to her.

"I'm sorry that this debate is reaching such an unfortunate level of incivility," she said, without getting up from her chair. "But a critical point has been raised by this outburst. Douglas Morgan *has* committed treason against us. There's no other word for his actions, even though I counted Doug among my closest friends on the day he left for Earthside. The question is, why did he do such a horrible thing? Why did he turn against us? Is there some factor in his psychological makeup that—forgive me—might have been inherited by his son? Or is it . . ."

Alec shot to his feet without thinking about what he was doing. Barely controlling his voice, he said, "I will not sit here and listen to my mother and myself being discussed like two specimens in a biology lab."

The Councilor at his right reached for his arm, but Alec pulled away and started walking around the table toward Catherine Demain.

"Since I volunteered for this expedition I have been subjected to every possible physical and mental test that the medical staff could devise. My record is available to all of you for the most intense study."

He stopped at the Councilwoman's chair. She had to turn and look up to see him. Clutching the chair's high back and looming over her, Alec asked, "Have you studied my record?"

"Yes, of course I have."

"Is there any indication of any unbalance whatsoever?" Alec found that deep inside him his anger was being supplanted by another emotion: not joy, exactly, but a thrill, an excitement, the tingle of *power*.

"No," Catherine Demain replied softly. "All of your tests were . . . well, you got excellent ratings."

"You yourself ran many of those tests," he said, looking down at her.

She nodded and turned away from him.

Alec swept the room with his eyes. "I know that I'm young. I know that my father failed us all—but he failed no one so badly as my mother and myself. And I also know that I've scored higher in every test, from word-association to heavy gunnery, than any citizen in this community. If my name were Kobol, or LaStrande, or Nickerson, you wouldn't have had the slightest hesitation in approving me to head the expedition. That is the truth and we all know it."

"You are out of order," Lisa said firmly. "Apologize to the Council and return to your seat." But her eyes sparkled.

He grinned at his mother. "Sorry. I beg the Council's indulgence."

As he went back to his seat, one of the younger women Councilors called for the floor.

"Councilor Dortman," Lisa acknowledged.

Sylvia Dortman had been a strong supporter of Alec's nomination, one of Lisa's most dependable allies.

But now she looked troubled. "There's no sense trying to ignore the problem that's bothering all of us," she said. "And that problem, quite simply, is trust. We trusted Douglas Morgan and he failed us. Deliberately. Can we trust his son?" Before anyone could reply, she quickly added, "I'm not questioning Alec's loyalty or strength of purpose. I'm not questioning his physical or mental abilities. I'm not even questioning his intentions. But the basic fear remains. His father was just as capable and well-liked and respected—more so, from what I've been told. And Douglas turned traitor. We don't know why. Equally, we don't know what Alec will do when he reaches Earth."

For long moments no one said a word. All the Councilors turned to Lisa, waiting for her reaction. Alec sat rigid with tension, staring at his mother like the rest of them.

At last, Lisa said very softly, "We are beginning to hear repetitions of previous discussions. A motion has been made to put the question to a vote. Who will second the motion?"

"One moment, please." LaStrande again. "I suggest that we change from our usual voice vote to a secret ballot. To assure complete freedom of choice."

"Very well," Lisa said. Her eyes closed and her voice sounded infinitely weary. "If there are no other objections . . ."

Why? Alec raged silently at her. Why vote now, before these stupid arguments have been laid to rest? Then he saw the withering look Lisa was firing at Sylvia Dortman and he suddenly understood. She wants to get the vote in while she still has the majority. She's afraid that our support is crumbling away.

The Councilors voted by pressing the appropriate button on the tiny panels set into the table at each of their places. Their votes were registered by the computer and displayed on the viewscreen on the wall. Fifteen Council members, eight votes needed to carry the election.

The screen flickered and showed: COUNCIL VOTE. SIX VOTES FOR MORGAN. FOUR VOTES FOR KOBOL. FIVE ABSTENTIONS.

Twisted around in his chair to read the screen,

Alec felt fear for the first time. Five abstentions! They could swing the vote to Kobol. Just four of them could!

"We'll have to take another ballot," Lisa said.

"Madam Chairwoman."

It was Kobol. He had stayed silent through the debate so far, as propriety demanded. But now he rose to his feet, a lanky unfolding of knees and elbows.

"There's been enough debate," he said slowly, nasally, "to convince me that further discussion could split the Council into antagonistic factions and cause divisions among us that might not be healed for years. I think the time has come for a compromise, in the interests of peace and unity."

"What do you have in mind?" Lisa asked.

With a humorless smile, Kobol replied, "If we look only at the various physical and mental tests that we've all been subjected to, there's no question that Alec is the best qualified man to head the expedition Earthside. What we're arguing about here is a question of trust—or guilt, really."

Alec could not take his eyes off Kobol's face. Something was going on behind the mask he wore.

"No one wants to head this expedition more than I do," Kobol continued. "I think I'd do a good job of it, despite my limp. I've been Earthside before, I know what to expect. I'd be prepared to fight off any opposition we might meet—even if it was Doug Morgan and his barbarian army."

A sigh of understanding went around the table.

"But I also know that for me to insist on heading the expedition could cause irreparable damage here: friend against friend, jealousy and hatred instead of harmony and cooperation."

What's he driving at? Alec ached to know.

"So I would like to withdraw my name from consideration as the expedition's commander . . ."

The Councilors gave a collective gasp.

". . . providing I can be named deputy commander, serving under Alec."

Alec felt as if he'd been led up to a mountaintop and then pushed off. The whole Council seemed stunned, but soon enough they recovered and began to murmur, nod heads, look back and forth at one another. Kobol sat down while they chattered. Lisa called for order.

LaStrande asked to be recognized. "I've never seen such a generous, unselfish move in this chamber. I suggest that we name Alexander Morgan commander of the expedition and Martin Kobol deputy commander—by unanimous voice vote!"

Everyone cheered. The actual vote was a formality.

Smiling, relieved, happy that the impasse had been broken, the Councilors filed out of the chamber. Each one of them shook Alec's hand—and Kobol's. Alec stood by his chair, still in turmoil inside, until no one was left in the room except himself, his mother, and Kobol.

Lisa stood behind her chair. It struck Alec that she was using it like a shield, keeping it between herself and Kobol.

"Is that what you wanted?" she asked him, in a low voice.

Kobol grinned at her. "Not entirely. But it's a step in the right direction."

Alec started around the table for his mother.

She said to Kobol, "Martin, I want to . . . thank you. It took a considerable amount of sense and courage to suggest this compromise."

"I'm always willing to settle for half a loaf, when it looks sure that I won't get any if I don't compromise."

Alec reached her side, but she was still focused on Kobol, who had also come closer. Now he was only a pace or two away from Lisa, within arm's reach.

"You're still determined to rule the Council,

aren't you, Martin?"

"The Council—and everyone on it."

She smiled at that. "And you believe you can use this expedition to enhance your position? Even as deputy commander?" Lisa put a subtle emphasis on the word *deputy*.

"Of course," he answered. "Why do you want Alec to head the expedition so badly? He'll be a Council candidate, won't he, when he comes back? Someday you'll try to maneuver him into the chairmanship, after you decide to step down."

"Why not?" Lisa said.

"Because *I'll* be chairman by then," Kobol said, with iron certainty in his voice.

She laughed. "You're dreaming, Martin."

"Some dreams come true," he replied, shrugging. "You've dreamed big dreams, god knows. And now one of them's coming true. Your son's going to avenge your husband's treason. Clear the family name. Preserve your power on the Council."

Lisa reached an arm out toward Alec. He took her outstretched hand, and she pulled him close to her.

"That's right," she whispered back to Kobol, in a low, breathless hiss. "Alec is going to achieve greatness. And you can't stop him."

"Stop him?" Kobol chuckled. "I'm going to help him. I've voluntarily placed myself under his command, remember?"

"Yes," she said. "Of course you have."

For a nerve-stretching moment the three of them stood there: Alec by his mother's side, Kobol facing them both. Alec saw that his mother had locked her gaze on Kobol, whose eyes were hidden, unfathomable. But the fire in Lisa's eyes was something Alec had never seen before, something beyond fear, beyond malice, much stronger even than hatred.

At last Kobol took a step backward. With a

muttered, "If you'll excuse me . . ." he headed for the door.

After the door slid shut behind him, Lisa turned to her son. "He'll try to ruin you, subvert your authority, perhaps even wreck the expedition."

"I know," Alec said. "He'll try to kill me."

She shuddered and grasped his arm tightly. Alec pulled her to him and let her lean her head against his shoulder.

"No, no, he wouldn't . . . Martin wouldn't go that far." But she looked up at him with real fear in her eyes. "I shouldn't have pushed you so hard. I shouldn't have forced you . . ."

"You didn't force me to do anything."

Her eyes closed wearily for a moment. "Alec, you're still a child. You don't understand any of this. I can manipulate you, the Councilors, everyone . . ." She looked away, toward the closed door. "Almost everyone."

"I can take care of Kobol," he insisted.

"Can you? Will you know what to do, when the time comes?"

"Yes." He was dead calm inside now. "When the time comes, I'll kill him."

"No! It mustn't come to that! I don't want you even to think that way. If it comes to violence, he'll kill you. He'll strike when you least expect it. He could be a thousand kilometers away and he'll still be able to reach you. It mustn't come to violence, Alec, or you'll end up the dead one."

Alec pulled away from her. "I can take care of myself. And him. And you, too."

She gazed at him, the expression on her face slowly changing, shifting, as she appraised her son.

"And your father?" she asked. "What about him?"

The old sickening wave of hatred rose inside Alec again. "I can take care of him, as well."

"He'll come looking for you, as soon as he learns

that we've landed an expedition on Earth."

"Let him," Alec said. "If he doesn't, then I'll go looking for him."

"And when you two find each other . . .?"

Alec's fists were clenched so tightly that his fingernails were cutting into his palms. "When I find him, I'll kill him."

Lisa Ducharme Morgan smiled. "Tell me again," she said softly.

"I'm going to kill him," Alec repeated. "For all he's done to you, Mother. I'm going to find him and kill him."

CHAPTER 11

He was born in a ditch alongside the road that twisted through the hilly wooded territory between bombed-out Knoxville and abandoned Oak Ridge. His mother left him half-immersed in rain water that had accumulated in the muddy bottom of the ditch. Her only act of mercy toward him was to bite off the umbilical cord and knot it. He never saw her.

If a pair of scavengers had not passed by a few hours later he would have died. If the woman of the pair—girl, actually, she was barely past fourteen—had not lost her own week-old baby a few days before they would have left the infant squalling there in the mud. As it was, the man scowled and grumbled when his woman took up the red-faced, naked baby.

"Leave 'im fer the varmints," he told her.

But her eyes welled up and she started sputtering and he relented.

They had been following in the wake of a larger band of raiders, a few dozen ragged men and women who scoured the countryside, picking it clean of everything edible, wearable, or tradable. The band had a few guns, a clever hard-faced leader who knew how to set up an ambush, and the desperation of hunger. The two scavengers had tried to join the band, but had been rebuffed angrily and threatened with death if they got close enough to be seen again.

So the two of them hung well behind the band, gleaning what they could from their leavings. It was not much. When the band attacked a farm or village they usually burned what they could not carry.

"Yer maw must've been one o' them raiders," the girl told her foundling child, once he was grown up enough to halfway understand her. "Prob'ly her man din't want t' be saddled with a newborn baby and made her leave yew fer us t' find."

Her man would nod and mutter to himself when she crooned the story to the youngster. Feeding an extra mouth was not to his liking. Besides, the baby's crying meant they had to stay even farther behind the raiders than they had before. He wandered off one day, less than a year later, as the autumn rains began to strip the trees of their leaves. Two weeks later she found him nailed to a tree, his gut sliced open to make a nest for teeming maggots. From the look on his face he had still been alive when they did it.

She stopped wandering then and built a crude hut of sticks and mud for herself and her baby. They nearly starved that winter; only her forays into the shattered, haunted remains of suburban Knoxville saved them. It was pure desperation; everyone new that the buildings and streets were poison. Lingering agonizing death lurked in them, invisibly. But she slunk through the shadows night after night to take the cans of food from the abandoned store shelves that others were too frightened to touch.

By the time he was six, she was obviously dying of cancer. She hung on for four years of pain and terrifying strange growths that twisted her body horribly. He buried her and faced the world alone, a skinny pinch-faced ten-year-old who knew how to run and hide in the woods, but little else.

After months of living alone, trapping small game and avoiding all human contact, he was snared by a wandering gang of teenaged boys. They had split off from a larger, older band of roamers and were on the prowl for food, fun, and women when they found him with a brace of rabbits tucked into his ragged shorts. Their first thought was to take the rabbits and roast him along with them over a hot fire. But their leader, wise beyond his years, asked the emaciated youngster how he caught the rabbits.

Once they realized how much he knew about hunting and surviving in the woods they adopted him into the band. He was officially named *Ferret*, partly because of his looks, partly because of his quick furtive movements, but mainly because he killed small game by biting through their throats.

Ferret he was, and by the time he was twenty years old he had risen to second-in-command of the band, which now numbered more than fifty men and their women. It was the most feared band of raiders throughout the rolling, wooded hills around Oak Ridge.

* * *

The satellite station revolved at a steady one *g*.

Alec had spent at least one hour a day over the past five years in the lunar settlement's big centrifuge, feeling six times his normal weight. His Earth-gened muscles had always responded to the full one-gravity load without complaint.

But here on the space station, after nearly a solid month of six lunar gravities, he was worried. He woke in the mornings tired and aching. His back felt sore, the sullen kind of pain that never quite goes away. His pulse drummed in his ears after the simplest exertions, such as climbing a ladder from the sleeping deck to an observation blister.

At least the blister was in the zero-gravity hub of the satellite station. Alec warned himself against spending too much time there; it would be too easy to allow his complaining body to subvert the purpose of his will.

Kobol was already there when Alec poked his

head up through the hatch in the blister's floor. The older man was sitting at one of the observation ports, safety belt latched loosely across his lap, peering intently through one of the stubby telescopes built into the bulkhead.

The observation blister had four such ports, spaced around its circular perimeter, and a fifth station dangling from the center of its domed ceiling. Taking up most of the floor space was a horseshoe set of consoles and viewscreens, where an observer crew of three monitored all the automated sensors that kept watch on the Earth.

Alec floated weightlessly up through the hatch. Touching his slippered feet to the bare metal floor, he bent over slowly and pushed the hatch shut. The action made him drift toward the horseshoe console. Reaching for the console's edge, he pushed off and glided toward an empty port.

The sight of Earth so close still made him gasp. A huge curving blue immensity streaked with dazzling white, constantly changing as it drifted past the observation port, colors shifting, different textures revealing themselves as it slid past his widened eyes. It's so huge, Alec thought. And so . . . alive.

"That's the east coast of North America," Kobol's voice drifted to him, like an ancient woodwind playing in its upper register, too refined to be impolite, but condescending, bored by the need to explain everything to inferiors.

"I know," Alec snapped. "And our prime target area . . ."

"Look through your number three 'scope," Kobol said. "I've got it slaved to mine."

Alec sat lightly on the swivel chair and leaned toward the little telescope on his right.

"Clouds . . ." Kobol muttered.

Through a break in the white, Alec glimpsed brown and green ripples like old lava flows along the edge of a ringwall. But there were no craters in view. These ripples were razorback ridges, hundreds of meters high. Or so he had been told.

"There . . . in the clearing . . ."

Alec caught a glimpse of gray, a slightly lighter form that looked like a lopsided letter X.

"That's the airport," Kobol explained as clouds covered the scene again. Alec pulled away from the telescope and turned toward Kobol, who was still talking. "The Oak Ridge complex is only a few kilometers from the airport. If it's still intact, that's where we'll find both processed and raw fissionables—enough for half a century, at least."

Nodding, Alec pushed away from his seat and glided to the monitoring consoles.

"Any activity in that area?" he asked the youth sitting in the center chair.

He turned to face Alec. "Nothing much . . . at least, nothing we can detect. No vehicles, of course. No fires or signs of life that the infrareds can pick up. The area's heavily forested; I don't think we'd be able to detect small numbers of people moving around in there."

Alec glanced at the fifty-odd screens that blinked and glowed across the curving bank of consoles. The other two technicians were steadily watching the screens, touching dials, making notations.

"We've got the strength to handle small numbers of raiders," Alec said. "You keep your sensors alert for larger bands."

The youth smiled. "Yessir. We'll do that."

The smile irritated Alec. He's only a year or so younger than I am, but I'm in command, by order of the Council, so he has to call me "sir." He wouldn't grin like that at Kobol.

Then he noticed Kobol watching him, face impassive behind his brows and mustache. Abruptly, Alec went back to the hatch and made his way down to the living and working area of the station.

Speed. Speed and firepower. Those were the keys. Alec lay on his bunk and watched the tapes play out on his viewscreen. His compartment was no bigger or better than anyone else's: a bare little cell with a bunk, a desk, a chair, and a viewscreen.

We've got to get in and out before anyone realizes we've landed, Alec told himself. He knew that his fifty men, armed with automatic rifles and lasers, could deal with any ragtag band of barbarians that might stumble across them. But the observers had occasionally seen larger groups, more organized, marching along the crumbling old highways. Some on horses. Even a few mechanical vehicles now and then.

Suppose they have Oak Ridge defended? Douglas knows the value of those fissionables. He might attempt to keep them from us.

Why?

Alec stirred uneasily on the narrow bunk. The fabric beneath him was wrinkled and cut into his bare skin annoyingly.

Why is he doing this? Why didn't he return to us? Why is he trying to kill us all?

Then a new thought struck him. What if he doesn't show up? That had not occurred to him before. What if I have to choose between returning to the Moon and finding him?

He lay there in the bunk, eyes watching the scenes of Tennessee's rugged hill country unfolding on the viewscreen. "Speed and firepower," he said aloud, trying to force his mind to focus on the mission. "Terrain is the key to speed. Get in and out before they know you've arrived."

Do that and you'll never find him, he knew.

Angrily, Alec reached out and punched the viewscreen's OFF button. He turned over on the lumpy, wrinkled bed and tried to force himself to sleep.

Briefings. Exercises. Examinations. Training. The days in the satellite station blurred into a continuous round of automatic routine. Morning briefings on tactics. Physical therapy, mainly running along the central corridor of the satellite for an hour. Then medical exams. After lunch, training: weapons, communications, hand-to-hand combat.

"You're losing weight."

The medic was a woman, a handsome woman. Alec had watched several of the men make fools of themselves, trying to impress her. She was big, with a broad Slavic face and strong, big-boned body that she kept in perfect shape. Her white coverall strained across her bosom and hips.

"It goes with the job," Alec answered. "Soon I'll start turning gray."

They were sitting in the tiny alcove off to one side of the medical compartment. The main section of the compartment was filled with the automated examination booth and its sensors and computer terminal. Sitting across the flimsy desk from her, Alec realized why the men chased her. But she was looking at him with coolly professional concern.

"What's bothering you?" she asked.

You are, he started to say. But instead, "I'm responsible for the lives of fifty men who'll be going Earthside with me. And for the life of the entire settlement, if we don't bring back those fissionables."

"But you sought out this responsibility."

"That doesn't make it any easier."

She eyed him for a long moment, tapping her finger lightly on the tiny desktop, then turned slightly to study the data screen on the wall at her side.

"I think," she said calmly, "that you are full of shit. Either you're trying to con me, or you're conning yourself."

Alec broke into laughter.

"You find that funny?"

"Sure, why not?"

She pursed her lips in obvious annoyance.

"Look," Alec said, "Dr. Sinton . . . um, what is your first name, anyway?"

"Lenore."

"Lenore?"

"As in Poe."

"What?"

"Never mind. Am I to assume I may call you Alexander, instead of Commander Morgan?"

"Alec."

She still had not smiled. "Very well, Alec. You are losing weight, even though you're not turning gray. To what do you attribute this medical phenomenon?"

"Are you a psychiatrist as well as a medic?"

"No. Please answer my question."

Alec leaned back in the flimsy chair. "The answer is—I don't know."

"I think you do."

Without raising his voice, Alec said, "I really don't give a damn what you think."

Now she smiled. But it wasn't sweetness. "You had better. Because you're not going Earthside until I'm satisfied that your physical condition is up to it."

Alec glared at her, feeling the heat rising inside him. "The tyranny of the medics."

She shrugged. Despite himself, he found the movement delicious.

For a strained, silent moment they sat there trying to stare each other down. Finally she said, "Shall I tell you what my opinion is?"

"You're the doctor." Alec tried to make it sound casual, but his fists were clenched in his lap.

"You're not sleeping well. You're not eating properly. You're edgy, moody, irritable."

"That's your opinion?"

"No," she said easily. "Those are my observations. Now the opinion comes. The reason for your condition is that you're," she hesitated a barest half-heartbeat, "scared."

Alec fought down an urge to get out of the chair and walk away. He could feel the color flaming in his face.

"Not in the sense of physical cowardice," Lenore added quickly. "You've been dragging around here under a steady full-Earth *g* and feeling lousy. All of us have. But you're worrying about how you'll perform on Earth. You know about the heavy atmosphere, the heat, the terrific humidity, and it's got you worried. Too much imagination. Like Lord Jim."

"Who's he?"

"God! Don't you read anything?"

"Sure—military history, meteorology, geography . . ."

Shaking her head, Lenore said, "Your problem is that you don't know how to unwind."

"That's your diagnosis?"

"It is. And I've got a prescription for you." She pushed away from the desk and stood up. Alec realized again how desirable she was.

"Prescription?" he asked as he got to his feet.

"Yes," she said, and now she was really smiling. "Tonight I'm going to fix a special dinner for you. In my compartment. Twenty-hundred hours. Be there. Doctor's orders."

Alec grinned at her. "The tyranny of the medics."

She *did* fix a special meal. Somehow, out of two standard dinner trays from the galley she managed to add spices, some sort of delicious sauce for the soymeat, and even a golden concoction that tasted almost like lunar brandy.

"I raided the galley and the medical stores," Lenore admitted.

She was sitting on the bunk. Alec had the compartment's only chair. Lenore was wearing shorts and a pull-over top, standard off-duty clothes. She filled them magnificently.

"I like your prescription," Alec said. He spoke slowly and carefully, the brandy was that strong. "I haven't felt this relaxed in months."

"The treatment's just starting," she said, patting the bunk beside her.

Alec took his glass to the bunk.

"You do feel good?" she asked.

Nodding, "Maybe too good."

"What do you mean?"

"I want to go to bed with you," he said.

"Well," she said, "why not?"

"I don't know. I'm not sure that I ought to."

"Are you afraid that I deliberately ensnared you? Manipulated you into this?" She was smiling.

"No, not . . ."

"Well I did," Lenore said. "I've been planning this for several days."

"Really?" Something in the back of Alec's mind told him that he should be upset about that, but it was a distant warning. He ignored it.

She went on, "Ever since I noticed how uptight you were starting to look."

"I see. I brought out your maternal instincts."

"Not exa . . . why did you say that?"

He shrugged. "Dunno. What?" Alec drained his glass and reached for the bottle on the desk.

But she asked, "How many women have you made love to?"

He grabbed the bottle. "Thousands. I used to keep a list in my desk back home but it got too long. Had to put it on the computer."

"Come on, really." She held her glass out and he started to refill it. The liquid flowed so fast under one-g that the tiny plastic cup overflowed and brandy splashed down onto her bare leg.

"Hey!"

"Hell! I'm sorry . . ." Alec put the bottle down

and took one of the napkins from the desk. He dabbed at the wetness on her leg.

"That's nice," Lenore said softly.

He kissed her, but that warning note still sounded faintly off in the back of his head.

"Why did you want to know how many girls I've been to bed with?"

"H'mmm?" she murmured. Then, pulling slightly away from him, "Oh . . . just professional curiosity."

"Professional?"

"Medical," she said. "Psychological."

"I thought you said you weren't a psychologist."

"I'm not. But still, it's interesting how people are sexually attracted to those who remind them of their parents."

He backed off completely. "You don't look anything like my mother."

Lenore smiled. "And you don't look anything like my father, either. But you have that same coiled-up animal power in you. Just like he did. And I tend to be aggressive, just like . . ."

"That's bullshit!"

"Such strong language! Really getting to you?" She seemed amused. "Would you have invited me to your place for dinner? Would it even have crossed your mind?"

"I thought about it," Alec said. "But you seemed busy enough."

"I haven't gone to bed with anyone since we arrived here at the station. Do you believe that? Six women and eighty men, and I get to fondle each man at least twice a week . . . and I waited for you."

Alec didn't know what to say.

"I even turned Martin down. Twice."

The warning alarm rang in his head. "Kobol?"

She nodded. "Twice."

"Why did you say *even?*" Alec demanded.

"I don't know. I guess because he's sexy. Dark

and mysterious. Deadly earnest. He warned me about you . . ." She looked as if she would giggle.

"Me?"

"Yes. He said you wouldn't be interested."

"Did he?" Alec felt the tide of rage building up in him. "What else did he say?"

Lenore looked at him quizzically. "Nothing," she replied quietly. "He didn't say anything else . . ."

"No?" Alec gripped her arm. "He didn't say that I'm a classic Oedipal? He didn't tell you that I'd like to screw my mother?"

"No . . . Alec . . ." Her eyes were wide and frightened now.

Alec threw his cup down on the floor and stood up. "I don't know what your game is, but you can tell Kobol or anyone else that I'm not afraid of anything. I'm not weak and I'm not scared! Of anything!"

He turned and reached for the door. She sat huddled in the corner of the bunk. "Alec . . . what did I . . ."

With one hand on the door handle, he said to her, "For all I know, Kobol put you up to this—to see if I have any balls at all!"

"Do you?"

Suddenly he wanted to hit her, smash her face, throttle her. Instead he grabbed her, pulled her off the bunk, tore the clothes from her body. She gasped and swung at him. But it was clumsy, hampered by the torn clothing that hung on her arms. They struggled against each other. She was a big woman but he was furious with a murderous rage. He ripped the rest of her clothes off, pushed her onto the bunk. When she tried to get up he cuffed her, hard, with the back of his hand.

She recoiled back onto the bunk, then reached for the bottle on the desk. By that time Alec had his jumpsuit unzipped. He knocked the bottle away, turned her on her back and fell on top of her. She snarled at him, teeth bared, "I'll bite your prick off!"

"Try it."

She struggled briefly, then stopped trying to push him off. "Wait . . . wait . . . at least . . ."

But he exploded inside her, then pulled away and got to his feet.

"Tell Kobol I'm not dead yet," he said.

And he left her there.

CHAPTER 12

"And I say we go now!"

They were sitting in the satellite station's tiny mess hall, which also served as a conference room. There were only four tables in the cramped metal-walled room. At this time of night, the other three were empty.

Sitting around the table with Alec were Kobol, Ron Jameson, and Bernard Harvey. Jameson was one of the few real military men of the settlement, an expert in weapons and tactics who had been a twenty-year-old soldier on duty at the lunar settlement when the sky burned. He had gone Earthside on every expedition since then, and now served as the commander's chief aide, the man who translated strategy into order to the men. He was tall, utterly calm, flat-stomached, with unflinching gray eyes set in a hawk-nosed, hunter's lean face. A hard man to panic. Harvey was a round, soft-faced, balding Councilor who would return to the settlement as soon as the expedition touched Earthside.

"But the schedule," Harvey objected, "calls for your leaving three weeks from now."

Kobol steepled his fingers in front of his face, hiding his mouth. "That's when the spring rains will be over and the ground dried out," he said. "Travel across country will be a lot easier then."

Alec said, "If we land at the airport we'll only have to travel a couple of kilometers, over paved roadway. We can be in and out overnight."

"But your own battle plan . . ."

"Ron, what do the pilots say?" Alec asked Jameson.

"They'd prefer the airport," he said in his easy drawl. "We've put the high-mag 'scopes on the airfield every time since you suggested it. Runways are in a sorry state, but there's plenty room for both shuttles. It'd be a lot better than trying to land in open country."

"The shuttles will be sitting ducks at the airfield," Kobol said. "That's how we lost the last one, at an airfield."

"Any sign of barbarian bands around the airfield?"

Jameson shook his head.

Tapping the table with a forefinger to make his points, Alec said, "The spring rainstorms keep the natives holed up, prevent them from travelling. In another three weeks those forests down there will be teeming with them and we'll have to fight our way into Oak Ridge and back out again. Right now the only natives who could be there are the locals, who aren't much of a threat. And no matter where we land the shuttles, they're going to be vulnerable."

Kobol looked impassive; Harvey upset.

"If we go now," Alec insisted, "land at the airport, we can have the entire mission accomplished in two days, max. Before any barbarian hordes have had time to mass and reach us."

"But that's not the way the mission was planned," Harvey pleaded. "It's your own plan! The Council . . ."

"The Council gave me command. My decision is that we go now. Tomorrow, if possible. The next day at the latest."

"It's a mistake," Kobol said flatly.

"Maybe," Alec countered. "But it's *my* mistake."

They sat there under the bluish fluorescent light panels of the ceiling for a silent few moments.

"All right," Alec said. "That's it. Ron, please get

the men ready for boarding as soon as possible. Inform the pilots and maintenance crews."

Jameson nodded.

Turning to Harvey, Alec said, "You can report this back to the Council, if you want to."

Visibly sweating, the Councilor said, "I guess I'll have to."

Alec got up from his chair, nodded to them, and walked out of the mess hall. The station's main corridor was dimmed down for night. As he walked through the shadows to his own compartment, Alec told himself, At least I won't have to see her anymore.

It took two days.

Two days of checking out the weapons, the communications gear, the food and clothing they would need. Two days of carefully observing the weather patterns across North America and predicting that the Oak Ridge area would be dry and clear. Two days of frenetic calls back and forth from the satellite station to the lunar settlement. Men who thought they had three weeks suddenly telescoping their homeward conversations into forty-eight hours. Questions from the Council. Technical data from the settlement's main computers to the station's.

Two days of innoculations and medical checks. Alec put off his final medical exam until the last possible moment. Lenore was all business with him, impersonal, clinical. Except as he got up to leave, she said calmly, "Good luck, Alec."

He mumbled a thank you and hurried out of the infirmary.

They filed into the two shuttles, fifty men and four pilots glide-walking through the narrow access tunnels that connected the station's hub to the waiting shuttles' hatches. The pilots went in first, in their usual blue coveralls. Then came the troops, looking weirdly out of place in olive drab uniforms and metal helmets, with bulky packs on their backs and slung weapons poking awkwardly. They shuffled uncertainly through the tunnels, hands outstretched so that their fingertips could touch the fabric-covered walls for balance.

Alec hovered at the station's main hatch and watched his men as they passed him, silent and grim-faced. The only sound was the occasional clink of metal or plastic, the shuffling of booted feet. When the last of them had disappeared into the tunnel, Alec pushed himself in, made his way through and stepped into the shuttle.

Two dozen men were strapping themselves into their seats. Packs and weapons were unslung and stowed in the special compartments overhead. Alec stood at the hatch for a moment. He had inspected the shuttles a dozen times over the previous weeks, but this was the first time he'd seen one occupied since they had arrived at the satellite station. The usual odors of lubricants and plastic and ozone were overwhelmed now by the smell of human sweat and gun oil. As he made his way up to the empty double seat at the front of the passenger compartment, Alec realized with a pang just how old the shuttles were. The plastic flooring was worn thin, the metal walls so scratched that they were starting to look almost polished. The shuttles had been built long before the sky burned, and kept in repair by the lunar engineers with a tenderness that approached blind religious faith.

Our link with Earth, Alec knew. And our only link back home again.

As he stopped in the aisle beside the seat and slipped off his own bulky pack, Alec wondered if he should say anything to his men. Many of them would have preferred Kobol's leadership to his own, he knew. Many of them resented, even questioned, his speed-up of the mission schedule.

"With any luck at all," he said, loudly enough to make them jerk with surprise, halt their whispered conversations, and look up at him.

"With any luck at all," Alec repeated, "we'll all be back aboard this bucket in thirty-six hours or less. That's why I speeded up the schedule . . . so we could *all* make it back, quick and safe."

They grinned, they nodded. They returned to their buzzing conversations, but it was brighter now, looser. Alec sat down and strapped in.

"Separation in five minutes," said the pilot's voice over the intercom. "Ignition in seven minutes."

Despite himself, Alec tensed. And if we do get in and out so quickly, what chance do I have of finding my father? But somewhere deep in his guts Alec knew that he and his father were going to meet down there on the surface of Earth. One way or another, they would meet. And one of them would die.

The separation and ignition were so gentle that if the pilot had not told them about it on the intercom Alec would have questioned their occurrence. There were no windows in the passenger compartment, and he felt only the slightest pressure and vibration of the retrorocket firing.

"We're on our way, on trajectory, and all systems are on the mark," the pilot reported happily.

Alec unstrapped and stood up gingerly. With one hand on the grip set into the bulkhead in front of him, he tapped on the hatch that separated the passenger compartment from the cockpit.

The copilot opened the hatch and Alec squeezed into the cramped world of green-glowing panel lights and data displays, two stripped-down control chairs, and dials and switches that literally surrounded the two pilots, spreading in front of them, to their sides, across the console between their chairs, even overhead. Through the narrow windshield windows Alec could see the vast brilliant bulk of Earth sweeping past them.

"Everything on the mark," the copilot said cheerfully. "We'll be buttoning up for re-entry in about ten minutes."

Nodding, Alec asked, "What about Kobol's ship?"

"Just got a buzz from them; all okay."

"Can we see them?"

"Not visually." The copilot pointed to a circular screen in the panel between the seats. A luminous yellow arm swept around it; a single fat dot hovered in the lower right quadrant. Other dots, smaller and fainter, stood out toward the edge of the screen.

"That's them, right behind us," the copilot said. "The other blips are the station and smaller satellites passing this area."

"I see."

"Sorry we don't have room for you up here," the pilot said, without taking his eyes off his instruments.

Alec got the hint. Commander or not, the pilot was in charge here and Alec was in his way. Grinning, he answered, "I'll be too busy to say thanks once we land, so I'll say it now. Good flight!"

"Thank *you*," the copilot replied, with a big smile.

Sitting back in his seat in the passenger section, Alec repeated to himself: Speed. Speed and surprise. If there is an enemy out there, don't give him time to think. Don't give yourself time to have second thoughts.

But he had his doubts, just the same. What if I freeze up? What if I get to the hatch and I can't step through?

He glanced at Jameson, sitting across the aisle, so relaxed that he seemed almost to be sleeping. Abruptly, Alec pushed himself out of the seat and unlatched the overhead bin. Guiding his weightless equipment before him he glided down the aisle to the seat nearest the hatch.

"Would you please take the first seat, up forward?" he asked the startled youngster sitting on the aisle seat. "Take your gear with you."

Clearly puzzled, the young man did as he was told. Alec stowed his own gear and strapped in next to an equally-surprised-looking kid. He said nothing.

"Re-entry commencing in one minute. Strap down tight," said the intercom voice.

It got rough enough to drive other fears from his mind. Alec *felt* the shuttle biting into Earth's heavy, turbulent atmosphere; felt the *g* forces that made the straps cut into his suddenly-heavy body. His hands were too massive to lift off the armrests. His neck and shoulder muscles cramped under the strain of holding his head up. His palms started to sweat. It began to feel stiflingly hot inside the shuttle.

Nonsense! Alec told himself. It's your imagination. But every man there knew that the outer skin of the shuttle was bathed in fiery air, heated to incandescence by the speed of their re-entry.

Makes a perfect radar target, he thought. Do they have radars working?

The shuttle lurched, staggered. Alec felt himself driven deeply into his seat, then suddenly dropping, his stomach nearly heaving.

"Sorry," the copilot's voice came over the intercom, no longer cheerful. "Kinda bumpy out there. We're through re-entry and flying in the lower portion of the atmosphere. Not too smooth, but nothing to worry about."

Swaying, bouncing, shuddering, they sat in suffering, frightened silence for an eternity of about five minutes.

"There's the airfield! Touchdown in two-three more minutes. Might be rough."

With a terrifying roar the landing wheel hatches opened beneath them. Despite their training, most of the men were clearly startled.

"Get ready for the landing," Alec shouted over the din of the rushing wind. "As soon as the pilot gives the word we pop the hatch and start moving."

The impact of hitting the ground was unmistakable. The shuttle bounced once, hit again, then rolled onward with a wild screeching of brakes and roar of retrorockets. Alec leaned against his shoulder straps, felt his head pushing forward.

Then abruptly the noise and motion ceased.

"Okay. We're down," the pilot reported tersely.

Behind him, Alec heard the main hatch crack open. He took one fast breath, then grabbed at his harness buckle. Standing up and reaching for his helmet, pack, and machine pistol, he commanded the others, "All right—let's *move!*"

The man from the other side of the aisle swung the hatch open. Alec gestured him back as he hefted his light gun over his shoulder.

"The steps are jammed," the man grumbled.

Alec nodded once, then without even thinking about it he jumped from the lip of the hatch. He barely had time to realize how fast he was falling when he hit the ground with a solid thump that buckled his knees. He put his hands out to brace himself and managed to keep from toppling over.

Unslinging his gun, he stepped away from the shuttle quickly. The other men were jumping behind him with a steady succession of *thumps* and *oofs.*

"All right, you know your positions," he waved his free arm at them. "Spread out and form a perimeter."

They hustled outward, a few limping noticeably. The steps finally creaked out of their slot below the hatch and dropped into place. The final ten men scrambled down them and got to work on the equipment bay hatches. Jameson was the last man out, looking as unruffled as if he were coming out of chapel after attending a friend's wedding. Except that his heavy automatic rifle was resting on his right hip, muzzle pointed outward, ready to fire.

Alec strode to the nose of the shuttle to watch the other men swing open the cargo hatches. Abstractedly, he noticed that the ship's nose and underside were charred slightly and streaked from its burning journey through the atmosphere.

And then it hit him. I'm on Earth! I'm standing, moving, breathing on Earth!

He spun around. The sky was gray, not blue, and the Sun was hidden behind the clouds. It was nowhere as bright as Alec had expected, so he kept his glare visor up inside his helmet. It wasn't even particularly hot, about the same temperature as the living quarters at the settlement. But there was something else, something strange: air moving across his body, like standing in front of one of the circulation fans. Except that this was gentler, softer, and nowhere near as steady. It stopped and started again, playfully.

The shuttle had landed not on the cracked concrete runway, Alec saw, but on the green grass alongside the runway. The concrete was broken and pocked with holes while the grass was reasonably flat, though bumpy. The shuttle's many-wheeled bogeys looked undamaged; they could get out again.

The whole area around the airport was open and unobstructed. The land seemed to go on forever; the horizon was much further away than it should be. Off in the distance were dark undulating hills, farther away than Alec had ever seen any landscape features before.

"Alec."

It was Jameson, who had come up beside him.

"Perimeter's established, and the heavy stuff's

been rolled out of the cargo bay."

"Good." Alec glanced at his wristwatch; five minutes since touchdown. "Very good. Get the laser trucks up along the perimeter. A couple dozen men can't keep this field secure with nothing but hand weapons."

Jameson grinned tightly. "Sound observation." He turned and started shouting orders.

A shriek split the sky and Alec looked up to see the second shuttle coming in, trailing a plume of vapor behind it. It circled the field once, then came down on the opposite side of the broken runway, screeching and roaring, blowing out tongues of bluish gas from its retrorockets, tossing clumps of sod and chunks of rock and concrete before it.

Alec hurried to the shuttle as soon as it ground to a halt. Before he could reach it, the ladder came down and men were pouring out to take their assigned positions. Last to emerge was the lanky figure of Martin Kobol, his limp much worse in Earth's heavy gravity.

"Welcome to Earth," Alec called to him.

A burst of machine gun fire punctuated his greeting.

CHAPTER 13

Ferret was checking his traps when the sky seemed to crack open with a terrifying screaming sound. He dropped the dead rabbit he had been holding and instinctively dived into the bushes. Too frightened even to open his eyes, he clawed as deeply as he could into the brush and then froze. He held his breath and tried to stop trembling.

Minutes later, the same roaring, screaming sky shook the world. Birds went silent. The whole forest froze with fright. Ferret pushed his face deeper into the damp earth and tried to become totally blank, nonexistent, so that whatever monster was shaking the woods would not find him.

He stayed there for a long, long time. Or so it seemed to him. Gradually the woods returned to normal. Birds took up their songs again. The breeze made the leafy trees sigh. Something slithered past his bare leg. Slowly, very cautiously, Ferret looked up. He saw nothing unusual, nothing to be afraid of. The monster had apparently gone away.

Still, it might not be far off. On his belly, Ferret slithered through the brush toward the edge of the woods, where the old cement buildings and long empty cement paths lay. If a giant monster was thrashing around through the woods, maybe he could spot the thing from there.

He risked getting up on all fours and scampering the few yards from where he was safely hidden by the brush to the bole of a large tree at the edge of the clearing. When he finally worked up the courage to peer out from behind the tree, he was startled by what he saw. Two weird silvery things, huge, shaped something like bullets, were sitting out on the cement runways that had been empty earlier that morning. They didn't look like monsters.

Then his eyes went even wider. There were men standing around the silver things! Men just like himself. They were dressed better and they had strange metal pots on their heads, but they were men, sure enough. And they carried guns. And there were wagons, too, that the men climbed onto and drove around on fat, soft-looking wheels.

An invading band of raiders here in our territory, Ferret thought. Billy-Joe's got to be told about this. But he'll want to know *how many* men, and what kind of weapons they have.

Every fiber of Ferret's wiry little body wanted to get up and run deep into the woods, away from these fearsome strangers. But he could see the expression on Billy-Joe's face when he reported incompletely. And when Billy-Joe started heating his knife over the camp fire, all other fears fled from Ferret's mind, even though he had never felt that punishment himself.

Swallowing so hard he nearly choked, Ferret sneaked out from behind the protective tree, crawling slowly, ever so carefully, toward the shelter of one of the big cement buildings, closer to the invaders. It seemed like hours, but the shadows thrown by the Sun had hardly moved at all by the time he reached the corner of the nearest building.

Members of the invading band were spreading out, forming a screen around their strange silvery things. The wagons were trundling here and there. They had incomprehensibly weird contraptions atop them. The men on foot carried guns, heavy, big-bore, long-barrelled guns. Ferret ached to have one for himself. Maybe Billy-Joe would let him take one as a reward for ambushing these strangers.

Ferret licked his lips and remembered that the only weapon he carried was a hunting knife—with a loose, wobbly handle, at that. He had seen enough. Time to get back and make his report.

As he turned and started creeping away from the building, a burst of gunfire crackled behind him. Concrete chips flew off the corner of the building and Ferret flattened himself against the grassy ground.

Kobol looked just as startled as Alec felt. All the men seemed to freeze in place.

"What was that?" Kobol asked, unconsciously taking a step back toward the shuttle.

Alec swung the microphone down from his helmet. "This is Morgan. Who fired and why?"

In his earphone he heard a tinny reply. "Kurowski. I saw something moving beside the buildings here on the west flank."

"A man? Did you hit him?"

"I don't know. It was something—I can't see it now."

Kobol had one hand up on his helmet, listening to the radio report. "It could have been an animal," he told Alec. "There are all sorts just wandering around loose, you know."

Alec grimaced. "Kurowski, what's your position?"

"As assigned. A hundred meters from the shuttle, on the west flank. Not much cover here, I'm on my belly in some sort of cement-lined rille."

"That's a culvert," Kobol said. "For carrying rainwater."

"All right," Alec commanded. "Hold your position. The others will be out there in a few minutes with heavier equipment. If you see anything else, don't fire unless it looks hostile. Conserve ammunition. But call me immediately."

"Yessir."

"I want those buildings searched," Alec told Kobol.

"It'd take every man we have to search them."

"We can spare half the heavy weapons men, once we have the trucks spotted around the perimeter."

"That's only six men."

"That's all we can spare. I'll lead the search as soon as the weapons are set up on the perimeter."

Alec headed off toward Kurowski's position, leaving Kobol to supervise the weapons set-up. He could see the buildings, gray and low, with holes in them for windows. A tower surmounted the central building, but its top was broken and charred. Someone could hide a hundred men in there. And a thousand more in those hills, he thought.

Kurowski was lying in the culvert, white-knuckled hands gripping his gun. Alec crawled down beside him.

"See anything else?"

"I'm not sure. Something was moving out there for a while. But it was heading away from us, and it didn't walk like a man."

Nodding, Alec said, "All right. We're going to get a search party together. Let's both watch the area until then."

It was actually pleasant. Lying there wasn't too uncomfortable, and Alec started to get a feel of this huge world called Earth. The breeze made noises, strange sighings and whisperings. Memories of old poems from his childhood school days started to make sense to him for the first time. And there were other sounds too. Alec had been told what bird songs and insect buzzings sounded like, but he had never heard them before.

"Look at that!"

Kurowski pointed six centimeters in front of his nose. In the stubby grass an insect was scurrying busily.

"I think that's what you call an ant," Alec said. "Or maybe a bee."

"Bees can fly, can't they?"

"Only the queens."

The heavy weapons carriers finally trundled into position. They were six balloon-tired armored trucks, driven by smooth-humming electric engines, mounting high-powered lasers. Some of the men hustled up on foot, laden with heavy rocket launchers and machine guns. They began clicking the sections of their weapons together, quickly surrounding themselves with a bristling arsenal of gunbelts and finned rockets.

Alec led six men on a cursory, fruitless search through the gutted buildings. They found nothing but burned-out walls, crumbling floors, shattered roofs. And a few startled raccoons and other small animals that had claimed parts of the abandoned buildings for themselves. One of the troopers fired a burst from his automatic rifle at a brown furry something that simply blew apart when the bullets hit it.

"Glad it wasn't a skunk," muttered Beardon, who had made a special study of troublesome Earth animals as part of his preparation for the mission.

By mid-afternoon Alec gave the word to extend their perimeter. Most of the rocket launchers and heavy machine guns were repositioned on the roofs of the buildings, together with infrared sensors for night vision. One laser truck was parked in front of the central building. The others prowled the farther limits of the airfield, while troopers patrolled on foot alongside them, cradling their automatic rifles in their arms.

Back inside the first shuttle, Alec reviewed the situation with Kobol. The older man sat heavily in a padded seat, looking tired and wary. Alec leaned against the chair's armrest.

"We've got to assume we've been spotted,"

Kobol said.

"Right. It's the safe assumption to make," Alec agreed, thinking to himself, I never realized the shuttles made so much noise! The entire countryside must know we're here.

"The shuttles would have been a lot easier to hide if we had landed in one of the valleys nearby," Kobol went on.

With a shake of his head, Alec countered, "They're safe enough here. None of the barbarians has weapons that can reach us from the edge of the airfield."

"Really?"

"And there's still no report from the satellite of a large number of barbarians moving our way. So we're safe from a mass attack. For a day or two, at least."

Kobol looked skeptical, but said nothing.

"All right," Alec said. "We move out tonight. I . . ."

"Tonight? In darkness?"

"Right. We have infrared sensors. The barbarians don't. We can move in darkness. They can't and they won't expect us to. I want a dozen men and one of the laser trucks. We have aerial maps of the region, the road between here and the Oak Ridge complex is clearly marked. We can be there before dawn and surprise any possible defenders."

Kobol shook his head. "The men won't want to move at night. And those who're left here will be scared even worse, knowing that one-quarter of their strength is off in the dark."

"Martin, I'm not in here to engage in debates," Alec snapped, getting to his feet. "The men will follow my orders. By this time tomorrow we'll be on our way back home."

Shrugging, Kobol acquiesced. "You're in charge. I presume you'll want to lead the trek to Oak Ridge yourself."

"That's right. And I'll want you along too."

Kobol's shaggy eyebrows rose a centimeter. "You don't want to leave me here with the shuttles?"

"Jameson can hold the airfield," Alec said, almost smiling at him. "I want you with me—to identify the fissionables."

"Oh. I see." Getting up slowly from his seat, Kobol said, "You know, if you're not careful out in the dark, you could get shot by one of your own men."

"You're right," Alec replied, keeping his voice even. "I've already thought about that. If it happens to me, though, there's a chance that the same thing could happen to someone else. A better than fair chance, in fact."

Kobol broke into a toothy grin. "That's about what I would expect."

"As long as we understand each other," Alec said, unsmiling.

The night was different.

It wasn't merely a turning down of the lights. It was *dark*. And alive.

Alec rode perched on the front fender of the laser truck, which trundled along quietly carrying the dozen men, including Kobol and himself. The driver, burrowed in the armored cockpit between the fenders, was groping along the winding road using the infrared lights and sensors. Up here in the open night air, all the ancient tales of ghosts and werewolves seemed only too real.

It's absolute nonsense, Alec told himself.

But still, there were things out there in the dark. Things that croaked and groaned, things that sighed, sudden cries and strange ghostly hootings.

"Bet that's what they call an owl," said a voice behind Alec.

The clouds had started to lift just before sundown, giving Alec and his men the most heart-catching sight they had ever seen: an earthly sunset, vibrant with reds and flame-orange that slowly paled to blue, then softest violet, and finally to star-strewn darkness.

The sky was clear now, and except for their disturbing twinkling, the stars seemed very normal. Where the highway swung close to the trees, though, even the stars were blotted out. All that Alec could see were the twisted black branches rustling in the moaning wind, swaying across the faint brightness of the sky. He shuddered, and not merely from the growing chill.

The truck braked to a stop so suddenly that Alec almost lurched off the fender.

"What is it?" he whispered urgently into his helmet mike.

From inside the armored cockpit the driver replied, "Something moved out there."

"Something? What?"

"Don't know. It threw off enough heat to register on the scope. Big as a man. Maybe more than one."

Alec swiftly considered the alternatives. "All right. We're not going to stop. All you troopers get off the truck and walk alongside. If you see movement, tell me on the intercom. Don't fire unless fired upon. Joe, keep the truck apace with us on foot. Let me know what you see on that 'scope."

"Right."

The ride down the broken, abandoned highway slowed to a walk, a crawl. Alec hefted his machine pistol and snapped its wire stock into place, so he could rest the base against his hip. He walked a few paces out in front of the truck, well off to the right shoulder of the highway. The road was broad enough for several trucks to pass side by side. But the brush and trees came right up to the edge of the cement and even invaded the cracks in the paving. An army could hide in here, Alec knew. But he saw nothing.

"Something up ahead!" the driver's voice sounded shrilly in his earphones.

"I saw something!" a trooper agreed excitedly. "It went across the road from left to right. Fast."

Alec said, "Gunner—spray the right shoulder of the highway . . . how far up ahead, Joe?"

"About fifty meters, I'd say."

"Fifty meters, gunner."

The truck stopped. The low hum of its electric motors was replaced by the high-pitched whine of the special generator that drove the laser. In the darkness Alec could barely make out the oval metal mirror of the laser as it turned slightly in his direction, catching a glint of starlight on its polished copper surface.

Then the whine rose to a harsh crescendo and the woods some fifty meters ahead burst into sudden flame. It sounded like a dull whooshing explosion, then a roaring crackle, as the invisible laser beam poured infrared energy into the brush. In the lurid light of the flames two large animals leaped onto the highway and bounded across it and into the brush on the other side. They were four-footed, with graceful slim legs.

"Deer," someone said disgustedly.

"Deers have horns on 'em."

"Not all the time!"

"Cease firing," Alec commanded.

The flames disappeared as abruptly as they had sprung up, leaving a patch of dull red embers at the side of the road. Alec smelled an oddly pleasing odor. It made him want to cough, yet it touched a cord so deep inside him that he had never known it was there. Burning wood? Why should it smell so good?

With a shake of his head, he ordered, "All right, everybody back on the truck. If there were any people there, they've taken off by now."

Kobol climbed back up on the left front fender with a grunt, then said loudly enough for everyone to hear, "Well, there's your ambush—two scared deer."

They all laughed as the truck started up again. But Alec couldn't help thinking, He's out there. Somewhere he's out there waiting for us. And he's not alone.

He checked with Ron Jameson back at the airport twice over the next few hours. No activity there; a quiet night with no movement. The men were sleeping in relays.

Alec found that his own men were dozing off as they rode, clinging to various parts of the truck, sprawling wherever they could find enough flat surface. He took over the driving himself, after his second call to Jameson, and let the driver catch a nap on the fender. Even Kobol seemed to be drowsing, chin on chest, head bobbing gently as they drove.

In the infrared scope before him, the highway showed clearly as a band of orange stretching out ahead, crisscrossed by cracks and breaks. The foliage to either side was pink, except for a small scurrying animal here and there, which showed a bright red.

"Who's on the gun?" Alec asked softly into his helmet mike.

"Gianelli."

"You wide awake?"

"Depend on it. Got my IR goggles on—they're so damned heavy they're giving me a headache. I couldn't fall asleep if I wanted to."

"Good."

"Glad to hear you're worrying about me, chief."

Alec grinned to himself. "You just keep a sharp eye out, especially to our rear. I'm watching up front."

"Right. I've been doing that. Nothing moving except a few more deer."

"You're sure they're deer?"

Gianelli laughed softly. "Unless men bounce

across the road on all fours."

"All right."

Alec was still driving when they topped a rise and the heat-radiating buildings of the Oak Ridge complex came into view on his scope. Almost automatically he slowed the truck to a gradual, gentle stop. Then he glanced at his wristwatch. The Sun will be up in another hour and a half.

For a moment he debated waking the sleeping men. Instead, he fished in the pouch at his belt for a stimulant capsule and swallowed it dry, with a hard gulp. Then he swung the overhead cockpit hatch open.

Climbing out into the breeze-murmuring night, he stood on the top deck of the truck and stretched his cramped arms and legs. Sleeping bodies sprawled everywhere, barely visible in the darkness. Another weird hooting sound floated out from the woods, sending a shiver along Alec's spine.

Stepping over one of the dozing men, he reached the laser gun mount. "Gianelli?" he whispered.

"Yeah."

"Take a nap. I'll stand watch."

Gianelli did not argue. Alec climbed into the gunner's jumpseat and silently took the infrared goggles from his hand. The laser was humming softly, set on wide-beam scan, acting as a searchlight instead of a weapon.

The goggles *were* heavy. Alec had to make a conscious effort to keep his head erect as he slowly swung the gun mount around in a complete circle. The faint whine of the drive motors sounded almost comforting against the strange night noises from beyond the truck.

The trees appeared ghostly white in the goggles, the concrete buildings of the complex down in the valley below were a hotter shade of orange. The buildings were set out in an open area, with the closest trees many meters away. The land around the buildings looked dark, lifeless. Maybe some grass, but not much else.

As Alec swung the laser around slowly, scanning in a complete circle around the truck, he began to get the uncanny feeling that someone was watching him. At first it was nothing more than a vague uneasiness. But gradually the feeling grew, became a prickling along his spine, a cold fear pressing into the back of his neck.

Maybe I should wake a few of the men, he thought. Then he answered himself, No! You're just nervous. Scared to be out here alone.

Clenching his teeth, he continued to turn the gun mount slowly, feeling colder every minute. Straight ahead was the road and down on the valley floor, the buildings. Turn and the trees came up, closer, closer, mysterious white branches reaching out toward you, grasping, lifting themselves up into the sky. Keep turning, the road again, the trail back to the airport, the shuttles, safety. Then the trees again, and finally the buildings.

What if he's out there? Does he have IR detectors? Goggles? If he does, then we're sitting here like a beacon, a big fat bright target.

Abruptly, Alec kicked on the foot pedals to reverse the mount's rotation. The electric motors shrilled for an instant, the mount jerked, then swung in the opposite direction.

There! In the trees!

It was gone before he could be sure of what it was. Hot spots, several of them in among the trees. They vanished from his field of view just as the laser beam exposed them.

Animals, he told himself. But are animals sensitive to infrared illumination?

He glanced at his wristwatch. Still an hour before sunrise, but already the sky beyond the Oak Ridge buildings was beginning to pale. Could our sunrise times be wrong? Then, remembering the lingering beauty of the previous night's sunset, and the briefings he had received from Dr. Lord on terrestrial atmospheric effects, Alec realized that the daylight actually started before the Sun itself appeared above the horizon.

For a tense fifteen minutes he continued to scan around the truck, moving the beam back and forth randomly, trying to avoid a predictable pattern. He saw nothing. Then it was light enough to snap off the laser and remove the heavy goggles.

A couple of men stirred as the light grew brighter. Alec didn't know which made him feel better, the fact that he was no longer alone, or the end of the dark, threatening night.

They made their way toward the buildings in good order, Alec walking up front on the right point, Kobol taking the three-man rear guard position, the truck in the middle of the spread-out formation of armed, wary men.

The ground around the buildings was barren. Scrub grass straggled here and there in thin patches. Large stretches of ground immediately outside the buildings were bare, broken cement and blacktop. There were some areas of gravel, as well, Alec saw.

As they approached the buildings, Alec began to understand why Kobol had volunteered for the rear guard. He was the only man who had been here before, the only one who knew the area. Alec wanted to ask Kobol if the buildings looked the same, but to do that he would have to bring Kobol up to the point position with him. In front of the men, he would have to show that Kobol was the man who knew what's what.

Screw that! Alec paced steadily toward the lifeless, gaping buildings, gripping his machine pistol in his right hand, feeling the welcome pressure of its strap riding firmly on his shoulder.

It was a longer walk than he had anticipated.

The morning was deathly quiet. No breeze. No bird songs reached them from the distant trees. The Sun was barely over the crest of the hills, yet already it was much hotter than the previous day had been. Does the heat come from the buildings? Alec wondered. Fears about radioactivity sifted through his thoughts. But he kept marching steadily, glancing back at his men and the trundling laser truck only occasionally.

When they reached the edge of the cement walkways that surrounded the buildings he called a halt. Faint dark streaks and strains mottled the walls.

"Stop the truck here, where it can cover the whole area. Form up in front of the truck."

Kobol limped up to him, thin chest and underarms of his coveralls dark with sweat. He looked slightly foolish with the heavy helmet clamped bulbously over his head.

"What do you think?" Alec asked, gesturing toward the buildings with his pistol.

Kobol hiked his shaggy brows enough to make them disappear inside the helmet. "It's been a long time since I was here. But everything looks pretty much the same."

"That's the main entrance, isn't it?"

Kobol nodded.

"All right. Gianelli, take two men and follow us. The rest of you stay here and stay alert. Keep a sharp watch all around."

The five of them walked slowly toward the building, tension mounting with each step. Alec could see that the windows gaped emptily, they had been shattered long ago. The doors were gone too, and the walls were streaked with the sooty reminders of old fires. The interior of the building was completely in shadow.

He could feel his heart hammering as they climbed the steps to the open, dark doorway. His hand felt slippery on the gun's handle, but inside himself Alec felt cold, not hot.

The interior of the building was littered with broken shards of cement, plaster, dried leaves and debris. The room was large and bare, stripped of everything except the litter on the floor.

"Reception area," Kobol said. "Everything in here was looted or burned long ago."

A sudden fear struck Alec. "The fissionables?"

Kobol laughed bitterly. "Don't worry. They're too hard to get at, even if the barbarians knew what they were and wanted them. Which they don't. There are all sorts of legends and taboos about radioactive material. They're scared to death of the stuff."

They walked through an empty, desolate building. The rooms were huge, but blackened, charred. Most of the roofs were gone, and the still-climbing Sun lit their way through the moldering shambles. Nothing stood except a few sagging partitions. No sign that human beings had ever occupied the area. Everything caked thick with grime; here and there the tracks of small animals. Kobol pointed to some dried grass wedged into a crack high up on a cement wall.

"Bird's nest," he said.

"Creepy," said Gianelli in a low, awed voice.

"The barbarians took everything they could from this building," Kobol explained needlessly, "and burned the rest."

They reached a metal door that opened onto a long tunnel ribbed with I-beams.

"This is the connector tunnel between the main administrative building, here, and one of the processing plants. That's where they produced the fissionables from low-grade natural ores." Kobol's lecturing voice twanged irritatingly off the metal walls of the tunnel as they walked through it. "You'll see plenty of heavy equipment in the next building, and beyond that are the storage vaults."

They opened the door at the end of the tunnel.

The room was huge, vaster than any enclosure Alec had ever seen. Sunlight filtered down slantingly through the shattered roof. It was eerie and still.

And empty.

The giant processing building had been looted even more thoroughly than the administration area. Nothing remained except the bare walls and a few dust motes drifting through the shafts of sunlight.

Kobol's jaw fell open.

"There's nothing here!" Alec said.

"It's been cleaned out." Kobol's voice was strained, shocked.

"The fissionables!"

They ran, the five of them. Kobol in the lead, they raced across the huge empty room, boots clumping dully on the cement floor. To Alec it was like a nightmare, running endlessly across the barren, torn-up expanse, this giant cement box they were trapped in. He ran as hard as he could but seemed to be getting no closer to the far end of the one-room building and the metal door that they had to reach. Almost subliminaly, Alec noticed that the floor was studded with metal fixtures where equipment had once been bolted down to the solid cement. The fixtures looked bright and clean; the equipment had been removed only recently.

They dashed, gasping, up to the heavy metal door. It was slightly ajar.

"The vaults . . ." Kobol puffed, wide-eyed, as he strained to swing the door open. Alec and Gianelli leaned into it, helping him.

The room on the other side was small, barely big enough to allow the five of them to squeeze in. It was lined with dull gray metal. Three walls were filled with box-sized compartments, like metal bookshelves, but with many thick separations along each shelf.

"Empty!"

Kobol was panting hard, his face white. "No . . . barbarians . . . did this."

Alec turned to face him.

"Only one man . . . knew what . . . the fissionables were worth," Kobol said. "Your father."

CHAPTER 14

Alec forced himself to breathe deeply several times before answering.

"You think he deliberately cleared out this place?"

Kobol's eyes were glaring. "Who else? Barbarians couldn't organize the men and machines you'd need for this. They wouldn't even know what all this was. They're scared as hell of this place."

Gianelli kicked at the wall. "Chrissake! We came all this way for nothing."

"Your father," Kobol made it sound as if he were accusing Alec, "knew we need the fissionables. So he's taken them away. He's trying to kill the whole settlement."

Alec asked levelly, "How long can we go on what's left in the settlement?"

"A year. Maybe eighteen months. What difference does it make?"

"By that time we'll have the fissionables. If I have to tear this planet apart, I'll find them."

Kobol didn't reply. He merely made a derisive, snorting sound.

They trudged slowly back out of the vaults and through the empty processing building, heading for the entrance they had come through. The tired march of defeated men, Alec said to himself. But somehow he did not feel defeated. He was excited, almost happy. Father's forcing me to seek him out. His first mistake.

They were halfway through the connector tunnel when Alec's earphone crackled: "There's somebody . . . toward us . . ." The radio voice was weak and masked by heavy sizzling interference.

"What?"

". . . lone person . . . walk . . . us here on the truck . . ."

Alec hurried through the tunnel and got out of the metal-walled area in time to hear, "Hey, it's a girl!"

They quickened their pace. Once outside, Alec could see a lone, slim figure heading for the truck, walking slowly but deliberately from the distant woods toward them. By the time he and his men reached the truck, she was almost in hailing distance.

"She's unarmed," Kobol observed.

"And good to look at," said Gianelli.

Small and slim, wearing a stained white blouse and long slacks that fitted the curve of her hips snugly. Longish, serious, big-eyed face. Long blonde hair wisping in the breeze. She shrugged it back away from her face as she came up to the truck.

Alec said, "Looks like she's got a definite reason for coming here."

"Maybe she's lonesome," Gianelli snickered.

"Not for you, big nose," one of the other men said.

"Can't see anyone else around," Kobol said, scanning the woods with binoculars. "But there could be an army out there among those trees."

Like Hannibal's army at Lake Trasimene, Alec thought.

He watched the girl as she calmly approached them. A stubborn face, frowning slightly in the sun. Strong jaw, prominent cheekbones, thin patrician nose. Mouth set in a determined line. But the eyes were searching, a bit uncertain, perhaps a bit frightened.

He could feel the tension among the men as she walked closer. Ridiculous! A dozen men armed to the teeth, staring nervously at a lone unarmed girl. The firing bolt of a rifle snicked mechanically.

Scared to death of one girl! Alec almost smiled.

"Gianelli," he said softly, "keep an eye on the buildings. She might be a decoy."

"Watch the flanks, too," Kobol said to no one in particular.

"I'd rather watch her flanks," Gianelli muttered.

The girl raised her right hand, palm open, and stopped some twenty paces from the truck. Alec walked out toward her. He knew without looking over his shoulder that Kobol was right behind him.

"My name is Angela," she said. No smile. Her voice was unemotional, matter-of-fact.

"I'm Alec, and this is . . ."

"Alexander Morgan and Martin Kobol," she said.

"You know my father." Alec wasn't surprised.

"He sent me here. To warn you."

For an instant Alec felt as if the entire world hung suspended in time. He could feel the sun on his shoulders and neck, see the bright sky and the new green woods in the distance, hear the girl's soft, wary voice. But it was all as if he were really somewhere else, far more distant than the Moon, watching the scene remotely.

"We're not frightened by warnings," Kobol said.

"Wait," Alec snapped. To the girl, "Warn us about what?"

She pushed a strand of hair from her face. "There's a raider band heading for the airport. They saw your ships land . . ."

"Why would they head for us? Aren't they frightened . . .?"

A smile toyed at Angela's lips. "Scared of a few dozen men? You know how many men the raiders can put together?"

"We have enough firepower . . ."

"I know," she interrupted. "They know, too. It's your weapons they're after."

Kobol stepped up to her. "You're lying. We would have detected a large group of men moving through this territory. We have sensors . . ."

"No shit?" She turned back to Alec. "Look, your father told me all about the platform you've got up in the sky. They can't see the raiders—not down under the trees. There's at least a couple hundred of them linking up together a few klicks from the airport. We're trying to keep them off balance . . ."

"It's a trick," Kobol insisted.

She scowled at him.

"Where is my father?" Alec asked her.

Angela waved a hand. "Up north . . . seven, eight hundred klicks from here."

"And the fissionables?"

"The what?"

So he hasn't told her everything. "The machines and things that were in these buildings. My father has them up north with him?"

She shrugged. "I don't know. These buildings have been empty for years."

I'll bet. "Come on," Alec said to Kobol, "we've got to get back to the airport. If there really are several hundred . . ."

"There can't be," Kobol said.

"I don't like being called a liar," Angela snapped. "Especially by a fughead who doesn't know a tree from a turd."

Alec bit his lip to keep from laughing. Kobol staggered a step backward; a lanky, helmeted, booted, armed man retreating from this tiny girl.

"Come on," Alec said, forcing his voice to remain serious. "We can't afford to ignore her warning. And there's nothing left here for us. Let's move out." He reached for Angela's wrist. "You can come with us."

She pulled back slightly. "I can make it on my own."

Holding onto her wrist, Alec said, "We've got the truck here. It's faster than walking."

She stopped arguing.

Once they piled aboard the truck and got rolling, Alec radioed Jameson. "Everything's peaceful here," his calm voice replied. No sign of movement except for a few birds."

"Check with the satellite," Alec ordered. "Have them make the most intensive scan of this area that they can."

"They're halfway on the other side of the globe now," Jameson answered. "Won't be back over here for another four hours."

"Damn," Alec muttered. "Well, keep a sharp watch. Protect those ships."

"You betcha," Jameson said.

Ferret quivered with a mixture of excitement and fear as they crouched in the brush, watching the strange ships sitting on the airfield runway and the handful of men guarding them.

"Now remember," Billy-Joe whispered, fingering the scar across his chin the way he always did just before a fight started, "once we knock off all them guys, we got to grab their weapons *fast*. There's a dozen other gangs spread around this-here airport and they're all lickin' their chops over them fancy guns."

Ferret nodded and bared his teeth in what passed for a smile. But inwardly he was sick with fear. It was one thing to overrun the men standing around those weird flying machines. But the real battle would be among the rival gangs once the strangers had been wiped out.

Grab a gun as quick as you can, he told himself, and then hide in the woods. Stay hidden until Billy-Joe gives the word to get back to camp.

The first sounds of battle came to Alec's ears while they were still several kilometers from the airfield.

"What's that?"

It was an odd, muffled sound coming from beyond the ridge ahead of them. Soft thumps, almost like an airlock hatch slamming in a distant corridor.

Alec was sitting up on the laser mount, his legs dangling over the edge of the turntable platform. Angela sat beside him.

She tensed at the sound. "Mortars. Will must've made contact . . ."

Alec yelled down at the driver, "Top speed! Get this truck back to the ships!"

The electric motors whined and strained, but the overloaded vehicle did not seem to move any faster as it labored up the grade to the crest of the ridge.

Angela said over the rushing wind and another trio of distant explosions, "Will Russo . . . he's one of your father's friends. He's got a small group of us here, trying to tie up the raiders long enough to give you a chance to take off."

"William Russo," Kobol snapped. He'd been squatting cross-legged behind them. "So he didn't die after all; he turned traitor along with Doug."

Alec twisted around and squinted up into the noon sun to see Kobol. "We ought to put out flankers," he said. "These woods could be swarming with barbarians."

"No, not on this side of the airfield," Angela said.

It was a tense ride. The truck was agonizingly slow, and it seemed to take forever to get through the spots where the tangled trees and undergrowth crowded up to the very edge of the highway. The men kept their weapons in their grips, straining their eyes on the foliage. Alec saw that they were sweating despite the cool shadows of the trees and the wind blowing against them.

He kept watching Angela. She seemed concerned, but not frightened. She's not expecting trouble here, he reasoned, so neither should we.

But his palms still felt cold and slippery.

Kobol stayed in constant touch with the ships by radio. Alec had taken his helmet off and hung it by its chin strap on the platform railing.

"Do you know my father well?" he asked Angela.

She nodded. "He's my father, too."

Alec felt as if she had kicked him in the stomach. There was no air left in his lungs. He could not speak.

"Stepfather," she added, oblivious to his plight. "He and my mother, before she died . . ." Her voice trailed off and she looked away, into the distance.

With a struggle, Alec sucked air into his lungs. He realized that his teeth were clenched together so hard the pain shot to the top of his head.

Angela turned back to face him. "He loved my mother very much," she said. "It wasn't just a man taking a woman. They were like man and wife. And he's taken good care of me ever since I was a little girl."

Alec said nothing. The knot inside him tightened with every heartbeat.

"You really live on the Moon?" she asked.

"Yes." His voice sounded like a dying croak, even to himself.

"Did I say something wrong?"

"No. Nothing." He shook his head. "I . . . it's just that . . . I didn't expect to meet a stepsister. My mother will be very interested."

"Oh. Yeah, I guess so. I see."

"Do you?"

"Yes, I do." Her chin went up a notch.

Alec shook his head. "I think not."

"There's the airfield," Gianelli's voice rang out. "Hot damn, those ships look *beautiful!*"

Alec scrambled to his feet just as an explosion erupted in the trees on the far side of the airfield, billowing black, flame-streaked smoke into the sky. The thundering roar reached his ears a split-second later. It felt almost like a physical blow.

"They're getting closer," Angela said. For the first time her voice sounded tinged with fear. "Will won't be able to hold them back much longer."

The truck was plummeting down the highway now, descending from the ridge crest and racing full tilt for the ships. They were still parked together, gleaming silvery in the glaring sunlight, looking strangely out of place in this land of soft greens and gray-brown concrete.

The other laser trucks were gathered in a semicircle on the far side of the shuttles. But as far as Alec could see, no weapons were being fired.

Alec turned to follow a trooper's outstretched arm and saw three men who had just emerged from the woods off to the right side of the ships. Even without binoculars he could make out the angular shapes of guns slung over their shoulders.

They stopped and waved their arms over their heads.

"Wait!" Angela yelled as the men on the truck swung their weapons toward the trio. "That's Will! Don't shoot!"

Before anyone could stop her she jumped off the truck and ran toward the three men.

"Hold your fire," Alec snapped. He pushed up to the driver's cab and rapped on its roof. "Get over there, where those men are." Turning to the troopers, he commanded, "All of you except Kobol, off the truck and get to the ships. Now!"

Their faces showed they didn't like what was going on, especially trotting a kilometer or two in the open, with those dark woods nearby. But they obeyed Alec's order.

The truck pulled up alongside Angela. She stopped running and the three men walked easily toward her. They wore nondescript, ragtag clothes: cut-off shorts, ancient gray shirts, one wore a vest, only one had boots. But their weapons were clean and each of them was laden with bulging cases of ammunition slung on straps across their shoulders.

Alec clambered down from the truck to meet them. Kobol stayed up on the laser mount, with the heavy copper mirror of the weapon pointing its shining face at Alec's back. He could fry us all in half a second, Alec knew.

Angela was smiling like a child. She reached for Alec's arm, as if to drag him an extra step or two toward the advancing men.

One of them had already stepped ahead of the other two. Angela said, "Alec, this is Will Russo . . . Will, Alec Morgan."

"Oh-ho! So you're Doug's boy!"

There had never been a dog or a puppy in the lunar settlement. Alec had seen tapes of children's shows, though, years before. Suddenly the image of a huge, friendly St. Bernard puppy flashed into his mind: he remembered how it had overpowered everyone else in the story with well-meaning enthusiasm that knocked down grown men and destroyed furniture. Will Russo was a big, shambling, grinning, happy St. Bernard pup. Like many truly big men, he was slightly stooped at the shoulders, from leaning over to deal with men smaller than himself. His face was round, with slightly protruding eyes, ruddy cheeks, reddish curly hair that was matted down with perspiration, an easy soft chuckling grin.

"It's a pleasure to meet you," he said. His voice was the velvet tenor of a balladeer. But he grabbed Alec's hand in a massive paw and pumped it heartily. "Sorry we have to be so brief, but there's a lot more of *them* than there are of *us*. We can hold them off for you for maybe another half-hour . . ."

Another explosion punctuated his words.

"The woods are swarming with them. Those

weapons of yours are really a prize they want."

"Casualties?" Angela asked.

Russo frowned. "Some. It's been mostly hit and run until just now. Just starting to get serious."

Another explosion. Closer. Alec's ears rang.

"Wait a minute," Alec said to Russo. "I've got to know a lot more about what's going on here . . ."

"Good Lord, this is no time for explanations. You've only got . . ."

Alec planted his fists on his hips. "I'm not budging until I find out . . ."

A high, sighing noise like the rushing of air through a punctured bulkhead.

"Incoming!" one of the men yelled.

Russo dove into Alec, knocking him down. Before Alec could say or do anything a series of explosions blasted the universe into flame and unbearable noise and shock. The ground heaved beneath him. Clods of earth pattered down. Alec could *taste* acrid smoke.

He was on his belly, face down in the damp grass. Head buzzing, he slowly looked up. Angela was on her knees, a trickle of blood wending a thin red line down her arm. Russo was squatting on his heels alongside her.

"Looks like you're right," he said, without the slightest sign of fear or anger. "You're not leaving."

He pointed, and Alec saw that one of the shuttles was in flames.

CHAPTER 15

It had turned into a bloody mess. Ferret scrambled up the steep side of the ridge, trying to get away from the screams of the dying.

Billy-Joe was down there, along with most of the rest of the band, blown into bleeding twisted blobs of blackened flesh by the explosions. Ferret himself was almost untouched; just a few scratches here and there, and a long painful gash down his left leg.

Something had gone very wrong. Instead of the usual rush, where all the gangs attacked the strangers, fighting had broken out among the gangs themselves. First. Right at the beginning. It had never happened that way before. He didn't understand it.

Now Billy-Joe and the others were all dead. Somebody had blown them into little pieces. The noise of the explosions still rang in Ferret's ears.

But he was still alive. That was the important thing. Still alive. Bleeding, but still alive. He could stand the pain. That didn't matter. The thing he had to do was to get away. Hide as far away from the fighting as he could. If one of the other gangs found him alone, they'd spend the whole night making him die. Slow. Not like Billy-Joe. Not like the others.

Choking, his eyes blurred with tears, the ringing blast of the explosions still echoing inside his head, his bleeding leg going numb, Ferret clawed at the foliage along the steep slope of the ridge, dragging himself away from the fighting, anyplace, anyplace except where the others could find him alone and helpless.

He reached the top of the ridge, gasping and too weak to move further. He rolled over onto his back, panting and blinking into the bright blue sky.

"Well lookey what we got here," a voice said from somewhere behind him.

"Looks like dead meat t' me," another voice said.

"Not yet. But he will be. He will be."

Ferret closed his eyes and waited for the agony to begin.

Alec stared at the burning shuttle. A huge gash was torn in its side and flames flickered in the dark smoke that was pouring out of it.

"We've got to silence that mortar," Will Russo said urgently, "or the other shuttle will get it, too."

Alec leaped to his feet and sprinted for the truck. Kobol was already screaming into his helmet microphone, "Get the shuttle the hell out of that area! When the fire gets to the propellant tanks it'll blow both of them sky-high!"

Scrambling up onto the laser mount, Alec motioned Kobol to silence. He grabbed his helmet and jammed it on his head, speaking into the mike. "This is Alec Morgan. Get every possible man into the undamaged shuttle and take off at once. Do you understand me? *At once!*"

Kobol argued, "One shuttle can only hold . . ."

Alec brandished a fist under his nose, and Kobol lapsed into silence. "Acknowledge that order!" he snapped. "Who's in charge down there?"

His earphone hummed meaninglessly for a moment. Then, "This is Jameson. One shuttle can't take more than thirty-some men, even if they're lovers."

"Pack them in. No time for arguing. Leave the trucks and equipment."

Staring down at the airfield, Alec saw the intact

shuttle start to taxi away from the burning one.

Jameson's voice came on again. "We've got three wounded men here. Both the shuttle pilots were killed when the ship was hit."

"Get the wounded aboard the good shuttle. I want a dozen volunteers to stay here with me. The rest can squeeze into the bird any way they can. Use the cargo space. The trucks stay here."

Russo and his people, including Angela, came up to the truck. The big redheaded man looked up at Alec, squinting into the brightness of the sky, grinning.

"Say, would you let us use some of these weapons to drive off the raiders?"

"Come on aboard," Alec said. He ducked under the laser mount's guard rail and kicked at the driver's roof. "Get us moving. Fast!"

Hanging onto the rail as the truck lurched into motion, Kobol leaned his worried-hound's face to within a few centimeters of Alec's. "I'm going out with them, on the shuttle. I'm not staying."

"Fine," Alec snapped. "Just make sure you keep in touch. I'll tell you when to come back and pick up the rest of us."

"Right," Kobol said.

They stared at each other for a long moment. He has no intention of coming back for me, Alec thought. And he knows that I know it.

The truck bounced crazily across the grassy field. Two more shells landed near the runway, but too far from either shuttle to do anything more than churn fresh craters in the ground. The smoke from the damaged shuttle seemed to have almost died away, it was only a thin gray haze now.

"Maybe the fire's gone out," Angela yelled over the noise of the rushing wind and the occasional explosions and gunfire coming from the woods.

Russo shook his head. "Doubt it."

Alec stood behind the driver's cab and watched

his men streaming toward the good shuttle, now stopped at the farthest corner of the field, its nose turned into the wind. The laser trucks made a thin wall between the shuttle and the woods where the fighting was going on. But they were not firing. The troopers from the Moon milled around them, peering toward the woods, gawking like spectators, trying to decipher the strange goings-on.

Alec's truck pulled up alongside the shuttle. He started shouting orders and the men began clambering into the rocketplane. Kobol was nowhere in sight. Probably already aboard, Alec thought, and waiting for the takeoff.

The silvery finish of the shuttle's fuselage looked pitted and stained now, dirty, soiled by the base elements of Earth. Jameson was standing at the bottom of the ladder that ran up to the hatch.

"They're just about loaded," he reported. "Fifteen men volunteered to stay with you; I've got them with the trucks. The pilot's checking the ship's systems to see if there's any damage that'll prevent takeoff."

Russo grasped Alec's shoulder and half-turned him around. "Lookit, I don't want to butt into your affairs," he said, pawing with his free hand at his nose, "but if you don't start using your lasers to clear out the woods at the far end of the runway you're not going to be able to get this shuttle out of here."

"All right," Alec agreed. He called to Jameson, "I want a driver and two gunners with each truck."

Jameson said, "I'll get them moving."

"You're staying?"

"Yep."

Alec grinned at him. "Good. Thanks."

Kobol appeared at the shuttle's hatch. "You still insist on staying here?" he shouted.

"Yes. Somebody's got to."

"No," Kobol called. "Listen. There's enough room in the cargo bay for the rest of the men, if the trucks are left behind. The bay's pressurized."

"I'm staying," Alec shouted up to him.

"To find your father."

"To keep those raiders off your back, so that you can get away. And to get my hands on the fissionables that we came for."

"I don't see any raiders," Kobol yelled. "Only mortar fire. It could be *his* mortar."

Will Russo shot Kobol a disgusted look and turned away. Alec started to say, "Listen, Martin . . ."

"No, you listen. We both know why you're staying. I hate to see you killing good men for your own personal reasons."

Alec wanted to run up the ladder and seize him by the throat. Instead, he hollered, "Then why don't you volunteer to stay with us, and let one of those good men get away safely?"

Kobol grinned his toothy mirthless grin. "If you want to be a fool, don't expect me to join you. I'm going back to the satellite station. From there I'll make a full report on your activities. I'm sure the Council will be interested. So will your mother."

The hatch started to slide shut. The last sight Alec had of Kobol, he was still grinning. The smile of a man who had just outmaneuvered his enemy.

"Alec," Ron Jameson called to him from the other side of the truck. "We're ready to roll."

It took Alec a moment to refocus his thoughts. He turned and saw that Will Russo was sitting on the front fender of his truck. With a deep breath of exasperation, he banged on the roof of the driver's cockpit and yelled, "Let's get moving!"

"I've spotted my other men on two of your trucks," Russo told him. "They know the territory pretty well."

The truck lurched forward as Alec tightened his chin strap. "All right. You can call the shots." As they rolled out past the shuttle's stubby wing, he asked, "What happened to the girl? Where is she?"

"Angela?" Russo blinked his big watery eyes. "I sent her on ahead. She'll tell our people to fall back, so they won't get caught in your fire."

The truck was picking up speed now, jouncing across the broken runway. Alec noticed that the firing seemed to have died down. No more explosions or gunfire came from the shadowy woods. Could Kobol have been right? Is this all some elaborate trap my father's laid out?

"Better steer wide of that damaged bird," Russo was saying. "No telling . . ."

The shuttle exploded with a violence that nearly tore Alec off the truck. The vehicle itself bounced and slewed as a huge ball of white-hot flame burst out and reached for them. Alec could feel its heat searing his face.

The driver swung the truck around viciously, away from the fireball. Hanging onto the laser itself for support, Alec watched the fireball transform itself into a dark tower of uprushing smoke that ballooned into a mushroom shape, far overhead.

"By golly, she really blew," Russo said, in an awed voice.

Within a few moments they were again racing as fast as the truck's electric motors would push them toward the woods. For the first time, Alec could see figures scurrying in the distant foliage, through his binoculars.

They looked ragged, furtive, no two of them wearing the same kind of clothes. Mostly bare-armed and bare-legged. But they each had weapons, and they were forming a skirmish line at the edge of the woods.

Alec passed the binoculars to Russo. "Are those your people?"

He glanced quickly. "Nope. They're raiders. And they've got grenade launchers, looks like, so I'd start squirting them with the lasers at the longest range possible."

As Alec started giving the necessary orders over his helmet radio, three quick, dull popping sounds came from the woods.

"Mortar fire," Russo said calmly.

He wore no helmet, he had no body armor. He simply sat there in the jumpseat, ludicrously big for it, hanging over the edge of the laser mount with the ground rushing past less than a meter below his moccasined feet. He looked completely at ease, smiling happily.

Three mortar shells burst up ahead of them. Alec winced at the explosions.

"Aren't you scared?" he yelled at Russo.

Will shrugged. "Guess so. But I learned a long time ago that it doesn't help. So I ignore it."

Alec stared at him.

"Say." Russo's expression changed to purposefulness. "If we swing this one truck up that way and head into the woods," he pointed to the far left, "we could probably sneak up on those mortars and get 'em."

Alec heard Kobol's voice in his head once more. You trust these people?

"All right," he said slowly. He reached for his helmet mike.

Russo wagged a finger at him. "Better not use the radio anymore. They might be listening to us now."

Another set of mortar shells exploded, one of them close enough to make the truck bounce. Alec crouched involuntarily and heard shrapnel *ping* against the side of the truck. A roar of flame geysered up ahead of them. The other trucks started to fire their lasers. He heard distant screams as the woods burst into flame.

Leaning down toward the driver's cab, Alec gave instructions to swing off to the left.

Ten minutes later they were climbing slowly

through a narrow lane in the foliage, edging up a steep grade toward the top of a ridge.

"How do you . . ."

"Shh!" Russo put a finger in front of his lips.

Alec inched closer to him. "How do you know," he whispered, "where the mortars are?"

"I'm guessing," Russo whispered back. "But they don't have much range, so they must be up here somewhere."

The truck's motors were almost completely silent at this crawling speed. The foliage was thick enough to brush against Alec's legs as he squatted on the laser mount platform. The back of his neck burned; it hurt when he tried to move his head. A tree branch dipped close, caught momentarily in the laser's cooling fins, then sprang loose as they inched past.

It was impossible to see farther than a few meters ahead in this brush, and not even that far along the flanks. We could get ambushed anywhere along the line, and there are only the three of us. Far behind them, Alec could hear the crackling of flames and the staccato of gunfire. The trees over their heads blotted out most of the sky, but to Alec it seemed to have turned gray. Smoke?

Then there was a roar like far-off thunder. But instead of grumbling into silence, it grew, it increased, louder and louder until the truck itself began to vibrate.

"The shuttle's taking off!"

Alec stood up full height and strained for a glimpse of it through the heavy foliage. A flash of silver roared by overhead, and then the thunder diminished, dimmed, grew fainter and fainter until . . .

The monstrous crack of a sonic boom split the air. Alec had never heard it before, but he smiled despite the shock and pain. "They've made it. They're on their way."

"Good." Russo bobbed his head happily.

Kobol's going back to the satellite. He could return to the settlement and be with my mother in another few days. Even sooner, if he pushes it.

Russo put a big paw on Alec's shoulder. "Listen!" he whispered urgently.

The soft popping sound of a mortar firing.

"Stop the truck."

It stopped. The mortar sounds came again, off to their right. Somewhere in the thick foliage. The trail they were following curved in the opposite direction.

"We have to leave the truck," Russo whispered. He checked the action of his rifle. It moved smoothly, with a deadly-sounding *click-click*.

Alec bent down over the driver's rearview slit. "Stay here and stay buttoned up. If anybody bothers you, fire the laser by remote control."

"Right," came the muffled reply from inside the armored cab.

Alec swung his machine pistol off his shoulder. It was an ugly, short-muzzled weapon with a long magazine built into the handgrip and a wire brace that could be rested against shoulder or hip. Russo was already on the ground, poking at the bushes alongside the truck. Alec jumped down beside him.

"Got your safety off?" Will asked.

Looking down at the gun, Alec saw that it wasn't. Red-faced, he flicked the catch with his thumb.

Russo grinned at his embarrassment. "Don't want to run into some strangers without being able to say hello right away."

They started into the brush, walking crouched over, Russo in the lead. The foliage was thick and scratched at Alec's face, arms, legs. The mottled sunlight made his neck burn even more now that he was bent over. Insects droned everywhere, and within a minute Alec felt itches and stings he'd never known before. It didn't seem to bother Russo at all, so Alec fought down the urge to swat and scratch.

The popping sounds were getting louder, more frequent.

"They've got a lot of ammo," Russo whispered over his shoulder. "Using up their whole winter's production in hopes of getting your stuff."

"I hope they haven't hit any of the trucks," Alec answered.

"It's the trucks they're after," Russo said. "If one of those gangs can grab off a truck or two, they'll run merry hell through the countryside—until the laser runs out of fuel or the truck breaks down. Those trucks of yours are like Christmas presents for them."

Alec nodded with new understanding.

"And your other weapons, of course. Everybody likes to get nice new guns."

Barbarians, Alec told himself. They're all nothing more than barbarians.

They flattened out onto their bellies and crawled under some tangled low-lying vines. Suddenly Russo hissed, "Freeze!"

Alec stayed absolutely still. He could feel his heart pounding, feel the ground slightly moist and yielding underneath him, feel the damp heat soaking into his body. He was sweating, beads of stinging salt dripping into his eyes.

Russo slid back alongside him, whispering, "Up in that big tree, at the top of the ridge . . ."

Alec lifted his head, making his burned neck hurt anew. In the tallest tree, standing out against the sky, its enormous arms spread widely, newly leafed and bright green, a man was crouching on one of the lower branches. He held a pair of binoculars to his eyes.

"Spotter," Russo whispered. "The mortars must be within shouting distance of him."

"Let's get him!"

Russo put a hand on Alec's shoulder. "If we pot him before we know exactly where the mortars are, all we'll be doing is warning the mortar crew. Come on, follow me."

Slowly, quietly, slithering like snakes, Russo led Alec down away from that spot. They started to make a wide circle of the area. After several minutes, Alec realized what he was doing. He's swinging around behind the spotter. Behind the mortars.

It took at least a quarter-hour, Alec judged. He didn't get a chance to look at his wristwatch, they were too busy moving. Finally Russo got cautiously to his knees, looked around, then rose to his feet. They were on the reverse slope of the ridge now, standing in waist-high brush. The big tree that the spotter was using was barely visible; only its crown poked above the ridge line.

"Are you sure that's the same tree?" Alec asked. "They all look alike."

Russo said, "Not after you've been here a while."

"All right. Now what?"

"Now we take a couple of deep breaths, then run like hell for that tree. Shoot the spotter as soon as we see him and spray the mortar crew when they come into sight."

"You're sure they're there?"

Nodding, Russo said, "Yep. Although I haven't heard any firing for the last few minutes. They might be packing up to move out."

Alec looked down to check his gun.

"Ready?" Russo asked.

"Yes."

"Okay . . ." The redhead sucked in a deep breath. *"Now!"*

They dashed up the remaining few meters of waist-high brush, Russo in the lead. At the top of the ridge Alec saw him bring his rifle up to armpit level and squeeze off a three-round burst. The sudden noise of the gun made him jump, despite himself.

Something fell from the tree, a blur that Alec noticed out of the corner of his eye because now he was at the top of the ridge and there were eight men frozen in mid-motion, dismantling the mortars. The tubes and bipod supporters and a half-dozen remaining shells lay scattered around them as they looked up, some crouching, some standing, one of them ridiculously mopping under his chin with a red cloth.

For a split instant Alec saw it all displayed in front of him. Then the men dived for their weapons. Alec felt himself firing his machine pistol. It kicked and clattered in his hands. Sprays of dirt sprouted in the midst of the startled men. Four of them jerked backward immediately, arms flung crazily and mouths open. Two others seemed to stagger, reach for the guns that were resting on the ground, then fall over. Another pair dived for the brush and started scrambling downslope, away from Alec and Russo.

Alec realized he'd been firing from the hip, spraying the area with bullets. He straightened and brought the gun to his shoulder, sighting carefully at the nearest of the fleeing men.

Russo tapped him on the shoulder. "That's enough, let them go."

"But they . . ."

"Good God, man, what do you want? We've killed seven men and got their mortars and personal weapons. What else?"

For the first time, Russo seemed annoyed. Not angry, but annoyed the way a parent gets upset with a naughty child.

Alec put his pistol down. "How do you know they're dead?"

Looking at the bodies sprawled below them, Russo answered, "If they're not now, they will be soon."

Slowly he walked down to the scene. Under the big tree the spotter lay unmoving, blotches of red welling over his body, his legs crumpled beneath him, his face contorted. Alec turned and looked at the six men near the disassembled mortars. His stomach heaved.

They were broken apart. Huge gaping wounds ripped through their grotesquely flung bodies. One of them had no face, only an oozing mass of red and gray. Flies buzzed over them.

One of them was groaning. Alec turned his back and tottered away from the sight and smell. Everything was going blurry. Still, he could hear.

"Please . . . please . . ."

"I'm sorry son, there's nothing I can do for you."

A single shot.

Alec leaned against the tree and threw up.

After what seemed like hours, Russo came up beside him. "First time you've seen men killed." It was not a question.

Alec mumbled, "First time . . . I've been responsible."

"Okay . . . You take their weapons back to the truck. Take it slow and easy. You'll need to make a half-dozen trips. I'll bury them."

"You'll . . . what?"

With an almost bashful shrug, Russo said, "Someday somebody's going to kill me, and I wouldn't want to be left aboveground to feed the maggotts."

"But you killed them. I mean, we did."

"Yep. And now they need burying." He paused a moment, then explained, "You kill your enemies when they're in a position to kill you. If they're running and weaponless, you let them run. If they're dead, you bury them. And you don't take prisoners unless you've got a good reason to."

"Those are the rules of war here?"

"The rules of survival."

Alec nodded to show that he understood, even

though he could not agree. He began to gather together the rifles and carbines that the dead men had left scattered on the ground. Russo took one of the corpses off along the tree line, carrying it in his arms almost tenderly.

"Hey!" he suddenly called. "Come here!"

Alec was running toward him instantly, slamming a fresh ammunition clip into his pistol as he moved.

Russo had dropped the corpse at his feet. Hanging from the outstretched limb of a tree, dangling by his thumbs, was a ragged scarecrow of a kid, wide-eyed with pain and terror. His thumbs were swollen and blue. A filthy rag had been stuffed into his mouth. A long gash was oozing blood down one bare leg.

Russo whipped a knife from his belt and cut the boy down, then pulled the gag from his mouth. He collapsed into the big redhead's arms.

"Must've been a prisoner of the mortar crew's," Russo said, "or one of the other gangs nearby."

The kid's emaciated face was hollow-cheeked, his chin stubbly with the beginnings of a beard. He stared at the rifle slung over Russo's shoulder, then at Alec and his drawn pistol.

"No, no . . . " he whimpered.

Russo loosened the ropes knotted over his thumbs as the kid winced with pain.

"What do we do with him?" Alec asked. "What are your rules for this?"

Holding the skinny youngster by his shoulders, Russo asked, "Can you stand?"

The kid nodded and hobbled a few steps away from the big redhead. Russo shook his head and looked back at Alec. "He'll never make it by himself."

"Please," the youngster whined. "Okay. Okay."

"Can you talk?" Alec asked sharply. "What's your name? Why are you here?"

"Ferret. Live here. In woods. They . . . caught

me. Gonna kill me. Later. Slow."

"No guns on him," Russo said. "Not even a knife."

Studying the painfully thin youngster, Alec realized that they might both be the same age. This kid is just a runt, Alec thought. He must have gone through his whole life half-starved.

Alec heard his own voice say, "We've got medical supplies in the trucks."

Russo started to reply, but Ferret sank to his knees with a barely-suppressed groan.

Frowning, Russo said to Alec, "You remember what I said about prisoners?"

"I've got a good reason. He knows the territory around here. He could be useful to me."

"Don't expect him to be grateful," Russo warned. "Don't trust him at all."

But Alec stepped over to the emaciated young man and helped him to his feet. "Come on," he said. "We'll have that leg fixed in no time."

When they got back to the airfield, the battle had long been over. Russo left Alec at the edge of the woods, saying he had to check his own men, and he would be back before sundown. Alec rode the truck back to the runway, with Ferret lying silent but wide-eyed at his side.

Jameson eyed the wounded prisoner with obvious disdain, but gave orders to have his leg attended to. Then he gave Alec an account of the battle. "They kept melting back into the trees. We couldn't follow them in there with the trucks, so we just kept patrolling around the edge of the woods, squirting at them to keep them from getting any closer. They lobbed a lot of mortar rounds at us, but didn't do much damage with them."

Two of the trucks had been clawed by shrapnel, but were still running. Several of the men were hurt, none seriously.

Jameson peered into the woods, his face the image of a hunting hawk. "This man Russo is with your father, is he? Are they on our side, or what?"

Shrugging tiredly, Alec replied, "Today they were on our side. I'm not sure of what happens next. Keep everyone on the alert. Post guards."

"And your prisoner?"

"Keep a guard on him at all times."

"When does the shuttle come back for us?"

"When I call it."

Alec could see that Jameson was skeptical about that. But after a moment's hesitation, the big man simply said, "I'll set out the guards." He strode away, leaving Alec standing alone.

He leaned back against the cab of the truck and surveyed the landscape. Out in the middle of the airfield lay the blackened smoking skeleton of the destroyed shuttle. The forest was silent now. Shadows were creeping across the open ground as the sun settled toward the west.

Alec realized that they were completely alone on an alien, dangerous world.

CHAPTER 16

The sun had already sunk behind the trees when Will Russo appeared again. He walked alone out of the forest and toward the semicircle of trucks parked at the edge of the runway.

Despite himself, Alec was glad to see the man. When Jameson told him that Russo was coming, Alec almost ran out to the guard perimeter to meet him.

"You're not bedded down for the night yet, are you?" Will asked, right off.

"No, not yet."

"Good, good." He looked genuinely pleased. "We've made camp up on top of the first ridge," he waved vaguely in the general direction, "and I think it'd be a good idea for you to camp there with us."

Alec said nothing.

"What's left of those raiders are still skulking around here somewhere," Will explained, "and with our two forces camping together we'll be strong enough to discourage them from trying anything during the night. We'll both be able to sleep easier."

My trucks and lasers and your experienced woods fighters, Alec thought. Nodding, he asked, "Can the trucks get up there?"

"Oh, sure, I'll show you the trail."

"All right." Alec turned and called for Jameson.

Will grinned boyishly. "Fine. Wonderful. In union there is strength."

The trail up to the top of the ridge was narrow and tricky. One of the trucks slipped in a rain-sliced gully alongside the barely-visible trail and it took nearly an hour to pull it out again. The men had to use primitive muscle power to lift the truck's rear wheels out of the foliage-choked gully. The other trucks' electric motors began to overheat when they tried to winch the stuck truck free.

For Ferret, the ride was wonderful. He lay on the back of a truck, behind the laser mount. His leg no longer hurt. These strangers had given him hot food and wrapped his wound with clean strips of something that looked like cloth, yet felt oddly slick and slippery. They were treating him like a king, and watched him carefully every minute.

It was full night when Alec's force finally reached the top of the ridge. Riding perched on the cab of the lead truck, Alec saw a meager handful of men and women sitting quietly around an open fire. One of them was Angela.

"Is this your whole group?" he wondered aloud to Will, who sat on the fender alongside the cab.

"Oh no! We've got twice this many set out as guards. Didn't you see them as we came up the trail?"

Alec shook his head, a gesture that was lost in the darkness.

The trees thinned out at the top of the ridge; there was ample room to park the trucks in a circle around the perimeter of the camp. Alec told Jameson to have the men sleep on the trucks, and to have one man awake per truck at all times.

"Are you sure one man per truck is enough?" Jameson asked quietly.

They were standing far enough from the campfire so that none of Russo's men was in earshot.

"What do you mean?" Alec asked.

"I don't want to be an impolite guest," Jameson replied softly, hitching his thumbs in the ammo belt he had buckled across his hips, "but—well, why should these people be so helpful to us? Especially if they're the same guys who stole the fissionables. Why did they stick their necks out to help us drive the barbarians away, and why are they offering to share their camp and their food with us? It doesn't add up."

Alec was forced to agree. "At least it's better than sitting down there in the open, alone. We don't have enough rations for more than another day or two."

Jameson's hawk-eyed faced scanned the men sitting around the campfire. "Suppose what they're really interested in is getting these nice, shiny new trucks for themselves? It wouldn't be too difficult for them to slit our throats while we sleep."

Somehow the picture of Will Russo murdering men in their sleep did not match in Alec's mind with what he had already seen of the man. Still . . .

"All right. Tell the men to sleep in the cabs of the trucks. Button them up and open them for no one except a recognized member of our group."

Jameson was silent for a moment. In the flickering light cast by the distant campfire it was impossible to read the expression on his face. At last he said, "Okay . . . but I still don't like this."

"Things could be a lot better," Alec admitted. "But they could be a lot worse, too."

"I suppose."

"Keep somebody on the radio. The satellite ought to be in range sometime tonight."

"Right."

Alec walked slowly toward the campfire. Angela was sitting there. He saw her long hair gleaming like hammered gold in the firelight.

The fire itself was strangely fascinating. Twisting, dancing, flickering hypnotically, the flames formed shapes and memories before his eyes. He stared at it, then realized that he was staring *into* the fire, deep inside the dancing flames, watching the logs glowing bright red and the flames licking up from them, orange and yellow and bluish and . . .

"Hello. Had any dinner yet?"

Alec pulled himself away from the hypnotic flames.

"What?" He saw that Angela was looking up at him. "Dinner? No, not yet."

"What's the matter? Are you okay?"

"I'm all right." He hunkered down on the ground beside her. "It's just . . . I've never seen an open fire before. It's fascinating."

"Oh. Yeah, I guess so."

Alec saw that there was a blackened metal container rigged on a set of poles, hanging over the flames. Angela called it a pot, but it looked to Alec as if it had started life as a gasoline tank. Now it was cut down, its corner battered and dented.

"Grab some stew and make yourself to home," she invited.

Alec got up and bent over the pot. Hot fragrant steam bathed his face; the smell was enticing. A simmering liquid bubbled in there, lumpy dark shapes poking out of the seething surface. Thinking of all the injections and pills he had taken before leaving the satellite station, Alec stirred the concoction with his knife, then jabbed at one of the shapes. He held it at arm's length, dripping and smoking, as he squatted awkwardly on the ground beside Angela once more.

"It won't hurt you," she laughed at him. "It was only a rabbit even when it was alive."

"A rabbit?" It was the first time he had seen her laughing.

With a nod, Angela asked, "Don't you have anything you can use for a plate? The stew's got plenty of good things in it: carrots and leeks and all sorts of herbs."

"Um . . . this is fine. I've got a messkit back at the truck, but just let me taste . . ." He bit into the rabbit. *Pain!* Alec had never felt anything so hot inside his mouth. Coughing, gagging, burning, he finally swallowed the chunk whole.

Angela was pounding him on the back, looking worried and shouting at him, "You want water? Are you okay?"

"I'm fine," he croaked, eyes tearing. "My mouth is a mass of second-degree burns and there's a lump of dead rabbit stuck sideways in my guts, but otherwise I'm fine."

The dozen people—mostly men—around the campfire were staring at him. But they quickly looked away and went back to their own conversations. Alec managed to down a few bites of the meat without further trouble, once Angela showed him how to blow on the chunks to cool them. He found that it was good. Good enough to make him want more.

"I'll go find my messkit." He started to get to his feet.

"Don't bother," Angela said. "Here, use my plate. I'll wash it off, okay? Then you won't have to go all the way back to the trucks."

She leaned forward to reach a small canteen of water that was resting on the ground near the fire. As she washed off the metal plate and spoon, Alec wondered, Why does she want to keep me away from the trucks?

He ate in wary silence, thinking vaguely about how long the immunizations shots they had given him on the satellite would protect him from local microbes. The stew was hot and strong, spicier than anything he had ever tasted in his life. Angela offered him water in a metal cup.

When he finished the meal he washed off the utensils himself and handed them back to her.

"Is your mouth okay?" she asked, grinning.

"I'll survive." In fact, with the hot meal inside him, Alec felt fine and strong. Except for the sunburn glowering on the back of his neck. And then, with a sinking feeling in the pit of his stomach, he remembered everything else: the stolen fissionables, the attack, the loss of the shuttle, the fact that he and his remaining men were stranded a quarter-million miles from home.

He closed his eyes and took a deep, shuddering breath. "I'd better be getting back to my men," he said to Angela, while a voice inside his head taunted, Failure! Failure!

She got up with him and walked alongside. Alec realized that the only weapon he was carrying was his knife. Angela was completely unarmed.

"Look." She pointed. The Moon was rising above the tree-fringed horizon. It was nearly full, bright and serene and glorious.

Alec stared at it. The lights of the settlement's surface domes could not be seen against its whiteness.

"What's it like?" Angela asked.

"What?"

"Living there . . . on the Moon."

"We don't live on it," he said. "We live in it, underground. You can't walk around in the open like this, you need a pressure suit and a helmet."

"Why?"

"There's no air."

Her eyes widened for a split-second, then went crafty. "Now wait . . . if there's no air, how can you live there?"

So they sat on a convenient rock, watching the Moon climb higher into the night sky, playing tag with occasional drifting silvered clouds, and Alec explained about lunar life to her. She really doesn't know, he realized as he told her what a dazzling sight the Earth is. Before long he found himself watching her, instead of the Moon. In the soft light from his home her face seemed to float pale and beautiful against the darkness. Lord, she's beautiful!

"This is the first time anyone's told me about these things," she said, her voice excited. "Dad—I mean, your father, never wants to talk about living there."

Alec felt his heart turn to ice.

"Strange," she said, still smiling but with puzzlement in her voice now. "It's kind of hard for me to call him Dad now . . . knowing he's your father."

"He never told you about the settlement?" Alec asked, his voice sounding cold and distant, even to himself.

Angela shook her head. "He'd always change the subject when I'd ask about that. After a while, I guess I just stopped asking."

Alec got to his feet. "I've got to check my men now. Good-night, Angela."

"Oh." She sat there in surprised silence for a moment, then stood up beside him. "Well, good-night, Alec." She turned and walked swiftly back toward the campfire.

He didn't trust himself to say anything more, to call after her. So he tramped in the opposite direction, to the trucks. Disregarding his own orders, he slept out in the open on a stretch of mossy ground near the trucks. He wrapped himself in a plastic tarpaulin and laid his machine pistol by his side. It seemed to take hours for his eyes to close, and when he finally did sleep, he dreamed of his mother.

Ferret slid off the back of the truck and tested his injured leg. It was all right. He could stand on it and walk. The food they had given him had made him strong again, and the leg would heal soon enough.

He limped around the truck and saw Alec stretched out on the ground, the shiny pistol at his side. Ferret crouched so that the guard inside the next truck could not see him, and stared at the pistol. He could snatch it and be off into the woods. They would never find him, and he'd have a wonderful gun for himself.

Dimly he remembered Billy-Joe and the others

of the band who had been killed. And his mother, feeding him, crooning him to sleep when he was a baby. They coulda killed me, Ferret said to himself. He coulda killed me. But he didn't.

The gun was an enormous temptation. But so was the food and medical care and wary but kind treatment these people had given him. I'll stay with them for a while, Ferret decided. This looks like a good gang to stay with. For now.

Stealthily he climbed back onto the truck and went back to sleep.

The Sun awoke Alec after what seemed like a mere few minutes of dozing. After checking with Jameson to see that everything was all right with the men, Alec walked stiff-jointed and aching to the embers of the campfire. It was smoldering low, but one of the women was putting fresh logs onto it.

"Well, you're up at last," Will Russo called to him jovially. He was standing a short distance from the fire, holding a steaming cup in one big hand. Walking around the fire to confront Alec, he said, "Here, have some herb tea. It isn't terribly good, but it'll help to start your engines running. If you'd like to shave . . ."

Alec shook his head blearily. He got the cup almost to his lips, then remembered the searing pain of the previous night's stew. His mouth still felt raw.

"Um . . . thanks." He handed the cup back to Will. "I'll just take some water."

Will shrugged. "Have you made contact with the satellite yet? Are they coming to pick you up?"

"Not yet," Alec said, going for the water canteen by the fire. "We've got someone on the radio now, but no luck so far."

He drank from the canteen, and again worried about catching some local disease.

"Well," Russo said, "I'd hate to leave you out

here in the woods by yourselves, but we can't hang around here much longer."

"I understand," Alec said.

He left Will by the campfire and strode quickly back to the trucks. Going to the cab of the first one he came to, Alec pulled the medical kit from its niche behind the driver's seat. The pills were all in neatly labelled vials, but the labels were not very specific. More than half the pills were already missing, besides. Trying to remember his medical briefings, Alec took three different pills and swallowed them dry.

"Oh, there you are." It was Ron Jameson.

Alec swung down from the cab. "What is it?"

"Radio contact."

Alec followed Jameson to the third truck. Gianelli was in the cab, a huge pair of earphones clamped around his head, squinting with concentration.

"Yeah . . . yeah . . . still coming through weak but clear. Okay, here he is now. Hold on . . ."

He took off the earphones and held them out for Alec. "The satellite's relaying a call from home. Kobol's back at the settlement already."

Fitting the earphones over his head and adjusting the lip mike that swung out from the right 'phone, Alec thought rapidly, Kobol! He'd pushed straight on to the settlement on the highest-gee boost he could get. Must have burned every gram of propellant between the satellite and the Imbrium mines.

The big, cumbersome earphones blotted out all sounds except for the hissing, crackling static of the radio. Alec could see that Gianelli was saying something to Jameson, but he could not hear their voices.

"Hello . . . hello . . . Alec Morgan?" The communications tech was a girl, that much Alec could tell. But her voice was faint and streaked with interference.

"Yes. Go ahead."

A pause, then, "Alec, this is Martin Kobol. Can you hear me?"

"Yes."

It took about two and a half seconds for Alec's words to get to the Moon and Kobol's response to reach back to Earth. A discernable pause.

"Good. Now listen. I've just arrived back at the settlement. The Council's going to meet in an hour. Everything's completely upset here—all our plans, everything. There's a threat of real panic through the entire settlement if we don't act carefully and reassure the people. They were all depending on getting those fissionables."

"I know that." Spare the political speeches!

Pause. Then, "We've got to work out another plan. Can you hold out down there on the surface for a few more days?"

Or a few weeks? Or months? "Yes, I think so."

"Good. Now listen. Stay where you are. Hold tight while we figure out the next move."

"No."

A long pause. Not merely because of the distance this time.

"What was that?"

"I said no," Alec repeated. "I know where the fissionables are. We're going to get them."

"You can't . . . I mean . . ."

"I can and I'm going to. We'll keep in touch with the satellite," Alec said. He counted, waiting for the response: one, one-thousand, two, one-thousand, th . . .

"This is psychotic! You're going to force us to pull another shuttle out of mothballs, track your movements . . ."

"Stow it, Martin. We came here for the fissionables and we're going to get them. Everything else is a detail."

Kobol's voice, when it came, was almost a woman's screech. "You can't travel across the continent and find him, you fool! You'll kill yourself and your men with you!"

"You'd hate that, wouldn't you?" Alec shot back. "Listen to me, Martin. We *can* travel across country. And we can live off the country, too. There's plenty of food here."

But Kobol was already saying, "I don't care what you do to yourself, your personal grudges are your business, not mine. But to risk the rest of those men without even giving them a chance . . ."

"Save your speeches for the Council, Martin. Tell them I'm following their prime directive: I'm going to get the fissionables."

The time lag between their statements was turning the conversation into two separate monologues. "And there's medicine," Kobol was saying, but more calmly now. He was more in charge of himself, obviously thinking fast while he spoke, "You'll be exposing those men to all the diseases of Earth . . ."

"I want to talk to my mother now," Alec said. "Please put her on."

"Your inoculations won't keep you protected . . ." Kobol stopped, then answered, "Your mother's busy preparing for the Council meeting. By the time we could get her here to the communications center the satellite would be below your horizon and out of range."

"Very well. Arrange for her to call me tomorrow."

The pause again. Alec could sense Kobol's mind churning furiously during the hiatus. "I'll tell her. In the meantime, I must warn you again that you should not endanger your men foolishly. The Council won't look favorably on any rash action. You should stay where you are until we've decided on the next step."

"Too dangerous," Alec countered. "We've already been trapped here once. I don't want to allow that to happen again."

Kobol's voice was starting to fade. "Your orders are to stay where you are."

Smiling tightly, "No good, Martin. We're in much greater danger here than we will be on the move. I'll expect a call tomorrow. From my mother. Now I'm going to put Gianelli back on. Give him the ephemerides for the satellite, so we'll know when you're in contact range."

Alec pulled the earphones off his head and handed them to Gianelli. "Quick, before the satellite gets out of range."

Gianelli took the earphones with a slight, quizzical grin. "Gonna make heroes out of us," he muttered.

Jameson said nothing. Alec left the truck and went searching for Will Russo. Halfway back to the campfire he spotted the big redhead striding toward him.

"Looking for you," Will said.

There was something about the man, his big gangling gait, the way his arms swung loosely at his sides, the innocent grin on his face—Alec found it impossible to distrust him.

"I've been looking for you, too," Alec said.

"Have you been in touch with your people?" Will hiked a thumb skyward.

"Yes. If you don't mind, I'd like to travel north with you. I want to find my father."

Will's grin broadened. "Good. Good. I just got a message from him. He's only a few klicks—eh, kilometers—from here, in a town named Coalfield."

"Here?" Alec suddenly felt weightless, all the breath knocked out of him.

"Yep." Will nodded happily. "We can be there in a couple of hours."

CHAPTER 17

Alec scarcely noticed the countryside rolling past as he sat on the fender of the lead truck, heading for the town where his father waited for him.

They came down out of the ridges and woods, all of his own men and all Russo's people riding on the trucks. They bumped onto a paved road; not a wide concrete highway like the one between Oak Ridge and the airport, but a narrow, twisting blacktopped road, cracked and potted beyond description. Weeds and grass sprouted in every crevice.

Behind him Alec could hear Gianelli talking with Angela. "You mean you walk all the time?" he was asking. "Carrying all your food and guns and all?"

She sounded almost amused. "Sure. We ride when we can find something to ride on. There aren't many cars or trucks still running—just a few electrics that run on solar batteries. Not much fuel left for gas-burners."

"So you walk?" There was amazement in Gianelli's voice. "And you carry everything on your backs."

"Unless we can find horses or other pack animals. I covered five hundred klicks on a cow last year, when I hurt my leg."

"Which one?"

"The right."

"Looks pretty good now." Gianelli's voice had a leer in it.

"It's fine. And you can keep your hands off!"

Alec turned and said evenly. "There could be five hundred raiders in those trees. Play some other time."

Gianelli's face reddened and his mouth squeezed down into a hard line. But he moved away from the girl. Angela looked at Alec for a wordless moment. Then he turned away.

Up ahead he could see the first buildings of the town. His hands suddenly felt clammy, shaky. He tightened his grip on the edge of the fender with one hand, shifted the machine pistol's belt across his shoulder with the other. He's here. Somewhere among these buildings . . . Every sense in him peaked, brightened. Alec could hear his pulse throbbing in his ears, feel his breath quicken. He's here! But deep within him, something was telling him to run, to get away, anything but this one place. Journey across the whole face of the planet, travel back to the Moon, get away, anywhere, anyplace.

Yet he was impatient to meet the man he had come to find.

Alec knew from his history tapes that this was a small town. Yet it still dwarfed the lunar community. All these buildings, aboveground, out in the open! And their variety: one floor, three floors, brick fronts, wooden slats, something that looked like stone blocks. Windows staring down at him, empty, mysterious, dark. Street after street after street, branching and intersecting every hundred meters or so.

But empty. Dead. No one lived here. No one was on the streets. No vehicles. Nothing in sight except the silent buildings and windblown dust billowing through the empty streets.

He looked across to Will, perched on the opposite fender.

"Town's been deserted since the sky burned," Will said. "People come by once in a while, but nobody lives here permanently. Too tough to grow food here; too hard to defend the town against raiders."

"How do you know which building my father's in?"

Will grinned hugely. "Oh, Douglas'll be in his usual place."

It turned out to be a one-story red-brick building with a sign spanning its width: U.S. POST OFFICE—COALFIELD, TENN.—33719.

Will suggested that the trucks be spread around the building in a defensive perimeter. Alec passed the order on to Jameson, then the truck he was on trundled into the parking lot behind the Post Office building. Nestled under a protective overhang sat a squarish, squat, open-topped vehicle. Alec recognized it from his teaching tapes as a jeep.

As he climbed down from the truck, Alec wondered where his father found the fuel to propel a jeep. If he can cover long distances in it, then he must have fuel depots spotted along the way. Then Will Russo came around, grabbed Alec by the arm and ushered him through a doorway that had long ago lost its door.

It was dark inside. They walked down a narrow corridor, turned a corner.

And there he was.

He was standing in the center of a big room, surrounded by empty shelves and broken, shattered wooden desks and tables. The roof was partially gone, so the sunlight streamed in, dust motes drifting lazily in the still air. The room was large and open, but Douglas Morgan seemed to fill it. He was big, hulking, broad-shouldered and thick-bodied. Will Russo was almost as big, Alec realized. But where Will was a grinning, happy oversized puppy, Douglas Morgan was a towering, lumbering gray bear.

His face was square-jawed and strong, with iron-gray hair rising in a bristling shock from his broad forehead and framing his powerful jaw with an iron-gray spade-shaped beard. His blue eyes were like gunmetal. They stared straight at Alec now, unblinking, pinning him where he stood.

I don't look anything like him, Alec heard his own inner voice saying. No wonder he hates me.

"You're Alec, eh?" His voice was strong, demanding, even in normal conversational tone. "You have your mother's genes, all right."

And not yours? Alec wondered. "I'm Alec," he said.

"Well, come over here and let me see you. I'm not going to bite you."

Alec walked slowly toward his father. The man was a giant, a mountainous man, with a powerful commanding voice to match.

They stood confronting each other. Neither offered a hand. Neither smiled. Despite the sunlight beaming down through the broken roof, Alec felt cold, numbed to his core.

"He's a good fighter," Will's voice broke the staring match between them. "Helped me take a nasty mortar nest. Handled himself very well."

Douglas nodded. "That's something."

"I vomited afterward," Alec snapped.

Douglas's heavy eyebrows went up. "Did you? A sensitive soul, eh? Well . . . killing a man's no joke. But be glad you were the one who was still alive to get sick, not the one somebody else got sick over."

Will said, "Why don't we sit down and have something to drink? It's been a dusty ride up here, and I sort of feel like celebrating."

"Celebrating what?" Douglas asked.

"Family reunion!"

"Oh. That." He smiled sardonically. "Sure. Obviously you've found some liquid lightning along the way. So uncork it and we'll have a little party. Just the three of us."

"It's in my pack." Will bounded back toward the door.

"Sorry we haven't had the place dusted and

decorated for the big occasion," Douglas said to Alec. "Eh . . . the furniture's a bit nonexistent. Care to sit over here?"

He gestured elaborately toward the floor next to a scarred, battered wooden counter that ran across the front of the room. Alec shrugged and dropped down onto his heels. He watched as Douglas stiffly, slowly sank down into a sitting position. He leaned his back against the sagging partitions under the countertop with an audible sigh.

"Caught a cold in my back during the spring rains," he said, without turning to look at his son. "Makes it merry hell to bend."

Will came back, holding a metal flask in his big freckled hand. He sat on the floor facing Alec and Douglas. Grinning, he unscrewed the cap of the flask and sniffed at its contents.

"Wow! Shouldn't keep this in the hot sun."

Douglas reached for it and took a cautious whiff. "I'll bet I could get fifty klicks to the gallon on my jeep with this stuff." He passed the flask to Alec. "Here. You're the guest of honor. You get the first shot. If you survive, maybe we'll try it."

"It's not that bad," Will said, trying to look aggrieved. "The farmer who sold it to me swore he brewed it last summer."

Alec took the flask and brought it to his lips. The fumes seemed to crawl right up inside his eyeballs, making them water. He took a sip. It stung and tasted sour. Don't cough! he commanded himself.

"Not bad," he said, his voice only partly choked.

Douglas took the flask from him. "Well, if you can stand it, I suppose I can too."

Alec watched his father take a long swallow of the liquor, while his own sip burned its way down toward his stomach. They passed the flask among themselves for another round before Douglas said:

"We have a lot to talk about."

"Yes, we do," Alec agreed.

Will said, "Maybe I ought to tiptoe out . . ."

"No, stay right here," Douglas commanded.

That eliminates talking about mother, Alec thought. Aloud, he said, "The fissionables are gone."

"Right. We took them north . . . er, for safekeeping."

"We need them."

"I know you do. I knew it before you were born."

"Then why did you take them away? Why didn't you bring them back yourself? Why did you turn your back on us and stay here in this mudhole?" All in a rush.

Douglas held the flask in his hand. He looked at it, then shook his head once, abruptly, as if he'd made a firm decision. "*That* is a long story. But it all boils down to one unavoidable fact. The lunar settlement cannot survive by itself. It needs Earth. Otherwise, it's going to die."

"Of course! We need those fissionables."

"It's not the fissionables." Douglas leaned an elbow on the sagging wooden shelf behind him. The wood creaked. "There's more than the fissionables involved . . . far more. The life of the settlement itself."

"I don't follow."

"Look—the settlement was never intended to be entirely self-sufficient. Right? When the Sun flared up they were suddenly thrust on their own. No more support from Earth."

Alec said, "And we've been on our own for more than twenty-five years now. Doing fine."

"Bull-hinkey! You *think* you're doing fine." Douglas's voice rose slightly. "But take a good, unbiased look at the settlement. You're still operating with the machinery that was there before the flare, right? No one's built new reactors, new processing plants, new solar panels, new shuttles, eh? No one's even tried to rectify the processing plants so they can run on the voltages that the solar arrays produce, have they? No! Instead you keep coming back to Earth to grab fissionables for the reactors."

"So?"

"So what happens when you've used up all the fissionable fuel you can find? What then?" Douglas demanded.

"That won't happen for centuries!"

"Centuries, millennia . . . what difference? The point is," Douglas insisted, "that it's going to happen one day, and unless you people have the knowledge and the guts to work out new devices—like fusion generators, for example—then you're going to die. All of you."

Alec said, "But that's so far in the future . . ."

"Then what about medicines?"

"We synthesize all the medicines we need."

"Oh sure you do. Certainly," Douglas sneered. "But how many people in the settlement are too brittle-boned to make the trip to Earth? How many of your own men are going to suffer sunstroke because they don't have enough melanin pigmentation in their skin? That's a beautiful burn you've got on the back of your neck, by the way."

Alec was starting to feel confused. "But those are hereditary traits. Medicine can't . . ."

"Exactly!" Douglas pounced. "What about the four or five people each year who die of cancer in the settlement? Huh?"

Bewildered, Alec replied, "Cancer's unavoidable . . . everybody knows that."

"Oh it is, is it?" Douglas glanced over at Will, then turned back to Alec. "It happens that cancer-arresting drugs were being manufactured on Earth before the sky burned."

"They were?"

Douglas nodded. "And the incidence of cancer in

the settlement is rising at a rate of five percent a year. In another generation or two . . . pfft!" He snapped his fingers.

"No!"

"I calculated it out myself. Cancer, birth defects, other genetic diseases—they're all on the rise in the settlement. Because of inbreeding. Before the sky burned, the inbreeding effect was masked because there was a constant flow of people coming and going from Earthside. But among the people who had lived on the Moon for years and intermarried, the hereditary effects were already starting to show up. Now that you've cut yourselves off from Earth, the genetic pool of the lunar community just isn't big enough to be viable."

"That can't be true."

"Can't it be? Do you think the computers tell lies? They don't. They have no pity. They don't care what you want the answer to be, they simply chug away at the problem and tell you what the answer *is*."

"I can't believe that," Alec said. "The answer you get depends on the data you put in . . ."

Douglas shrugged ponderously. "The data I put in was the medical records of the long-term lunar residents. The settlement is dying. It's too small and inbred to survive. Oh sure, maybe you'll get along for another generation or so . . . say, about fifty years. But I doubt it. There were already a lot of visible strains when I left. I'll bet there's a lot more tension in the air now. Nobody knows how to build new equipment; you've got some smart engineers and technicians, but no scientists to speak of. A few astronomers. And the genetic diseases are being quietly brushed under the rug because nobody knows how to handle them or what to do to get rid of them."

"He's right," Will said gently. "I was a physician up there, you know. What Douglas is saying is absolutely right."

Alec glared at the two of them. "So you decided to let the settlement die. You left with no intention of coming back."

"That's just about one hundred percent wrong," Douglas said. "The settlement will certainly die—*if it stays alone.* I'm trying to save it by forcing you people to reconnect with the rest of the human race, with Mother Earth. And to do that, I've got to build a viable civilization here on Earth. Right?"

A boiling tide of rage was rising in Alec's guts. "That's a fancy way of saying that you're carving out a nice little empire for yourself down here, and you want to force the settlement to become part of it."

Smiling sadly, Douglas replied, "I can see that your mother's been educating you." He spread his big, thick-fingered hands. "Call it an empire, a renaissance, an attempt to hold back the complete annihilation of the human race as a species—call it any goddamned thing you want to! But I'm going to bring the threads of civilization back together again, one way or the other. And I want you to work with me. You're my son and . . ."

"And someday I'll inherit all this?" Alec shouted at him. "The heir-apparent? The crown prince?"

"Something like that," Douglas muttered.

"Then you're a fool! Don't you know that crown princes spend their lives planning the king's murder?"

Douglas said nothing. He simply sat there on the dusty floor and stared at his son. Then, slowly, he struggled to his feet and walked out of the room. Alec watched him, unmoving.

Will Russo shook his head. "I shouldn't stick my nose into this damned thing . . . father and son, after all. But, by golly, that was a lousy thing you just did to him. He's been waiting twenty years to see you."

"So he saw me," Alec said, suddenly weary of

the whole thing. "What was he expecting? Congratulations for running out on us? A hero's medal for turning his back on the whole lunar settlement so he could play emperor down here?"

"There's a lot to this that you don't understand."

"No," Alec said, getting to his feet. "I understand him perfectly. He can rationalize all he wants to, but the simple fact is that he's a king down here instead of a responsible citizen of the settlement. And he's trying to make us submit to him by holding the fissionables. He knows we can't survive without them."

"You won't survive even with them," Will said gently. "That's the point he's trying to make."

The afternoon seemed infinitely long. Alec paced alone through the dead streets of the town, kicking up dust, watching the weeds and a few straggling flowers tossing in the warm wind. Trees grew tall and dark in all directions around the town, but for some reason the trees planted along the streets were nothing but dead bare skeletons.

It took him several hours to calm down, to regain enough self-control so that he could face his own men without being afraid that his hands would tremble or his voice would crack. My father's convinced himself that he's right, Alec thought. And he's convinced Will and the others, too. Everything mother told me about him is true. He's able to rationalize anything, everything: leaving us, not caring if we live or die. And he claims it's for our own good. The bastard!

The flaming beauty of sunset went unnoticed. Only when it started getting dark enough to worry him did Alec return to the trucks. He lost his way several times among the empty diverging streets, but finally he found the Post Office and his men. They were eating with Will's people, gathered around an open fire in front of the Post Office building.

"There you are," Jameson said as Alec stepped out of the shadows cast by one of the trucks. "I was starting to think I ought to send a couple of scouts out to find you."

"No need," Alec said.

His own men and Will's people were intermingling freely. The girls were laughing and charming the men. Angela was not in sight, though. Alec sat on the ground by the fire and shared their communal dinner. He didn't bother asking what was in the pot. It was tasteless—at least, he tasted nothing.

Angela showed up as he finished eating.

"Dad wants to see you," she said tightly.

He rose and started walking off with her. Despite her small size she kept pace with him. She's tough, Alec couldn't help thinking. Battle-hardened.

"Hey, chief, where you going?" Gianelli's voice called through the flickering shadows cast by the campfire. "Don't do anything we wouldn't do!" The laughter of several men followed them.

"He's not your father," Alec said grimly as they walked around toward the rear of the Post Office.

Her eyes flashed and she snapped, "More than . . ." Then she seemed to catch herself, think better of it. "That's right. He's not really my father."

"And you're not my sister."

"So?"

"So just remember that."

Her voice was brittle. "I'll keep it in mind."

Douglas was sitting in the jeep; it was still parked behind the building. The only light was from the stars; the Moon had not risen yet.

"Thank you, Angela," Douglas said softly. "If you don't mind, I'd like to talk to Alec alone."

"I don't mind . . . Dad." She put special

emphasis on the last word, Alec thought.

"Well?" Alec asked, standing beside the jeep. He could barely make out the expression on his father's face, in the darkness.

"What are your plans?" Douglas asked.

Alec hesitated, then lied. "I'm not sure yet. I have to talk to mother and the Council."

"She's still on the Council?"

"She chairs it."

Douglas grunted. "I might have guessed. Matriarchal societies need a queen bee."

Alec clenched his fists but said nothing.

"Listen to me," Douglas commanded. "In the next few days you and your men are going to come down with dysentery. It's not fatal . . ."

"We have pills for that."

"Bull-hickey! The pills won't do a damned thing for you, take my word for it. Once you start eating the local flora and fauna your gut bugs change and you get dysentery. It's inevitable. And although it won't kill you, it'll make you wish you were dead. You'll be in no condition to defend yourselves. Unless you're safely in the shuttles, you'll be helpless here. And I can't afford to have my people sitting around here for days on end, protecting you."

"So take off," Alec snapped. "We don't need your protection."

"You could come with us."

"And help you to build your empire?"

"Help save your mother and everyone else in the settlement!"

"I'll save them—by getting those fissionables."

Douglas shook his head, a ponderous negative motion. "No. That's something you can't do. They're too far from here, and too well protected. You'd be dead long before you got to within a hundred kilometers."

"I came here for the fissionables."

"You'll get yourself killed."

"You're going to kill me?"

"I won't have to lift a finger!" Douglas was starting to sound exasperated. "There are a thousand ways of getting yourself killed here: raider bands, injuries . . . hell, you could even starve to death, if you know as little about survival as I think you do."

"I'm going to get those fissionables, one way or the other."

Douglas suddenly turned sarcastic. "Oh are you? Well, you're going to find that that's just a leetle tough to accomplish. In the first place, when you talk to your mother, she's going to order you back home. I know her, and she won't have her precious son running around here in the open where he might stub his toe."

"You might have known her," Alec flashed, white-hot, "but you don't know me."

"That's true. And it's a shame I never will. Because you're either returning to the settlement or you're going to be killed inside of a week."

"We'll see."

"Indeed we will. It's a shame your education is going to prove fatal. You might have eventually turned out to be somebody worth knowing. You're stubborn enough to be my son, I'll give you that much."

With that, Douglas reached for the jeep's dashboard and twisted the ignition key. The motor purred to life. An electric motor! Alec realized, taken aback with surprise. Without another word Douglas put the jeep in reverse, backed smoothly out of the parking lot, and disappeared silently into the night.

Alec stood there for some moments, fingering the pistol at his side, before he realized that he might have killed Douglas then and there.

CHAPTER 18

Alec expected an argument from his mother the next morning, but he got none.

He sat buttoned into the armored cab of his truck, alone and isolated from the others. He reported everything that had happened so far, ending with his decision to head north and find the fissionables. His mother's voice sounded strangely faraway, much colder and more distant than the quarter-million miles between them.

"You must do what needs to be done," she said, metalically, icily, amid the cracklings and hisses of Sun-static.

"When I locate the fissionables you can send reinforcements to me."

He could sense other pressures, other emotions working in her mind. "Very well, Alec. The Council will accept your plan. I'll see to that."

"And Kobol?"

The hesitation in her voice was more than the lag of lightspeed. "There are ways of handling Kobol. He won't stop you."

"You'll need to bring out the other shuttles and make supply drops for us. We're going to need medicine and ammunition, fuel for the truck generators . . ."

She said, "That will take time. Several days, at least. Probably longer."

"All right. I'll keep in touch through the satellite. It might be a good idea to activate one of the automatic relay satellites in synchronous orbit, if you can. Then we can keep a communications line open all the time."

Her voice was fading, the satellite was passing out of range. "I'll try, Alec. I'll try."

"Take care, Mother. Be careful."

"And you, Alec. Do what needs to be done. Find him and do what needs . . ." her voice dimmed to an inaudible hiss.

Alec sat alone in the truck's cab for several minutes, feeling flushed and weak. Got to get a grip on myself, he thought. I'm responsible for fifteen lives. He reached for the door handle and a sudden stab of pain seared through his middle. His head swam.

Dizzily, he stumbled out of the truck. It was cooler in the morning air. He took several deep racking breaths and forced the pain down.

"You," he called to the nearest man, who was poking into the truck's fuel cell, behind the cab and under the laser mounting. He looked up. Alec recognized him but couldn't recall his name. "Find the medical tapes and read out the information on dysentery. Remind Gianelli to get all the available data on the subject when the satellite's in range again."

The man looked blankly at him. "The satellite won't be in range again for twelve hours, will it?"

Alec nodded, bringing up the dizziness again. "Right. Do it."

"Yeah, okay. Dysentery?" He started to look scared, rather than puzzled.

Slowly, fighting against the nausea that was gripping him, Alec made his way along the line of trucks, looking for Ron Jameson. He found him calmly sitting on the ground with his back against a truck's wheel, cleaning his automatic rifle. The weapon was spread on a plastic sheet in front of him, broken down into its many glittering metallic parts. Jameson was deftly oiling the firing mechanism.

Ferret stood about ten meters away, watching Jameson with gleaming eyes.

"I don't trust him," Jameson said, as Alec's shadow fell over the rifle parts. Then he looked up and saw Alec's face. "You've got it too."

"And you?" Alec sagged to a sitting position against the balloon tire.

Jameson nodded, keeping one eye on Ferret. "Had a siege last night. Not much fun."

"We're all going to come down with it. And Douglas is pulling his people out."

"I know. Will Russo was around here looking for you. He was pretty shame-faced about it, but they're all leaving before noon."

Leaning his head against the truck's cool metal fender, Alec closed his eyes. "That means we'll be on our own."

"With diarrhea and vomiting as our constant companions." Jameson said it flatly, with neither humor nor malice.

"What can we do?"

"They're not sending a shuttle for us?"

"No . . ." Another cramp made Alec gasp and fight for self-control. "We're going north to find the fissionables. As soon as we're able."

Jameson was silent for a long while. Through pain-blurred eyes, Alec watched him. He was scanning the streets around them, his hawk's eyes registering every detail of the buildings and intersections, his mind obviously working at top speed.

"Well then," he said at last, "I guess we'd better get these trucks inside of some of the buildings, where they won't be spotted so easily. And we'd better pick buildings that are set so that the trucks can support each other with crossfire, in case we *are* attacked. We've got to defend ourselves with a troop of sick pups."

He glanced at Ferret again. "And I wouldn't trust him further than I can spit."

"We've got the advantage of firepower," Alec said.

Jameson gave him a pitying look. "Won't do much good if the gunners are crapping their guts out when it comes time to pull the triggers."

Alec couldn't stand any more. He lurched to his feet and staggered off to find some privacy where he could be thoroughly sick.

The Sun was almost straight overhead when he forced himself back to the street where the Post Office stood. He was drenched with sweat, yet shivering. He stank. His knees were trembling with the mere effort of keeping himself on his feet.

A pair of strong arms grabbed him from behind.

"My God, you really do have it, don't you?" Will Russo said. His usually carefree face was dead serious now.

"I'll be . . . all right," Alec managed.

Will led him in to the Post Office and sat him down on the floor. Squatting on his heels next to Alec, he said, "Look, we've got to leave. There's a lot of going on further north that needs our attention . . ."

"Then go." Alec fluttered a weak hand at him.

"Let me finish, doggone it! I know you feel like you're going to die, but you won't. You'll be okay in a few days. The thing to avoid is fever . . . it weakens you to other infectious diseases. Now, do you have any anti-fever medicines—aspirin, anything like that?"

"Yes . . . but nothing much more."

"You don't need it. Gobble aspirin and use water baths to keep your temperature down. Same for everybody."

"All right." Far back in his mind Alec shrank from the idea of using water for bathing. Water's too precious.

"Okay," Russo said. "Now, I see that some of your men are still strong enough to start moving your trucks inside garages and store fronts and such. That's good. Keep out of sight and maybe nobody will bother you."

Alec said nothing.

"Now, the raider bands we tangled with have apparently scattered across the countryside. But they haven't left the territory, you can be sure. I've asked a couple of the local farmers to sort of watch out for you, warn you if any packs come into the area. The locals don't like the raiders and they've always worked with us pretty fairly. So they'll at least try to warn you, if they can."

"Good."

"But don't depend on them too much," Will warned. "They're not going to risk their own necks to help strangers. Stay alert. Especially at night."

Sure, Alec thought, stay alert. We'll be lucky if we can stay conscious.

"Well . . ." Russo clambered to his feet. Towering over the prostrate Alec he said, "Good luck. I hope you get through this okay and we can meet again under happier circumstances."

When we do, we'll be pointing guns at each other, Alec realized.

The first night wasn't so bad. Before the Moon rose one of the men thought he saw someone prowling along the street and fired a burst of automatic rifle fire at him. Everyone roused, the sick and the well, but the alarm was over just that quickly. Once the Moon came up and it was fairly bright, the town became absolutely still.

At least, as far as Alec and his men could tell.

The next day it clouded over and by mid-morning began to rain. Alec lay in absolute misery on the floor of the Post Office next to the two trucks that had been trundled inside there. The rain dripped through the broken roof, adding rivulets of soaking water and a chilling, soggy air to the agonies that they all felt.

Ron Jameson was the strong one among them. He was on his feet, moving from building to building, truck to truck, man to man, carrying medicine and discipline and—most important of all—morale. He kept a constant eye on Ferret, as well, but the pinch-faced youth never tried to run out on them, never strayed far from the trucks and the other men. He watched them, eyes darting everywhere, in their miseries.

Hunched over Alec's makeshift pallet as the rain drummed on the sagging roof and dripped through its shattered sections, Jameson said matter-of-factly:

"I wouldn't depend on any farmers to warn us of raider bands. From what Russo's people told me, most of them won't bother to help us as long as the raiders leave them alone."

Alec nodded weakly. "I guess that's so."

"And the way it's raining, the raiders could march in here with a brass band and we wouldn't see or hear a thing until they were right on top of us."

"How many . . ." Alec had to take a breath, " . . . how many men are on their feet?"

"They're starting to recover. We've got seven or eight who're as good as new, almost."

"Out of fifteen."

"The worst is over. I think you got the biggest dose of all."

Alec smiled wanly. "Good. I wouldn't want anybody else . . . to go through this . . ." He had been vomiting aspirin and antibiotics all day. The cramps and diarrhea were not so bad now, but he was cold and utterly weak. Nothing stayed inside him.

"We'll make it," Jameson said, with a grim smile. "Once the Sun comes out again we'll be okay."

Alec translated, If we get through tonight we might have a chance.

Alec drifted to sleep. When he awoke, it was dark. Rain pelted the roof of the cab he lay in, but it seemed lighter now, diminishing. Cramps again. He pushed himself up to a sitting position and the nausea washed over him in waves. Dizzy, he grabbed for the truck door handle and half-fell, half-slid to the floor of the Post Office room.

It was wet. The drizzling rain coming through the roof felt almost good on his head and shoulders. Clutching at his midsection, Alec staggered out toward the back door. If any of the men noticed him, they gave no indication of it. He saw no one stir.

He was fumbling with the belt of his pants when the first explosion came.

It lifted him off his feet and slammed him into the muddy ground ten meters from where he'd been standing. The back wall of the Post Office was a sheet of flame and it collapsed in surrealistic slow motion, crumbling in on itself. Sparks and flaming debris soared upward.

Alec rolled over on his back in the ice-cold mud. Gunfire. Men yelling. The high-pitched whine of an electric generator revving up to top speed.

He rolled over onto his stomach, fumbling for his pistol, but couldn't find it. Four men were running toward him. In the dancing light of the flames he saw that they were armed. Then a truck smashed its front end through a store window across the street. The running men turned to flame as the invisible laser beam hit them. Their clothing burst into fire and they jerked, screaming, hair and flesh ablaze. They fell and the ground bubbled where the invisible laser beam struck. The pencil line of boiling earth marched across the street to where Alec lay, close enough for him to hear the hellish hiss of it as he watched, paralyzed with fear.

Then the beam swung away. More explosions. Another truck started to pull free of a building that was collapsing, but the truck itself blew up, hurling pieces of men and machinery so high into the air that they were lost in shadow.

Alec couldn't move. He lay there soaked in mud and his own excrement as bullets zinged by, kicking up puffs of mud close enough to splatter his face. One truck seemed to be the only one fighting, and running, cursing men backed away from it, firing as they fell back.

Then another truck trundled slowly around the Post Office building. A dozen raggedly-dressed men charged at it, trying to capture it intact. The laser caught them in the open and they instantly became gibbering torches. More men appeared on the rooftop of the building where the first truck stood, but they must have been Alec's men, for they sprayed the street with automatic weapons' fire.

Bullets spanged everywhere and Alec knew he was going to be killed. Then he felt a tug at his ankles. Turning his head, he saw Ferret, lips pulled back over his yellowed teeth, bent over double to drag him through the muddy street over to the side of a building and a modicum of safety. Ferret knelt beside Alec, wincing with every bullet that whizzed near, obviously terrified.

Before Alec could find the strength to say anything, he saw a third truck coming up from the other end of the street. Its laser was silent and a gang of armed men crouched on the mounting platform, behind the armored cab. More men walked stealthily behind it. They've captured that one, Alec realized, but they don't know how to work the laser.

Jameson must have realized the same thing. Alec saw him standing erect alongside the first truck, pointing a straight unflinching arm toward the captured one. The laser generator shrilled and the captured truck was caught in its merciless beam. Men screamed and burned, tires burst and the truck slumped to a halt. Then the beam found the oxygen and hydrogen lines of the fuel cell and the truck fireballed, searing Alec and Ferret with its glaring heat.

Suddenly it all stopped. The truck burned sullenly, the Post Office was a twisted mass of smoking ruins. The shooting ceased. No more shouting. No more movement. The street was littered with bodies.

Christ! They wiped us out and I lay there like a turd.

Alec forced himself up to his hands and knees.

"Okay?" Ferret asked, his voice high with fear. "You okay? Okay?"

"Yes," he said, still nearly breathless. "I'm all right."

Two men jumped out from behind the corner of the building, guns levelled at them. Ferret threw his arms over his head and dived for the ground.

"Hey, it's Alec!" Gianelli's voice shouted.

"And that Ferret character."

"He's one of them," Gianelli said. "Shoot the bastard!"

Alec heard the *snick* of a gun being cocked. "No," he commanded, as loudly as he could manage. "He saved my life. Leave him alone. He wasn't with them. He pulled me out of the line of fire."

"You got hit?" Gianelli asked, striding to Alec. His face was grimy, streaked with soot. His partner kept his rifle levelled at Ferret.

"No," Alec said. "I'm . . . I wasn't hit."

After an hour of cleaning and changing clothes, Alec felt strong enough to look for some food. The other men were dragging off the bodies of the dead, tending to each other's wounds. The word had quickly spread that Alec's deepest injury was soiled pants. The men shied away from him.

He found Jameson by a small cookfire, near one of the remaining trucks.

"You're okay," Jameson said.

Alec nodded. "And you?"

"Broke a fingernail on the safety of my rifle," he said with utter seriousness.

"How many . . . did we lose?"

"Three killed, five wounded. Two pretty

seriously. The other three are just scratched. Could have been a lot worse."

We're down to a dozen men, Alec thought. "Did they get one of the trucks?"

Nodding, Jameson said, "It cost them twenty-two dead."

"And wounded?"

"They dragged most of their wounded away," Jameson said flatly. "The others died."

A single pistol shot cracked through the smoldering darkness.

"That's the last one now," Jameson said.

"I got caught between you and them," Alec mumbled. "Went out to . . . never got my pants down."

Jameson shrugged. "I hear Ferret dragged you to safety. Guess I'll have to start trusting him a little."

"Yeah. Maybe he can help us locate some food."

Jameson excused himself and left Alec alone by the tiny fire. While Alec tried to get some hot broth down, he heard one of the men grumbling:

"I don't care if he does hear me! He was crapping in his pants while Ollie and the rest of 'em were getting killed. Some leader!"

And then Jameson's voice, quiet, calm. "Maybe you don't care if *he* hears you but if *I* hear you make another crack like that I'll break your jaw. Understand? He was sick . . . still is."

The reply was mumbled too low for Alec to hear.

He leaned back against the metal of the truck and held the warm cup of broth in both trembling hands. A dozen men. Twelve against Thebes. Twelve of us and two trucks to cross the country and find Douglas and the fissionables. And most of the men think I'm either a coward or a madman. Or both.

He almost laughed. The only real friend he had among them was the half-witted Ferret.

Alec looked up. The first hint of dawn was lightening the sky to the east. It would feel good to have sunlight warming him again.

"All right," he whispered to himself. "Two trucks and twelve men. We start north. Now!"

BOOK THREE

CHAPTER 19

It was pleasantly cool among the trees. The Sun still felt hot, falling in mottled patches through the swaying branches and lighting up the grassy glades of clearings among the trees. The breeze had a tang to it as it gusted in from the northwest. The leaves were already falling, their colors fantastic. Alec had never seen such a profusion of reds and golds before.

But he was not paying attention to the autumn foliage now. He lay on his belly atop a carpeting of soft leaves at the rim of a hill, under the cover of the maples and birches. Out in the cleared valley below stood a walled village. A cluster of little huts with thin plumes of smoke curling from a few chimneys.

Ron Jameson lay beside Alec. "They picked a good location. Couple of klicks out in the open. Nobody can get to them without them seeing him first and closing their gates."

Nodding, Alec raised his binoculars to inspect the village's wall. Old cinderblock, mostly. Some newly made brick. Wooden gates, probably scavenged from one of the abandoned cities nearby.

He noticed a few men working in the cornfield between the woods and the village. No women were in sight, although they might have been in among the rows of two-meter-high stalks.

"They're greedy," Alec said quietly. "They've planted cornfields all the way from the edge of their wall to the edge of the trees. And they're trying to get a second crop in before the frosts come."

Jameson grinned. Perfect cover.

On Alec's other side, Ferret jabbed an excited finger. "Road," he said. "Carts. Wagons."

"They must be carrying on trade with other villages," Alec said. "That's too much corn for them to eat all by themselves."

"Maybe they supply Douglas's people?" Jameson suggested. "If he's got a sizable army and an organized base near here, he'd need supplies from villages like this."

Alec scanned the area again. A cloud of dust caught his attention, far down the road toward the horizon. "Truck," he murmured. "No, it's a wagon, pulled by horses."

"Wagon," Ferret agreed, nodding happily.

He handed the binoculars to Jameson. "Empty, heading in toward the village. Driver and two gunners."

"Wasn't there another one yesterday?" Jameson asked, adjusting the focus as he peered through the glasses.

"That's right. Gianelli spotted it."

"Just about this time, too."

Alec smiled. "We can make a Trojan Horse out of the next one."

"A what?"

"You'll see," Alec said.

All through the summer Alec had driven his tiny band northward, toward the area of Douglas's headquarters. Not that he knew where it was. Only that it was north, toward the lakes.

When he had first reported on meeting Douglas to his mother, she mused, "He was born up in the lake country. It would be just like him to make his home territory into the center of his empire."

She assigned the satellite observers to scan the area carefully and, sure enough, they reported extensive networks of roads, villages, farms in the area. It all appeared quite settled and serene, with no sign of marauding raider packs molesting the farmers or villagers.

Alec headed for the lake country.

The laser trucks ran out of fuel after the first few days. Alec burned them, rather than let them fall into barbarian hands. But with the loss of the trucks they also lost their only link with home, the truck radios which were capable of reaching the satellite station and, through relay, the Moon. Alec had one of the radio transceivers taken from a truck and carried along.

"Whenever we find a power source for it, we can make contact again," he told the men.

Gianelli grumbled at the extra few pounds. Jameson ordered the men to take turns carrying it. Alec talked with Kobol or Lisa or one of the other Council members whenever they could surprise a village or an armed outpost that had a suitable electric power supply. Lisa had supplies dropped for them, with zero success. The supply vehicles were unmanned and virtually unguided, catapulted from the Moon to the satellite station and then nudged into a re-entry trajectory by the satellite crew. They flamed to Earth like great meteors, either missing Alec's position by enormous margins or being reached first by barbarians who plundered the food, ammunition and supplies inside them long before Alec's men could reach them.

So they lived off the land. Ferret became invaluable, bringing in food where the lunar invaders could find nothing, slowly teaching them how to hunt, trap, *see* the landscape and the living creatures who dwelled in it. Ecology became a lifesaving study for Alec and his men. And they stopped thinking of Ferret as a halfwitted spy in their midst.

They also raided villages and took what they needed. Alec tried to do it peacefully whenever he could, but it was seldom possible to take the food people had grown for themselves, their ammunition, boots, or medicine, and do it peacefully. Especially when Alec had nothing to exchange for the goods he took except his thanks.

They lost three men on such raids. In one of them the seemingly indestructable Jameson took an arrow in his thigh that left a wound that infected badly. He still favored that leg.

Twice they tangled with other raider bands and fled for their lives. The raiders were bigger and knew the territory better. Like primitive tribes, each band had staked out a territory for itself and drove off trespassers.

Feudalism, Alec realized. They protect the villages and in return the villagers supply them with food. He shrugged to himself. Well, it's a step up from barbarism.

Alec himself was wounded slightly in the arm, and they lost a fourth man the one and only time they went into a city.

Their sporadic contacts with the satellite had at least provided them with information about the radioactivity levels of the cities. Many of the urban areas had not been bombed, and fallout levels had diminished over the quarter-century since the sky burned, although the eastern seaboard from Boston to Norfolk was still a glowing tangle of devastation for fifty kilometers inland.

They had reached the Ohio River, travelling mostly on foot since the trucks had failed. The summer heat was like a weight pressing on them, although they had adapted to the sunshine by tanning darkly. They commandeered trucks or cars wherever they could find them, abandoning them when they ran out of fuel. Once in a while they would find a few horses, but such animals were usually guarded more passionately than food or women by the farmers in the villages. And Alec found it very strange and difficult to ride a vehicle that had a mind of its own. It wasn't merely a matter of steering it; he had to fight a battle of wills to make the beast do anything at all.

Cincinnati was to their west and still dangerously radioactive, the satellite sensors showed, from the bombing of the big U.S. Air Force base in nearby Dayton. The cities along the Ohio River were mostly abandoned, emptied because the surviving people could not feed themselves inside their cities. And the diseases that had scourged the survivors had been at their worst in the cities.

But empty or not, the cities were treasure-houses of canned food, ammunition, clothing, maps, compasses, vehicles, and even fast fuel dumps that still held usable gasoline. But even after twenty-five years, most of the earthlings shunned all the cities with superstitious dread.

Most of them. The satellite sensors could not warn Alec about the few crazed, ghoulish lunatics who haunted the dead, empty buildings. Nor of the rats and diseases that lingered there with them.

Alec's band numbered twenty-three when they reached Pittsburgh. The newcomers were youngsters, several still in their teens, with only the faintest fuzz on their chins. They had joined Alec's band from the villages, for adventure, for safety, for loot or women or to get away from parents or for any of the ancient reasons that turn a boy into a would-be warrior.

When they staggered away from Pittsburgh only nine of them were left. The city was teeming with rats and ferocious, feral dogs—and with wild-eyed, half-starved ragged screaming things that could barely be recognized as human. They fought as madmen fight, swarming into Alec's men by the hundreds, oblivious to the murderous fire that mowed them down, piling up their dead on the broken filthy streets and still coming, clawing over the corpses to get at the living.

It took two days to get out of the city, and they had never penetrated close to the heart of it. Constant fighting, night and day, until the men and their ammunition were both exhausted. The only way they got out at all was to torch the buildings on all sides with the precious fuel they had discovered in a cargo truck. They built a wall of fire between themselves and the attacking barbarians, retreating slowly back toward the hilly countryside behind a curtain of flame and smoke.

They left Pittsburgh on foot, nearly unarmed, limping, bleeding, smoke-blackened, totally exhausted.

Of the fifteen men who had stayed with Alec at Oak Ridge, only six still lived. The three other members of his gaunt-faced band were newcomers: Ferret and two farm boys.

They moved northward again. They stole or bluffed or bartered meager possessions for guns and ammunition. Ferret kept them well-fed, by his own standards. There was no extra fat on any of them. When Alec felt strong enough, they raided a few small villages, mostly at night. They even picked up a few more recruits.

Alec learned from a woman in one village that the local raider band had been trailing them for several days and planned to destroy them. He retreated from the village hurriedly, leaving a plain trail for the raiders to follow. They walked into his forest ambush. Alec's fourteen men, using a mixture of weapons from automatic rifles to crossbows, killed eighteen and took the weapons from their bodies as their comrades fled in panic. Then he returned to the village and took what he needed.

Now Alec travelled with a heavy automatic rifle

either slung over his shoulder or cradled in his arms. Its weight was his comfort. He nurtured the weapon, kept it carefully oiled and working smoothly. It protected his life. He slept with it at his side, like a woman.

Now it was autumn. They were in the lake country, the area where Douglas had been born and to which he had returned to carve out his primitive empire.

Alec lay on the damp leaves with his rifle comfortably tucked beside him, watching the village down in the valley through his binoculars. He was convinced the village supplied Douglas with corn.

"We'll hit them tomorrow," Alec told Jameson. "Take the village and hold it long enough to replenish our supplies, get fresh horses, and question them about Douglas' headquarters."

"Maybe they've got a truck," Jameson said, almost wistfully. It was such a difference from his usual matter-of-fact tone that it startled Alec. He doesn't like riding horses any more than I do!

"Maybe," Alec said, keeping his smile inward.

"Tonight," Ferret hissed. "Go when it's dark, huh?"

Shifting slightly in his prone position, enough to make the leaves crinkle under him, Alec disagreed. "No. Tonight they'll bottle themselves up inside their wall. Probably they'll have dogs out among the huts that would set up a yowl as soon as we approached. I wouldn't want to try to climb over that wall while the villagers are shooting at me."

Ferret's narrow, pinched face pulled into a scowl.

"We'll hit them tomorrow, when the men are out in the fields working. We can work our way through the corn right up to their gate."

Jameson added, "We'd better also take that supply wagon while it's on the way into the village.

Don't want anybody riding off to spread an alarm."

"Good thinking," Alec agreed.

The Sun was high in the early afternoon sky. The day was warm and drowsy with the buzz of insects. An old man, paunchy, mustacheoed, sat on a chair in the open gate of the village wall, his head on his chest, snoozing gently. An ancient shotgun lay across his lap.

Alec lay prone at the edge of the cornfield, watching the old man, giving his other men time to work their way through the tall rows of corn. It had taken nearly an hour, inching through the field slowly, crawling on their stomachs, avoiding the men picking the corn down at the far end of the field.

Now they were ready. Alec got to his feet and stepped out quickly, head ducked low, and snatched the shotgun from the old man's hands.

"Huh . . . wha . . ."

Alec handed the gun to Ferret, on his left, as he hissed, "Not a sound, grandfather. We don't want to hurt anyone."

They stood him up and marched him inside the gate. "Close it," Alec ordered. The old man did it, with help from one of Alec's men. Alec left the youngster there to watch the old man and marched the rest of his troop past the quiet huts toward the center of the village. He could hear the horse-drawn wagon clattering and creaking up ahead, but could not see it because the narrow village street twisted between rows of huts. Then a man's deep voice rumbled, "Hey, what the hell's going on here?"

Quickening his pace, Alec made his way to the cleared area at the center of the village. Jameson was standing atop the wagon, an automatic rifle resting casually on his hip, its muzzle pointing at the handful of villagers who stood in the clearing, looking shocked and alarmed. Gianelli and the other men whom Alec had sent out to capture the wagon were already fanning around the edges of the clearing. Down the lane by which the wagon had come, Alec could see two of his young bowmen swinging shut the village's other gate.

Most of the villagers in the clearing were women. A few small children clung to their mothers, already frightened. A couple of older men were easing back away from the wagon, their eyes on Jameson and his gun.

From behind them, Alec said, "You'd better stand still, all of you."

They jumped with surprise, then froze. Alec walked past them, up to the horses that pulled the wagon. They stood stolidly, placid-eyed, neither knowing nor caring about the games the humans played.

"We don't want anyone hurt," Alec said loudly enough for everyone to hear. "We don't intend to hurt any of you."

Standing under Jameson's protective gun, Alec ordered, "Gianelli, take your men and search every hut. I want everyone out here in the open. If there's any trouble," he pointed to the three men who now stood glaring at him, "these three will be shot immediately. Then the others." Alec said it without looking at the women and children.

"There won't be any trouble 'less you make it," one of the women spat. She was lean and hard and splintery-looking as the logs from which the huts were made.

"Good," Alec said. "Then we'll get along fine."

They secured the village quickly, Gianelli's men rousting out another half-dozen old men and women and a few more children. Plus a fair-sized array of guns, including a carbine and a submachine gun. And many crates of ammunition, all new-looking. Made in the past year, Alec thought.

Then Alec had his men reopen the gates and stay

out of sight behind the wall, awaiting the return of the village men from their fields. The villagers were returned to their huts and ordered to stay quietly inside them.

Jameson, satisfied that everything was under control, jumped down from the wagon. "Not bad," he said. "Twenty minutes to seize, search, and settle the prisoners."

Alec relaxed enough to grin at him.

"Got a surprise for you," Jameson told him, starting for the back of the wagon.

"Did you have any trouble taking the wagon?" Alec asked.

"No. Driver and two gunners, same as the past few days. Coming in for corn and hay. They didn't put up a fight, they saw they were covered. Got them in here . . ."

He dropped the wagon's rear panel and pulled a ragged covering off the three lumpy shapes back there.

"Angela!"

She was lying on the wagon's floor with two young men, all of them bound with their wrists behind their backs, their ankles tied together. Gags stuffed their mouths. She looked furious.

"She was one of the gunners. Tried to shoot me, too, before the driver convinced her she'd only get all three of them killed," Jameson said, a respectful smile on his face. "I thought you'd want to talk to her."

Alec jumped up on the wagon and pulled the gag from her mouth.

"I should've shot you," she snarled at Jameson. "If I'd thought you'd do this to me . . ."

"Quiet," Alec snapped. "Ron acted under my orders. We didn't want the wagon crew to give the villagers an alarm." He started to untie her wrists.

"I would have, too!" She yanked her hands free of the loosened cords and sat up, reaching for her ankles.

"What are you doing on a job like this?" Alec wondered.

"What's wrong with a woman on guard detail?" she raged. "I was the only one with guts enough to fight." She glared at the other two prisoners, still helplessly bound and gagged.

"That would have caused a lot of shooting. Here in the village and out in the fields, too. A lot of people would've gotten hurt. We're not trying to hurt these people."

"Not much!" She pushed him away and scrambled to her feet. "You're just trying to steal their food and weapons. Leave them hungry and defenseless."

"No," Alec said firmly. "What I want is what I came to Earth for: the fissionables. We've fought our way across the country all summer to get here. I know he's not far from here, and the fissionables are here too." He took her by the arm. "Where is he?"

She looked at him. There was a silly scrap of straw clinging to her cheek. She brushed it away. "He's not far," Angela said. "And when he finds out what you've done *he'll* find *you*."

"That's fine," Alec said. "One way or the other, it doesn't matter. But I still want to know where he is now and where the fissionables are stored."

Angela shook her head. "It wouldn't do any good, even if I told you. You'd just get yourself killed. You can't storm the base with a dozen men."

"I can get more."

She turned away.

"All right." Alec hopped off the wagon, then turned to help her down. She jumped down on her own. Frowning, he turned to Jameson. "Find an empty hut and lock her into it."

CHAPTER 20

The Sun swung down and touched the western hills. In small groups the village men came back from their fields, to be taken and disarmed—their faces slack with shock—by Alec's men. By nightfall the entire village was safely under guard.

"Hey!" Gianelli shouted in the flickering light of the fire they built in the center of the village square. "We found the wine!" He waved a wicker-covered jug over his head, then put it to his lips.

Alec was sitting by the fire, eating with Jameson. "Better make certain that no more than a couple of those jugs are opened," he said. "Put the rest under guard or break them. And keep the villagers inside their huts. I don't want any of our men grabbing their women. I want to stay as friendly with these people as we can."

Jameson nodded, finished scraping his plate clean, then moved off into the shadows.

Alec spent a fruitless couple of hours questioning the village men. None of them admitted to knowing where Douglas' headquarters were, except that it was west of their valley. For years they had been sending grain over the western road in exchange for protection.

They spoke seriously and politely. They shared the wine from several jugs together. They would reveal nothing. They spoke of Alec's father as "the Douglas," like "the Lord."

"You can see," Alec said, being careful to allow a long time between sips of wine, "that he isn't keeping his end of the bargain. Where is your protection?"

"It will come," one of the elders said sullenly.

"Protection should protect," Alec countered, "not revenge. My men could have burned your village, raped your women, murdered all of you."

"Ahhh . . ." said the old man who had been napping by the gate. "The Douglas knew that you were no ordinary raiding band."

"What?"

"He told us weeks ago that his son might pass this way."

"Shut up, you old fool!" a younger man snapped.

But Alec waved him down. "Douglas came here and warned you that his son might raid your village?"

The old man looked troubled now, uncertain. "Eh . . . it was something like that . . . perhaps I've got it wrong . . . I forget a lot nowadays . . ."

So he's expecting us, Alec thought.

They changed the subject, or tried to. Alec steered it back to the location of Douglas's headquarters. Jameson joined the circle around the fire, but still the villagers would admit nothing. Finally Alec bade them goodnight; they got up and returned to their huts.

Watching them drift into the darkness, Jameson murmured, "Be easier to guard them if we packed them all into one or two huts."

"Let them sleep in their own beds," Alec said. "We have their weapons, and they don't want any trouble."

Shrugging, Jameson said, "They didn't tell you much, did they?"

"Not much," Alec admitted.

"We have the wagon crew. They know where Douglas' headquarters is."

"Yes."

"And they know that we know. A little persuasion would open them up."

Alec said nothing.

"I could . . . um, talk with them. The two men,

that is. I wouldn't bother the girl."

"I'll talk to her," Alec said. "Maybe I can convince her . . ." He let the thought trail off.

"Alec," Jameson said, his lean face hidden in the shadows, "What do we do if she tells us where he is? We can't just walk up to Douglas and expect him to hand us the fissionables."

"No—but we can call down as many men as the settlement can provide. And I think we can recruit some of the people around here. They can't all be totally loyal to Douglas. They'll join our side for a share of the loot, especially when they see the army we can put together."

"You really think Kobol's going to bring down an army for you?"

"Not for me," Alec said. "For the fissionables. They'll have to." And he added silently, to himself, Even if Kobol's gained complete control of the Council he'll have to come here for the fissionables.

In the dwindling firelight, it was impossible to see the expression on Jameson's face. He said slowly, "Listen, Alec . . . some of the men don't think we'll ever get back to the settlement. They think we've been written off."

"That's not true!"

"It's what they think," Jameson said. "And . . . well, they're not all that unhappy about it. This is a big world here. We could carve ourselves a nice chunk of it, if we wanted to. Some of the men have even been wondering why we don't join up with Douglas . . ."

Alec almost swung at him. At the last instant he managed to check himself, already leaning toward Jameson with his fists clenched and ready.

Forcing his voice to remain calm, Alec asked, "Join the traitor? Let the settlement die?"

"They've left us to die."

"They'll send all the help we need, when we're ready for it."

Jameson made a low, sighing sound. "It better be soon, if you expect to have any of these men following you."

"It will be," Alec snapped. He was blazing hotter than the fire now, not trusting himself to say any more. He started to walk away.

"Wait," Jameson called. He unbuckled his gunbelt as he walked up to Alec. "If you're going to go strolling in the dark, you'd better have at least a pistol. Don't trust anybody."

Alec's anger softened. "All right," he said. "Thanks." He strapped the gun to his hip.

Walking down a crooked lane between two rows of huts, Alec saw that the stars were gleaming brightly. He recognized Orion rising sideways above the southern horizon. It'll be winter soon, he thought. We've got to get the job done before the snows start.

He paced along the bare dirt path slowly, thinking, planning, trying not to think of confronting Angela and questioning her. I've got to find a power source for the radios. Douglas must have a few tucked away here and there, this close to his headquarters. Find one, make a raid, stay long enough to get a message off to the satellite.

A sound pulled him up short. A gasp, scuffling, heavy breathing. He flattened himself against the rough logs of the nearest hut and slid the pistol from its holster.

Again. A muffled sound, almost a groan, but stifled.

Carefully, Alec edged along the log wall. A dim light glowed faintly from a doorway in the next hut. He tiptoed for it. More gasps, whispers, then a low voice saying:

"C'mon cutey . . . come across . . . you won't look too good if you don't . . ."

Alec stepped into the hut, gun level at his waist.

In the wavering light of a single candle, he saw

one of his own youngsters holding Angela's arms pinned tightly behind her back with one brawny arm, his other meaty hand over her mouth. Gianelli stood in front of her with a long, slim knife. Her shirt was torn away and three long welling red slashes streaked down one breast to the nipple. Her eyes were wide with pain and terror.

"Gianelli!"

He wheeled around. The knife blade was red.

"You want to find out where your father is, I'll find out for you," Gianelli said, his voice low and shaking with excitement. "I'll get a lot more out of her, besides."

"Get away from her."

The kid let his hand drop from Angela's mouth, but still held her arms.

"Listen," Gianelli said. "I've had a bellyfull of your orders. I'll get what you want from her and then I'll get what I want."

The gun's blast was deafening in the tiny hut. Gianelli slammed back against the wall, his mouth open in a silent "Ooohhh . . ." He dropped the knife and slid to the floor.

The kid stepped away from Angela, toward Gianelli's crumpled body. "I . . . he told me . . ."

Alec fired once more and the kid's face dissolved in an explosion of blood. Angela screamed and Alec grabbed her, pulled her out of the hut into the clean night air, leaving the stench of gunsmoke and blood behind them.

"They . . . they . . ." she gulped.

"They're dead," Alec said. He still held the gun. His hand was trembling so badly that it took three tries to slide it back into his holster.

Jameson was the first to reach them, a carbine in one hand. Half a dozen other men pounded up right behind him.

"What happened?"

"I just killed two men who couldn't follow orders. Drag them out into the village square and leave them there."

They were a quiet and subdued group when they left the village the next morning. The villagers stood mutely around the two corpses as Alec lined his men together and marched them out the gate, down the westward road. Angela rode on the captured wagon beside Alec. Douglas' man, unarmed, drove the horses.

She still seemed dazed. "You're just going to . . . leave the bodies there?"

Alec had not slept all night. His head throbbed. "Let the villagers bury them in the fields. Make good use of them."

"Why . . .? You didn't have to kill them."

He turned on the hard wooden seat to stare at her. She looked as bleak as he felt. "Did you want me to leave them with you?"

"I . . ." Angela ran a hand through her blonde hair. "In some crazy way I feel like it's my fault. Partially, at least."

"I shot them. They deserved it. If I had to do it all over again, I'd do it exactly the same way."

She shuddered visibly. "Because it was me."

"Because they were acting like scum!"

"With me. If it had been one of the village women . . ."

"I'd have done the same thing," Alec said coldly. "Don't flatter yourself."

They rode in silence for most of the morning, heading for the hills that bordered the western edge of the valley, under a sky of rolling fat cumulus clouds that checkered the landscape with warm sunlight and sudden cool shadow.

"Jameson found out last night that there's a relay station for the horses over the first row of hills," Alec said to her. "Is that true?"

She hesitated, then nodded. "Yes. And it's built like a little fortress."

"Can you talk the people there into giving us fresh horses peacefully, or will we have to fight?"

"Why should I help you?"

"You've got a damned short memory."

"No. A long one."

"All right, be tough. We'll get the horses anyway."

Which Alec did, by the simple expedient of threatening to shoot Angela if the men holding the station didn't give them all the horses in their fortified corral. Alec held Angela on a knoll, far enough from the station so that the men could see her plainly enough. Jameson did the negotiating.

Angela fumed, "You're *using* me!"

"That's right," Alec replied, smiling. "But that's better than killing people, isn't it?"

She was too angry to answer.

Toward sunset, as they rode together on the wagon, he asked her, "Still angry with me?"

"Yes." But she looked more sullen than angry.

"Are you in pain?"

"No."

"There's no soreness?"

"Of course it's sore! But it hasn't bled anymore. And the bandage is still in place. Want to inspect it for yourself?"

"Dammit, *I* didn't do it to you!"

"You killed them. You shot that boy."

"You ought to be glad that I did."

"You're a murderer and you expect me to love you for it?"

"You wanted me to leave you alone with them so they could carve you into little pieces?"

"So it's my fault!"

He knew he was red-faced; he could feel his cheeks burning. The driver kept his eyes strictly forward, not daring to show any expression at all on his face.

Lowering his voice, Alec said, "Yes, it was your fault. You were right this morning. If it hadn't been you I wouldn't have killed them. I lost control. I couldn't stand to see them with their hands on you. I . . ."

"All right," Angela said soothingly. "It's all right. I've been a terrible bitch. I'm sorry."

They rode together in silence, Alec's mind whirling in confusion, until it grew too dark to ride further.

CHAPTER 21

Alec slept with her that night. Without a word of prearrangement they walked off together from the campfire and took their blankets from the back of the wagon. Side by side, still unspeaking, they moved off into the darkness.

He made love to Angela gently, tenderly, trying to avoid hurting her. She held him, touched him, kissed him, moved with him until they both forgot about her injury.

In the morning they bathed together in an excruciatingly cold lake that stretched several kilometers wide. Alec still could not feel at ease using water so lavishly. This world is so rich!

By the time they were dressed and heading back to the camp again, Angela said, "You'll have to go back to the Moon, won't you?"

He couldn't take his eyes from her gold-framed face: lovely, troubled, serious.

"Not without you," he said.

Nodding, she answered, "I know. I'll have to leave him . . ."

"Who?"

"Father."

You mean *my* father."

She almost smiled. "Is there such a thing as foster-incest?"

"Will you come with me?" Alec asked.

She did not hesitate at all. "Yes," she answered. But her voice was so low that he could barely hear her.

They reached the camp by the side of the rutted road. The men were milling through their morning routine, cooking eggs from the village, grooming the horses, cleaning guns.

Alec said to Angela, "I'll need a power source for our radio. Not for very long, an hour or two."

Angela thought for a moment. "You won't be able to get one without a fight. The closest power source I know of is at a perimeter firebase, about twenty klicks from here . . . up in the hills, off the road."

A horse neighed somewhere behind them. The Sun was up over the distant hills now, burning away the fog that hung over the lake. The valley floor was still lushly green, the wooded shoulders of the hills an unbelievable pallette of reds, golds, oranges, browns, set off here and there by the somber deep greens of pines and hemlocks.

Angela said, "If I help you get a radio for a few hours, you'll go back to the Moon?"

"With you?"

'You'll give up the idea of trying to get the fissionables and go back?"

He hesitated, then lied, "Yes. I will." She's only trying to protect him, he told himself, although a deeper voice insisted, She's trying to protect you!

Reluctantly, as if she knew she was doing the wrong thing no matter what she did, Angela said, "All right, I'll show you where the firebase is. They have a radio there that can reach headquarters, and that's about fifty klicks away."

"That should be plenty of power for our radio," Alec said, trying to keep his voice even.

"I don't like it," Jameson said, staring off into the distant hills, sniffing the air for danger.

He and Alec stood at the edge of a gently rising meadow that ended in a thickly wooded hillside. The road they had travelled was farther down the slope. The Sun was high overhead but the wind was cold enough to make Jameson push his hands deep into the pockets of his worn, tattered trousers.

"We're deep inside their territory. They've got

to know we're here, they're not fools. Now we're going in even deeper."

Alec disagreed. "You're missing the point, Ron. This is their territory, all right. But look how big it is. They don't have enough men to patrol every hectare. We can stay in the woods, keep on the move, until we rendezvous with the reinforcements."

Still scanning the distances, Jameson countered, "And you think he's going to let a few shuttles land within fifty klicks of his home base without opposition?"

"By the time he can get some opposition mounted we'll have seized enough territory so that the shuttles can land and take off safely. Before they can organize a big-enough counterattack we'll have reached his headquarters and found the fissionables."

"Maybe," James said. "With a large scoop of luck."

"Not luck! We don't need luck. Just enough men and good timing."

"Well . . ." Jameson looked at Alec at last, then stuck out his hand. "Good luck anyway. You're marching yourself right into the bear's cave."

Alec let his hand be engulfed by Jameson's. "I'll be back tomorrow. And inside of a week or two we'll be home."

"Yeah." Jameson's voice went dead flat, as if the word *home* was starting to take on a different meaning.

Alec thought about that as he and Angela rode through the woods that afternoon, heading up the gentle slopes of the hills toward the firebase.

Home is the settlement. The Moon. Where it's safe and clean. Where Mother is. But another part of his mind added, Where it's cramped and small. Where life is rigidly determined by the amount of air and water available. Where the colors are whites and grays or pastels. Where you speak with polite restraint and wait your turn in the hierarchy that governs all.

Twisting around in his saddle, looking over the glorious autumn plumage of Mother Earth and the even wilder grandeur of the flaming sunset, Alec could understand why some of the men might be tempted to remain here. A flight of birds sped far overhead in a ragged vee formation and Alec's heart leaped at the sight of them. Their queer honking sounds drifted across the landscape.

"Winter's coming," Angela said.

Alec nodded. The birds were heading roughly southward. He took another look at them as they faded into the distant purple-reds of the dying day.

It took an effort to force his thoughts back to the settlement. No winter there. No seasons at all. How is Mother holding out? Can she still handle Kobol? Is the Council still loyal to her?

But as he asked himself these questions Alec found that he was watching Angela riding beside him, swaying softly and crooning to her horse as it plodded up the leaf-littered hillside.

They reached the crest of the final hill and Alec saw the firebase. It was small; it couldn't hold more than twenty men. A wooden fence topped with metal spikes ringed it. The gate was open, but guarded by two alert youngsters with carbines slung over their shoulders.

Even in the twilight, they recognized Angela as she rode up.

"Angie! We thought you'd been taken prisoner down in the village. There's some raider scum in the area . . ."

"I'm all right." She smiled at them as she got down off her horse. "The raiders have left the village. This is Alec . . . he's from the village. He came along with me, for protection."

The two boys shook Alec's hand. They *were* boys, no more than fifteen. But they carried their guns well and eyed Alec carefully, despite Angela's lie.

Inside the pallisade, two ancient artillery pieces stood mounted on wooden wheels, their heavy snouts poking skyward. Alec had such weapons on history tapes. They fired lumbering inert projectiles that contained high explosives. Sure enough, there was a neat pile of shells next to each piece. It must take a pair of men just to lift one of them, Alec thought. He also noted that there were only six shells per gun. They must be as ancient as the guns themselves, or damned difficult to manufacture properly. There were plenty of smaller weapons in sight: machine guns mounted on the wall, small rocket launchers, cannisters crudely marked FLAMMABLE with hoses that ended in pistol-grip nozzles.

They unsaddled their horses and slung their bags over their shoulders. Alec's bag had the extra weight of the radio transceiver. One of the boys led the horses to a roofed shelter that was already stocked with hay.

The other boy escorted them down narrow earthen steps that went into a complex of bunkers that honey-combed the ground under the firebase.

The firebase commander was an older man, graying at the temples. "Your father's putting together dozens of search patrols to find you," he told Angela sternly, as if she were a little girl who had wandered off into the woods.

"I'd better radio him right away and let him know I'm all right," she said.

The commander nodded curtly and took them to the radio room. The equipment looked old and impossibly bulky to Alec. He stood at the doorway beside the glowering commander and looked over the power generator and its connections while Angela got the radio operator to put her in touch with headquarters.

At last she pulled off the headphones and looked up to Alec and the commander. "He's already out in the field with Will Russo. They'll send a rider out to tell him that I'm okay."

"Good," the commander said. "I suppose you'll be spending the night here." He made it sound like a cross between a challenge and a complaint.

"Yes, I'd rather not travel in the dark."

The commander gave Angela his own bunk, set into a curtained niche cut into one end of the bunker's main room. He showed Alec a cot among a dozen others in a separate room, connected to the main room by a low, narrow tunnel some two dozen paces long.

They ate in the main room with the commander and six other men. Everyone seemed to know Angela well, but no one questioned her in the slightest about what had happened in the village. After the meal they went their separate ways. Alec stretched out on his bunk and actually fell asleep, almost at once. His last thought was that this bunker was like home, in the settlement.

He awoke to the sound of snoring. The room was dark. Slowly his eyes adjusted to the faint glow coming from the tunnel entrance. Most of the cots were occupied now by sleeping men, and in the darkness Alec thought that the form next to him was the commander himself.

Carefully, noiselessly, Alec got up and reached into the bag he had slipped under the cot. The radio felt solid and reassuring in his hands. He ducked into the tunnel and went slowly to the main room. It was empty and lit only by a single bare electric bulb hanging from a wire overhead. The power generator hummed softly, bringing a smile to Alec's lips. Pulling a wrinkled, weathered, handscribbled timetable from his shirt pocket, he checked the numbers carefully. Another half hour before the satellite could possibly be above the horizon.

After a moment's hesitation, Alec quickly climbed the earthen steps and poked his head out of the bunker's only entrance. Four men were standing by the pallisade, slumped with boredom or hunched against the cold, looking outward into the night. Two more sat by the fire, talking to each other in low, serious tones.

Alec ducked back inside. Angela was sleeping behind the curtain that partitioned off the commander's cubicle. He nodded. Everything's as good as it's going to be.

He went swiftly to the unattended radio room and jammed the makeshift wooden door shut, as tightly as he could. There was no way to lock it. He put the transceiver down on the operator's desk and spent the next few minutes connecting it properly to the antiquated power supply. Then he sat at the desk, slipped the single earphone over his head and swung the tiny microphone next to his lips. He waited an eternity to hear the satellite's automatic beacon beep out against the steady hiss and sputter of cosmic static.

The eternity ended at last.

"Hello, hello," he called as loudly as he dared. "Come in satellite station. Answer. This is Alec Douglas."

Another eternity, seconds long, and then, "Alec . . . Alec! Is it really you?"

"Yes. Can you hear me all right?"

"Faint but clear. Go ahead."

Alec gave his approximate position, then said, "Get the Council to send the strongest force they can put together down here as soon as possible. Within the week, at most. We can locate the fissionables and take them if we move quickly. Tell my mother that one quick, decisive stroke can win everything for us. Airdrop me electric power supplies, weapons and ammunition. I'll find it if you can drop it within ten kilometers of me."

"All right, but . . ."

"No buts! I want a strong force down here as fast as the Council can put it together. Men, weapons, trucks . . ."

"That's what I've been trying to tell you!" said the voice from the satellite. "Kobol's already landed a force of a hundred men—almost two weeks ago. Trucks, lasers, rockets, everything. It took five shuttle flights to get them all on the ground!"

"Kobol! Two weeks ago? Where? Where did he land?"

"Far south of you . . ."

"Oak Ridge?"

"No, further south. Someplace called Florida, I think."

Alec sat in the harsh light of the overhead bulb, stunned.

"Hey, Alec . . . you still there?"

He nodded, then realized that it was a meaningless gesture. "Yes . . . Listen. Get this message through to my mother. Tell her I'm within a few hours' striking distance of Douglas' headquarters and the fissionables. Tell her to shuttle Kobol's forces here. Order him here! Remind him that I'm still the commander of this mission, by order of the Council."

"Yes sir." The voice went formal.

"All right. And get a power supply to me right away. Tear one out of the bulkheads up there if you have to, but it's vital that I re-establish communications within twenty-four hours and I can't do it without a power supply."

"Will do!"

Alec signed off. For many long minutes he sat there, his mind whirling, wondering what Kobol was doing and why. But he was too tired to think straight. Slowly he disconnected the transceiver, then stealthily edged the door back to its open position and stepped into the bunker's main room.

Douglas was sitting at the table in the center of

the room, making the bunker look crowded with his bulk. Angela stood beside him, staring at Alec in cold fury.

"You made it through the summer, I see," Douglas said. He was smiling, but there was no humor in his voice.

CHAPTER 22

For a stunned moment Alec didn't know what to say or do.

Douglas seemed to enjoy his surprise. "Do you really think you've been out of my sight for one minute since you landed on Earth?" He spread his massive hands in an all-inclusive gesture. "From the minute you touched down at Oak Ridge you've been under surveillance. I've been impressed. You learn very quickly. There were only three or four times when I was tempted to step in and help you."

"You haven't lifted a finger," Alec snapped. "We fought our way here on our own."

"That's right," Douglas agreed. "You spent the summer working out an experiment—in survival. The experiment was a success. You survived. You even helped us to polish off some of those raider bands." He laughed, and the underground bunker seemed to shake with it. "Lord, they'd get their attention all focused on your pitiful little gang and start licking their chops. Then Will would swoop in and clobber them. It was sweet."

"Glad to have been of help to you."

Douglas's laugh faded to a cocky grin. "I've never turned down help from any quarter. I'm not too proud to accept your help."

"As long as you can have things your way."

"Of course."

Still standing at the doorway to the radio room, Alec asked, "And what do you plan to do with my pitiful little gang now?"

"Will's going to speak to them in the morning. Offer them a chance to join us. Most of them will, I expect. The rest will be escorted out of my territory, politely but firmly. Maybe they can work their way south again and link up with Kobol." Douglas scratched at his iron-gray beard. "We, ah . . . overheard your radio conversation on the monitor in my jeep."

"We," Alec echoed, looking at Angela. She refused to meet his gaze. For the first time, anger began to seep in and replace the shock that had numbed him.

"Get yourself some sleep," Douglas said, hauling himself to his feet. "We travel at sunup."

He went to the stairs and started up. Angela followed him. She glanced over her shoulder at Alec for a fleeting instant, but said nothing.

Bitch! he snarled at her, silently.

Strangely enough, Alec slept deeply through the remainder of the night. Dreamlessly. He awoke with a slight sense of guilt at feeling so rested.

Douglas's jeep was parked just outside the pallisade. Alec was marched to it by an armed man as soon as he got up. No breakfast, no formalities; none of the firebase crew said a word to him. The morning was raw and chill. Thick gray clouds covered the sky from horizon to horizon, making the rolling hills seem somber and grim, muting even the wild colors of the autumn trees.

Douglas was already at the wheel of the jeep, a dark blue windbreaker over his nondescript clothes. Angela was talking with him, very seriously. A blanket was wrapped over her shoulders.

The guard sat Alec in the back seat of the jeep. Angela started to go around to sit beside him. The guard looked questioningly at Douglas.

"It's all right," Douglas said, his big hands gripping the jeep's steering wheel. "Let her sit back there with him. You ride shotgun up front. He won't try to run away. He's been waiting all summer to see our base. Right, son?"

Alec said nothing.

With a shrug, Douglas added, "Maybe, if you behave yourself, I'll even let you see where the fissionables are stored."

Angela climbed in beside him, the guard swung into the right front seat beside Douglas and laid his heavy black pistol on his lap. Douglas glanced at the threatening sky, then started the engine. The electric motor purred to life and the jeep started slowly, gathering speed as it jounced down the hillside, down the narrow trail.

The wind was raw and it sliced right through Alec's thin shirt.

"Here," Angela said. She pulled a thermos bottle from under the seat and took the top off. Steam wafted from its innards. Alec accepted it wordlessly and took a small sip of hot broth. Then a gulping mouthful. He handed it back to her.

"Thanks."

She nodded and pulled the blanket closer around her shoulders. For several kilometers they rode that way, side by side, silent and angry. Finally, Angela shook her head as if she had been arguing with herself, then unwrapped the blanket and offered part of it to Alec.

"Before you freeze," was all she said.

He hesitated a moment, then pulled the warm fabric across his shoulders. Automatically they slid closer together, huddling together under the blanket.

"You told Douglas where he could get me," Alec said to her.

Her face set into a stubborn frown. "You used me, didn't you? You had no intention of going back to the Moon without the fissionables. Did you think I fell for your lies?"

I fell for yours, he answered silently. Then he shook his head and said to her, "I guess I've been outsmarted all along."

"You've outsmarted yourself."

"We'll see."

"Why did you lie to me?" she asked, her tone

more hurt than angry. "Was it just to screw me or to get the radio? Which one?"

"I wasn't lying," he said. Before she could reply, he added, "I didn't tell you the whole truth . . . but I wasn't lying when I said I want you to come back to the Moon with me."

Angela's frown softened, but her eyes were still wary, searching. "You mean, after you've taken the uranium."

He nodded.

"You knew that wasn't what I meant when I offered to get you to the power supply."

"Yes, I knew."

"Then you were lying to me."

"And so were you," he countered, "when you offered to help me. You knew you were going to call Douglas and trap me."

"I know you'll have to kill him before you can get your hands on the fissionables."

"And you're protecting him."

"I'm trying to protect both of you," she said earnestly, urgently.

"And that's why you lied to me."

She almost smiled. "All right, I lied too. Feel better?"

"Yes." It *was* almost funny. They had both been sneaking around each other.

"But he needs you, Alec. What he's trying to do . . ."

He stiffened. "Douglas? He doesn't need anybody. He's got enough ego to cover the world all by himself."

"And you're blind!" she snapped.

Douglas' base was a shock. They drove up to a well-maintained wire mesh fence that seemed to wind clear across the landscape, over the rolling hills and as far as the eye could see. Where the road penetrated the fence stood a sentry tower, wooden beams weathered by sun and rain. Two men lounging at the base of the tower straightened the guns on their shoulders and opened the gate wide enough for one of them to step through. Douglas brought the jeep to a full halt and exchanged a few words with him.

They swung the gate wide. Alec saw that there were at least two more men up at the top of the tower. The grim snout of a heavy machine gun poked out over the railing up there.

After another chilly fifteen minutes of driving, with nothing to be seen but open countryside, they came to the first buildings.

"This used to be a base for the United States Air Force," Douglas called back from the driver's seat. "Makes an ideal headquarters for us—ready made. They used to call this area *Rome*. Appropriate name, don't you think?" He laughed; Alec did not.

They drove past row after row of neat wooden buildings, most of them looking as if they had been freshly painted. Barracks, machine shops, warehouses, mess halls, even a building marked BASE THEATER in barely readable faded lettering. The airfield itself was immense, huge swaths of concrete runways and ramps, hangars and maintenance buildings and office towers built of brick and stone. All in excellent condition. But not an aircraft in sight.

"The missile assigned to this base must've missed its target or been shot down," Douglas said. "It went untouched."

We could land the shuttles right here, Alec was thinking.

People were everywhere. Throngs of people, more than Alec had ever seen in his life. Walking, working, laughing; many of them waved to Douglas as he drove past. Hardly any of them carried weapons. Like the history tapes of the old cities, Alec saw.

They drove past the airfield, out to a more deserted sector of little knolls topped by small clumps of vividly colored trees. No buildings in sight out here, except one solitary concrete blockhouse standing on a bare grassy hill. Douglas drove straight to the blockhouse.

"This is where the fissionables are," he said, turning in the too-small bucket seat to face Alec. "Want to see 'em?"

Alec supressed an impulse to lick his lips. "Yes."

Douglas hauled himself out of the jeep and headed for the blockhouse door. The guard stepped out of his seat and turned toward Alec. He slid the pistol back into its holster, but kept his hand on its butt. Alec climbed out and turned to help Angela, but she had already jumped out on the other side.

Douglas had the heavy metal door open already, and Alec frowned inwardly at the realization that he hadn't seen if it had been locked or not. Doesn't matter, he told himself. We can blow it open if we have to.

Inside, the blockhouse was musty and damp. It was a small room, completely empty and dark except for the light sneaking in through the gun slits in each wall.

"Eh, would you mind?" Douglas gestured toward a metal trapdoor set into the cement floor. "I can't bend as easily as you can."

Alec reached down and grabbed at the metal catch at one end of the steel door. He tugged, then heaved. Nothing.

"It slides," Douglas said.

"Thanks for telling me before I ruptured myself." The door slid back smoothly. It's been oiled recently, Alec realized.

They clattered down a long metal stairway into utter darkness, groping along the wall and railing until Douglas said, "Wait a minute . . . the generator switch should be . . . here . . ."

A click, and then from somewhere in the darkness below them a rumble and whine from a diesel generator set. Alec smelled a whiff of machine oil. Then lights glowed into life.

He could see that the stairs went down another twenty meters and ended in a huge storehouse room. Spread across the floor were heavy, dull-gray metal cylinders, each bearing the blood-red three-sided emblem of danger and the printed words RADIOACTIVE MATERIAL. There were dozens of the cylinders, Alec saw, scores of them. A hundred, maybe more.

Enough to power the processing plants for a century, at least.

As if reading his thoughts, Alec said, "There's enough fissionable material here to blow up everything between the Greak Lakes and Cape Cod."

Alec turned to his father, standing two steps above him. "We need this . . . some of it, at least. We need it to live."

But Douglas shook his head. "No. If I let you take even some of this back to the Moon, we'd be killing them. You can kill people with kindness, you know. The wrong sort of kindness."

Alec could feel himself going tense, the skin on his face stretching taut. "In another year we won't have the energy to process the water and medicines we need. You can't . . ."

"Don't tell me what I can't do!" Douglas's voice boomed off the cement walls and metal stairs. "Those people can't survive up there by themselves no matter how much fissionable fuel they have. They can't live cooped up in their underground rats' nest. They've got to re-establish contact with Earth. Not just a raid every few years, but real contact—genetically meaningful contact!"

"So you can rule them!" Alec lashed back at his father.

Douglas's mouth opened, but no words came out. He broke out into a roar of laughter, instead.

They quartered Alec in a room of his own, in what had once been the Air Base's bachelor officers' quarters. The two-story brick building was an efficient but drab set of dormitory rooms. They were spacious, compared to what Alec had grown up with. His room was on the second floor, in a corner, so that he had two windows. There was a real bed, a desk, and a chest of drawers. Alec smiled at the furniture. He had nothing to put in the drawers, nothing to hang in the closet.

But there was a shower, and it worked! For a slothful long hour Alec luxuriated in the unbelievable pleasure of having actual water, steaming hot, sluicing over his naked body. Two large pieces of fuzzy cloth hung on a rack next to the shower; Alec used them to rub himself dry.

Someone tapped at his door. Wrapping one of the cloths around his waist, he yelled, "Come in," as he stepped from the bathroom in time to see Angela open the hall door, carrying an armful of clothes.

"Oh . . . " They said it together.

She simply stood there gaping at him. Alec clutched at the towel, holding it tightly around his middle, feeling foolish about it but embarrassed to let it slip.

"I was cleaning myself . . ." he said lamely.

She grinned at him, making his face redden. "So I see." She wore a pale blue dress that complemented her eyes and golden hair. The skirt was short enough to show that her legs were fine and graceful.

"You look very pretty," he said.

"So do you," she replied, with a giggle.

Flustered, he stood tongue-tied.

"I brought some fresh clothes for you from the supply shop," Angela said. "I hope they fit okay. If they don't, I can fix them for you."

"Thanks."

She dropped the clothes on the bed. Looking around the room she asked, "Is everything okay? Do you need shaving things?"

"No," he answered. "I won't need another depilatory treatment for six months or so."

"Oh. Okay."

"Is there someplace to eat around here? Have you had dinner?"

"The mess hall will be open in an hour. If you're really hungry I can fix you something at my place. It's not far from here."

"Uh, no, that's all right. Guess I'd better get dressed."

"Okay." She started for the door.

"No, wait." For Christ's sake, this is idiotic. We've made love together! "Don't go . . . Let's have dinner together."

She nodded and smiled at him.

Feeling utterly silly, Alec took the clothes into the bathroom and tried them on. Turtleneck shirt, dark blue and thickly ribbed. Gray slacks that were too large in the waist and so long that he had to turn the cuffs up twice. A pair of solid boots, good size. A belt to pull the pants tight. And they all smelled clean, felt soft.

"How do I look?" he asked as he came out of the bathroom.

She smiled and frowned at the same time. "I wasn't too good about the sizes, was I?"

"Only the pants. The rest fits fine."

They had dinner in the noisy, crowded, clattering mess hall, sitting on benches at long wooden tables surrounded by steam and pungent odors and other people who chattered their conversations, oblivious of Alec and Angela. They sat side by side, saying almost nothing to each other. The food was hot and solid, nothing fancy, but more of it than Alec had been able to get since leaving the Moon.

Outside afterward, it was dark and their frosty breaths hung in the air before them. The buildings were all alight. Why not? Alec thought. He's probably got nuclear generators buried underground somewhere, using the fuel we need.

They walked under the chilled stars to Angela's home, a separate little house at the head of a curved row of white wooden houses.

"I have some wine," she said. "The villagers make it."

Inside, the house was a combination of warmth and utilitarianism. Furniture was sparse. The front room was completely empty except for a single old wooden chair with a high straight back and a rug made from some sort of animal fur, rolled up in a corner. The fireplace looked cold and empty. Angela led Alec back to the kitchen, which had a table and three mismatched chairs, as well as a small refrigerator, stove and sink, all lined against one wall. Through another doorway Alec could see the bedroom. There was nothing in it except a mattress on the floor with a sleeping bag half unrolled atop it.

"You have this place all to yourself?"

"Yes," she said, reaching down to a cabinet under the sink and pulling out a dusty green bottle. "I just moved in a few weeks ago. Da . . . uh, Douglas said it was time for me to have a place of my own. He lives in the house down at the other end of the row. Will and most of the other leaders live here . . . or really, their families do. Most of the time the men are out in the countryside somewhere."

"Will has a family?"

She set the bottle on the table next to Alec and took two glasses from a cabinet. "He was going to marry a girl from one of the villages west of here.

But she was taken by one of the raider gangs. No one's been able to find her since."

Somehow that hit Alec like a physical blow.

Angela brought the glasses to the table. Sitting next to Alec, she said softly. "It happened years ago . . . he got over it."

"Did he?"

She shrugged. "He functions. He lives. He even sings, sometimes."

Alec let his breath out in a pent-up sigh. "It's a lousy world."

"It's the only one we've got."

No, it isn't, he answered silently.

Eyeing the wine bottle, Angela asked, "Will you pour, or shall I?"

He took the bottle and pulled the stopper out of it. Funny, spongy thing. Cork? he wondered. Somewhere he had heard about the substance. Very carefully, conscious for the first time in months of Earth's six-fold gravity pull, he half-filled the two glasses with bright red wine.

It tasted marvelous. Smooth and warm and warming.

He put the glass down firmly on the table. "It's not the only world we've got, Angela. There's an entirely different world, where all this insanity of raiders and killing doesn't exist."

"The lunar settlement," she said.

"Right. Civilization. Where you don't have to carry weapons all the time and worry if you'll make it through the night."

"But we have that here!" Angela said. "That's what Douglas has built for us here."

"Yes . . . by force, by war, by betraying the people who trusted him."

Her eyes flashed, but she caught herself and changed the subject. "Tell me more about the lunar colony. What's it like up there?"

With an effort, Alec pushed his own smoldering anger aside. "It's peaceful. Polite. People can be human beings instead of jungle animals. You don't have this heavy gravity pulling on you all the time. You can sail in the aerogymn and dance all the ballets ever written."

"Ballets?" Angela looked puzzled.

Never heard of them, he realized. "Up on the surface," Alec went on, "you can see real beauty. I mean, it's beautiful here on Earth, of course, wild and unpredictable and all . . . but on the Moon, watching the sunrise takes a whole day. And the stars . . . and Earth itself, hanging there blue and beautiful. You can go for a thousand klicks in any direction and never see another person, alone, just by yourself, with the whole universe hanging up there and watching you . . . ."

"It sounds lonely."

"No, it's beautiful. Watching the ice vents outgas right after the perigee quakes. There's just enough sulfur dioxide in the rocks to tint the vapor pink—the stuff puffs up and out like a ghost escaping from its grave."

Angela shuddered. "That doesn't sound beautiful to me."

"Wait 'till you see it."

"I'll never see it," she said. Sadly.

"Yes you will. I'm taking you there, remember?"

"No . . ."

He hunched forward in his chair. "God, you're beautiful. Let's go to bed."

She didn't look surprised. "There's more to it than that, Alec."

"What?"

"If Douglas finds out . . ."

He pulled back from her. "He means more to you than I do."

"No, it's not that," she said. "Alec . . . I don't mean anything to you. Not really. You can screw me one minute and try to trick me the next."

"You did the same damned thing!"

"Because I knew that's what you were doing! You didn't fool me, not for one minute."

"Then why did you go to bed with me?"

Her voice rising, "Because you saved me and I was scared and you were kind—no, you killed those two . . . oh, hell! I don't know. I did it because I wanted to."

"And you don't want to now."

"Yes, I do want to."

It took a moment for Alec to realize what she had said. Then, leaning back in his chair, he wondered aloud, "Then what are we arguing about?"

Angela shook her head. "You don't understand any of it, do you? Not a bit of it."

But she got up from the table and took him by the hand and led him into the bedroom.

The first light of dawn woke Alec. He lay with Angela's soft warmth beside him, her head cradled in his arm, and watched the day slowly brighten through the bedroom window. The sleeping bag was spread lumpily over them.

"Are you going to stay?" Angela asked very quietly.

"Huh? I thought you were sleeping."

She smiled at him. "I've been thinking for the past couple of hours."

"With your eyes closed?"

"Are you going to stay here . . . at the base, I mean?"

"Do I have a choice? I'm a prisoner."

Pushing away from him slightly, she said, "Oh, that. You don't have to worry. Douglas just wanted you to come here without any fuss. He wouldn't stop you from leaving. He does love you, you know."

"The hell he does."

"Don't be a fool. Of course he does."

Then why did he leave us? Alec demanded

silently. What kind of love is that?

"Well?" she asked.

"What?"

"Are you going to stay here?"

"Would you come with me if I left?" he countered.

"No. I couldn't."

"Because *he* needs you more than I do."

She laughed. "Don't be silly. Douglas doesn't need me. He doesn't need anybody except one person."

"Who's that?"

"You."

He huffed. "Don't be funny."

Angela sat up and pulled her knees up to her chin. The cover slid down to her ankles, and Alec shivered; not from the room's chill, but from the curve of her smoothly fleshed back and hip.

"Look," she said, "What you don't . . ."

"I'm looking," he murmured.

She intercepted his reaching hand. "Not now. You've got to realize a few things. Douglas is an old man . . ."

"Fifty-five. That's not old."

"It is when you've lived the way he has," Angela said, completely serious. "He needs help. Your help. That's why he brought you here. He was overjoyed that you made it all the way here from Oak Ridge. He bragged about how you got through the summer on your own."

"I'll bet."

"He wants you to join with him, help him bring the lunar settlement and his own territory here together. If the two of you can work together you can build a real civilization that links the Earth and the Moon. But if you fight . . ."

"Listen to me," Alec snapped. "He ran out on us. Not just on my mother and me, but on hundreds of men, women and children who depended on him, trusted him. He's stolen the fissionables that we need. Without them we'll all die. He won't let us have them."

"Yes he will!" Angela insisted. "If only you'll agree to help him."

"Help him make himself into another Genghis Khan? He can rot first."

"You just don't understand!"

"Wrong! I understand far more than you do. Far more."

She shook her head. "No, Alec, you're wrong. You're all wrong about so many things."

Instead of answering, he got to his feet. The bare floor was cold.

"Where are you going?" she asked.

"Back to my own quarters."

"Not yet." She slid one hand up the side of his leg. He turned and sank to his knees on the mattress.

"You don't have to go now," Angela said, almost in a whisper. "And stop pouting. What's going on between you and your father has nothing to do with what's going on between you and me."

Doesn't it? he demanded in his mind. Aren't you doing this to make me stay here, to get me to join forces with him?

But although he thought it, Alec did not say anything as Angela pulled him back into the warmth of the bed again.

CHAPTER 23

It was easy to slide into the routine of daily life at the base.

The leaves fell steadily from the trees, the grass turned brown and brittle. The wind came always from the north or west, cold and sharp enough to cut through the heaviest of coats. The sky turned gray as the days shortened. The Sun did not climb far above the horizon and the Moon seemed to have disappeared from the cloudy night skies. One titanic rainstorm stripped away the last of the leaves, blew off roofs and tore limbs from the bare trees. Alec's quarters stayed dry, although the heat and electricity went out for several days. Angela's house was flooded to a depth of ten centimeters in the cellar.

Then the weather turned fine and dry. Days were cold, invigorating. Nights were arctic. More and more, Alec slept with Angela. If Douglas knew about it, he said nothing, even though they dined together frequently in his house with Will Russo and others of Douglas's aides.

It was an easy time. The summer's fighting was over and everyone was preparing for the long winter. Trucks and wagons came in every day from the outlying villages, heaped with produce from the harvest. They went out with tools, guns, and ammunition that had been manufactured in the base's shops.

Troops of warriors came in from the hinterlands, reunited with families and friends that they had not seen all summer. There were parties, celebrations, even dramatic offerings by self-styled actors and singers in the base's mammoth, bare auditorium.

Alec found their efforts amateurish, but he attended every performance, sitting with Angela next to him. Douglas always sat front row center and it always appeared to Alec as if the performers were playing especially to him. He appeared to enjoy himself hugely, guffawing at the jokes and applauding every effort lustily.

Will had brought in a cache of whisky, "liberated" from a long-deserted city that his troop had detoured through. He rationed the stuff carefully, except for one long night when he gave a party and they all—even Alec—sang drunkenly until the Sun rose.

All except Douglas, who left early in the evening after a few drinks. And by the time they started singing "The Frigging Bird" for the fourth time, Angela slipped quietly away, too.

"I wanted to check on Douglas," she explained the next morning. "He didn't look too well when he left."

Through his thundering hangover, Alec said, "So you had to nursemaid him."

"You seemed to be having fun," she answered, smiling.

But I don't want you with him, Alec said to himself. I want you with me. And suddenly he realized that he loved her.

A few nights later they were walking arm in arm from the mess hall to her house, heavily bundled in thick coats and wool hats and gloves. The water in the nearby lake had a thin layer of ice over it, and the only birds still remaining around the base were hardy brown sparrows who puffed up their feathers and hopped over the dead grass looking for seeds or crumbs.

For the first time in weeks, Alec noticed the Moon. It was only a sliver sailing eerily among the clouds scuttling by.

"I wonder how my men are doing?" he mused aloud.

"Have you asked . . ."

"I've tried to get to them, but Will said it's better if I don't. He told me they're all okay, but I shouldn't ask anything more about them."

"Will wouldn't lie to you," she said.

Gazing at the thin slice of a Moon, he wondered, "Do you think Kobol's still in Florida? Or has he returned to the settlement? What's he up to? What's his game?"

Angela said nothing.

"He'll be back in the spring," Alec went on. "I'll bet he heads this way, next spring."

"Then there'll be fighting," she said.

"Plenty of it."

They had reached Angela's house. "And when the fighting begins, which side will you be on, Alec?"

He thought about it. "I don't know," he answered honestly. "I just don't know."

The first snowfall came early and caught everyone by surprise, Alec most of all.

He walked out into the howling wind, turning dizzily round and round to watch the strange white flakes bury the world in their clean coldness. They spattered against his face and hands as drifts built up against the buildings. He trudged to Angela's and dragged her out into the snow. She taught him how to make a snowball and they pelted each other until they laughed themselves into wet exhaustion.

Then they spent the rest of the day by her fireplace, not thinking of food or anything else except each other.

It was Will Russo who pulled Alec away for a few days.

After more than a week of steadily heavier hints, Will finally asked Alec if he would go with him into the woods on a hunting trip. Something in the way he asked implied that he had more on his mind than simply hunting. Alec agreed.

They set off across the solidly frozen lake early one morning, as the Sun was just starting to brighten the eastern sky. Alec felt plainly nervous about walking on ice, even though the snow atop it made the going easy. All that water below, he kept thinking. But Will chattered happily, even hummed to himself occasionally, perfectly at ease. So Alec shifted the heavy pack on his shoulder harness and tried to forget what would happen to them if the ice broke.

They spent the whole day up in the hills, moving straight ahead, following some inner sense of direction or purpose known only to Will. The snow was thinner up under the fir trees, barely a dusting on the ground.

"Will," Alec asked, pulling up alongside his long-striding companion, "what are we hunting for?"

"Three men," he replied, trying to replace his happy grin with a serious look. He was only partly successful.

"What? Men? With these?" Alec hefted the long-barrelled rifle Will had given him. It fired only one shot at a time.

"Well, maybe we won't have to use the guns. They might come peacefully."

"I thought we were going for meat . . . to eat."

With a swipe at his nose, Will answered, "Nope. Trappers bring in plenty game for the table. Oh, we might bag a deer or something on our way back. But only after we deal with the thieves."

"Thieves?"

Still striding along fast enough to force Alec to trot every few moments to catch up, Will answered, "They joined one of our scout parties late summer. I thought all they wanted was a safe, warm place to spend the cold months. But a couple weeks ago they took off with a wagonload of food, guns, and ammo."

"A couple of weeks ago? They could be in Asia by now!"

"Nope, they're not. They had to shoot their way past the gate guards, and one of 'em was wounded. Killed two of our guards, by the way. Other guards followed them for a while, and we've had relays of scouts trailing them—at a distance. Don't want anybody hurt unnecessarily."

That made sense to Alec. But now, "We're going to take them in?"

"Right. They're holed up in a cave, out of food. One of them's still in bad shape from his wounds, I imagine. The other two might listen to reason."

"And if they don't?"

Will hiked his eyebrows. "That's why we're carrying the rifles."

They camped in the woods overnight and ate from the food they had carried with them. Only a small fire. They slept in sleeping bags. Alec was shivering when he woke up next dawn.

By midmorning they were halfway up a barren hill. Underneath its coating of snow, where the wind had blown bare patches, it looked as if the ground had been scorched black. No trees grew on the hillside, and only a few stunted, gnarled bushes stuck their tortured bare limbs out of the snow.

"There's the cave," Will said, pointing with his rifle.

Up near the top of the rocky hill was a black fissure between two large boulders.

A clatter of pebbles behind them made Alec whirl around, rifle cocked and levelled. He saw a man, old and gnarled as the nearby bushes, whiplash thin, with a cold-whitened face that was mostly bones and eyes. His mouth was sunken, toothless, and his heavy fur hat was jammed down until it merged with the bulky collar of his rough coat.

"They're still in there," the old man said to Will as he advanced carefully toward them. "Haven't seen any signs of smoke or a fire for three days now." He said *fie-yuh* for *fire*, an accent Alec hadn't heard before.

"Not much firewood to be had around here, that's for sure," Will said.

"Eh-yup," said the scout.

"Okay. Good." Will wriggled out of his shoulder harness, reached inside the pack and took out two oblate metal objects. Grenades, Alec realized.

Pushing one grenade into each of his coat pockets, Will said to them, "You two stay here and cover me. I'm gonna see if they'll listen to some sense." He picked up his rifle and started scrambling toward the top of the hill.

Alec kneeled in the snow and clamped his rifle under his arm, pointing it in the general direction of the cave.

"They're bad poison," the scout muttered in his strange accent. "Caught Johnny Fullah last week and shot him through both knees. Left him crippled to bleed to death in the snow. Lucky I found him before the wolves did."

Alec glanced at the old man, then put the rifle to his shoulder and aimed it dead at the cave opening. Will was nearly at the edge of the big boulder on the left of the cave.

"Hello the cave!" he shouted.

No reply.

"We know you're in there. We know you're cold and hungry and your friend needs medical help, if he's not dead already. Come on out and we'll take you back to the base. I'm a medic, I can help your wounded man."

"And then hang us!" a voice shouted back. It sounded young and trembly to Alec.

"That's up to the jury. You'll get a fair trial."

"We ain't comin' out!" It was definitely a young voice, cracking with fear.

Will talked with them for half an hour, patiently, almost pleasantly. He pointed out to them the hopelessness of their situation, urged them to come out peacefully.

Finally the voice said, "Okay . . . okay, you win . . ."

Will grinned back down toward Alec, then rose to his feet. "Good," he said toward the cave. "I knew . . ."

The shot exploded, echoed by the cave walls, and knocked Will completely off his feet. He tumbled, flailing legs and arms, down the rough hillside. A yellow-haired figure darted from the cave mouth and dashed off toward the right.

Alec had let his rifle rest on his knee, but without thinking about it he snapped it to his shoulder and fired. The rock chipped in front of the fleeing blond. He skidded to a stop, pawing at his eyes. Alec fired again, slamming him back against the rock. Again, and the figure jerked once more and crumpled to the ground.

Alec swung his rifle back to the cave's mouth. Another shot boomed out, and the snow puffed a few centimeters in front of Will's sprawled body. Alec emptied the rest of his clip at the cave's entrance. The firing stopped. He scrambled up the few steep meters to Will's side. There was a spreading red stain across his coat front. His eyes were open, but hazy.

"Don't . . . don't . . ." Will mumbled. Alec heard more shots, from behind. He glanced over his shoulder and saw that the scout was aiming a smoking pistol rock-steady at the cave's mouth.

"Give them a chance . . . they're scared . . ." Will said weakly.

"I'll give them a chance," Alec said. He pulled the two grenades from Will's pockets. One of them was slippery with blood. Hooking a finger through their firing rings, Alec grabbed Will's rifle with his free hand and made his way, doubled over, toward the entrance to the cave.

There was no more firing. Flattening himself along the boulder beside the cave entrance, Alec yelled, "You've got five seconds. Come out with your hands up or I'll blow you all to hell."

The same high, cracking voice shrieked. "Wait! Gimme a chance . . . he's out cold . . . I gotta drag him . . ."

But Alec was counting, not listening. He reached five, glanced at Will still sprawled on his back in the snow halfway down the slope, then pulled the pin from one grenade and tossed it into the cave.

"Hey . . . wh . . . no . . . *wait!*"

The explosion sounded strangely muffled. Smoke poured from the cave and Alec heard a high, keening screech, long and raw and agonized. He yanked the pin and threw in the second grenade. The explosion blotted out all other sounds, and by the time the smoke had wafted out of the cave, all was silent inside.

Alec edged into the cave carefully, rifle cocked. It took half a minute for his eyes to adjust to the gloom. There was enough left of the two bodies to recognize that they had once been human. Barely enough.

He walked out and went to the blond he had shot. The kid could not have been more than fourteen. He lay where he had fallen. There was no gun or any other weapon near him.

The wind gusted. Alec looked up and saw that the scout was at Will's side.

"Don't look too good," the old man said as Alec joined them. "Think they got a rib. Mighta punctured th' lung."

"Can we move him?"

"Got to. Can't leave him hee-yuh."

They bound Will's chest as tightly as they dared, Alec tearing strips from his own shirt. Then Alec sent the scout on ahead to get help as he wedged himself under Will's arm, on his good side, and started to help him to his feet.

"What about . . ." Will sagged, nearly dragging Alec to his knees, " . . . those kids."

"Don't worry about them."

It wasn't as bad as Alec had feared. Although they barely made two klicks by sundown, trudging along with most of Will's weight on Alec's shoulders, just before it got truly dark a trio of scouts met them. They had a stretcher and the four of them carried Will to an overnight camp that the old man had set up. It was only a lean-to, but it sheltered them from the wind. They slept next to a big, hot fire.

The next morning a wagon came up and took Will and Alec back to the base. Douglas and Angela and half the base's people were at the first gate to meet them.

Two nights later, Douglas banged open the door to Angela's house. She and Alec had eaten dinner in the mess hall, then walked the snow-banked paths to her house. They were sitting in front of the fire, drawing a charcoal sketch on a piece of fabric together, when Douglas strode in without warning. Suddenly the little room was overcrowded.

"Well, at least you're dressed," Douglas said.

The two of them scrambled to their feet.

"Of course we're dressed," Angela replied cooly. "Now close that door or it'll be freezing in here."

Douglas nudged the door shut. "You're wanted over at Will's place, right away."

"What's happened?" Alec demanded.

"No time for explanations. Come right now."

Alec took Angela by the hand and the three of them trotted through the icy darkness down three houses to Will's place, while Alec's mind raced. An infection. Something's happened to Will. Maybe the wound was worse than they thought.

They burst into Will's house, and there was the big oversized puppydog, sitting on the sofa in the main room of the house with half a dozen half-drunk men and women sitting on the floor around him. A merry fire roared in the fireplace and they were all laughing and waving glasses.

"Oh-ho!" Will called as the three of them stepped into the house. "He's here! Give them all glasses and let's drink a toast to my companion-in-arms and rescuer."

Someone shoved a glass into Alec's hand. Someone else filled it eight centimeters deep with whisky. Everyone except Will stood and faced Alec as the big redhead intoned, with enormous seriousness:

"To Alec, who brought me back alive."

"To Alec," they all repeated.

The whisky was beautiful, smooth as free-fall and warmer than sunshine. But then, "What is all this?" Alec asked, slightly dazed. Angela looked puzzled too, but happy.

Will sat there grinning happily. He was fully dressed, but Alec could see the bulk of the bandaging under his shirt.

He said, "My medical colleagues have finally admitted that I'm out of danger and can be up and about . . ."

"In a few days," said one of the older men, trying hard to look dour. "In a few days, Will."

"Right. In a few days," Will agreed. "So I thought to myself, if I can be up and about in a few days, that means I can go back to Utica and hunt for more whisky. So why don't we celebrate my miraculous recovery with the bottles we already have on hand?"

"Sound strategic thinking," Douglas boomed, and the party was officially launched.

It went on all night. Toward dawn a few of the women disappeared, murmuring about getting breakfast together and hot, black coffee. Douglas was slouched on the sofa beside Will. Most of the others had bunched into little knots of conversation in corners of the rooms. Douglas pounded the empty space on the sofa alongside him and said to Alec, "Come here, son. Sit down." It was a command.

They were all drunk enough to drop most of the pretenses that people live with. So Alec, knowing that his grin was as unsteady as his walk, made his way past a quartet of men sitting cross-legged by the dying fire and dropped onto the sofa next to his father.

"Well," Douglas said, in the nearest thing to a quiet conversational tone that he could muster, "you've been with us for almost three months now. Still think I'm an ogre?"

Alec could see Will watching him, beyond Douglas' bulky form, grinning hugely as if he'd arranged a reconciliation between David and Absalom.

"No," Alec admitted, "I guess you're not a monster. I still don't agree with you, but I think I can see why you did what you did."

"Good!" Douglas raised both hands in the air, like a victorious gladiator. One of them held an empty glass instead of a sword.

"Now then," he went on, letting his hands drop, "there are a few things to be settled. First, I think you ought to marry the girl. She's like my very own daughter, and I'll admit I had mixed feelings . . ."

"Wait a minute," Alec said. "Marry Angela?"

"Of course."

"That's between her and me. You don't have anything to say about it."

"The hell I don't!" Douglas exploded. "She's practically my daughter. You *are* my son. If you think you're going to go fucking around and leave her pregnant, you goddamned better well think again."

"Now wait . . ."

"No, you wait," Douglas insisted. "You're going to marry her, and then head a delegation to meet Kobol. There are a few things I want you to make clear to him."

"I'm not sure I want to!"

"Not sure? What the hell do you mean, not sure? You can't have your cake and eat it, too. You're either with us or against us. There aren't any neutrals around here. You just said you're on our side."

"I didn't say that!"

"Then you're against us!" Douglas roared.

Will put a hand on his shoulder. "Hold on, Doug . . . just a . . ."

But Douglas shrugged him off and lumbered to his feet. Alec stood up beside him, barely coming up to his father's shoulder.

"Now you listen to me, son," Douglas said, his voice low and threatening. "I've let you sit around here and have your fill of food and warmth and shelter for three months. You've sneaked around behind my back to make it with my virtual daughter. And what have I asked from in return? Nothing! Not a goddamned thing. Except loyalty. And you refuse?"

Trembling white hot inside, Alec answered in a voice so choked and low that he himself could barely hear it. "That's right. I refuse."

"Then get out!" Douglas roared, pointing to the door. "Take whatever you own and get the hell out of here!"

"That's just what I'm going to do."

Alec started for the door. Everyone else in the house was staring at him now, all pretense of polite disinterest vanished. Will looked worse than when he had been shot.

"Just a minute," Douglas snapped as Alec reached the door. "You can take whatever you please from this base. But you leave Angela alone. You're not good enough for her, no matter how cleverly you've tricked her."

"I'll take what I want," Alec said.

"Try taking her and I'll have you hunted down like an animal and killed. I promise you!"

BOOK FOUR

CHAPTER 24

Alec stormed blindly out into the frozen night. He passed Angela's house, saw the lights and glimpsed a bustle of women inside. He guessed that they were preparing breakfast, talking together, laughing and gossiping.

He went on past. By the time he had put together his own few belongings and saddled a horse, dawn was streaking the eastern sky. But it was a dull, overcast day that arose, with a sky as grimly sullen as Alec's own thoughts. He rode beyond the checkpoints and the guarded fence gates, away from Douglas's base.

Riding most of the day, he camped up in the hills under a stand of firs. Their branches made a poor fire that burned too quickly, then smoldered without heat. By morning he was shaking with bone-deep cold. And hungry.

The only weapon he had brought with him was the automatic rifle he had come in with originally. It was heavy and cumbersome to use on small game, even when choked down to single-shot action. And Alec quickly discovered that his shooting was not good enough to hit a rabbit or smaller rodent as it scurried across the frozen ground. His dilemma was painful: squirt a clip of rounds at a rabbit and you might hit the animal, you might even have enough of it intact to gnaw on, but you'd be out of ammunition in a day or two.

On his third day of wandering it snowed, a heavy fierce blizzard that howled through the woods and blotted out everything except the very nearest trees. Alec was lucky enough to find a cave and enough hardwood to make a fire that lasted through the night. The horse needed it as much as he did. There was no forage to speak of, and the animal was weakening rapidly. Briefly he thought of killing the animal for food, but then he would be on foot in the middle of this snowy wilderness.

He spent two days in the cave, locked in by the blizzard. No firewood, no food, nothing but the stench of the horse and the moaning wind. When it ended and the sky shone blue again, the world was completely covered with white. Snow plastered the trees and made their laden branches sparkle crystalline in the newly risen Sun. Drifts heaped up against the mouth of Alec's cave waist high. The land beyond was a rolling featureless unmarked expanse of white.

He admired its beauty for several minutes. Then his hunger and his fear of dying drove him out into the snow's cold embrace.

The horse died that morning. It collapsed under him in a shuddering groan and floundered in the snow. Alec could feel the warmth of life seeping out of its body. Now he was totally alone. Nothing alive was in sight. There were no landmarks, no direction to aim for, no hope. He stood in the thigh-deep snow, wet and cold and trembling between despair and bleak fear.

He looked at the horse's emaciated carcass, flirted with the thought of carving off some flesh and eating it raw. But he couldn't bring himself to do it. Sleep, he told himself. That's what I need. Rest and sleep.

And the wind sighed, making the trees croon to him, Sleep . . . yes, sleep.

But then, from somewhere deep within his memory came a fragment of poetry that he hadn't realized he knew. It spoke itself in his mind, and he jerked erect. He muttered it to himself, then flung his head back and, arms outstretched, shouted it to the trees and wind:

"To sleep! Perchance to dream:—aye, there's the

rub;

"For in that sleep of death what dreams may come . . ."

That sleep of death. Alec repeated it to himself. And he hunched forward and fought his way through the snow. It was a bitter exhausting battle, as much against himself as against the elements. Cold, hungry, weary, he clamped an iron determination over his aching, protesting muscles and empty gut as he pressed forward.

There are villages all around here, he told himself. Look for smoke, or maybe a road.

He found a road first. He barely recognized it; there was nothing to distinguish it from the rest of the snow-covered landscape except a faint pair of ruts where sled runners had pressed down. It was easier to walk in the ruts, though, and thankfully Alec staggered along, heading slightly downhill, away from the base and toward the valley floor where the farmlands and villages stood.

It was nearly dark when he tottered up to the village. It was either the same one they had taken months earlier or another just like it. Then Alec saw the old man who sat by the gate. Underneath his muffling coat and heavy, pulled-down hat he was the same man. With the same shotgun across his lap.

They said nothing to each other. Alec stood by the gate on unsteady feet, clutching his automatic rifle feebly, numb with cold, puffing with exhaustion. The old man faced him, shotgun in his gloved hands, looking uncertain and red-faced in the last dying rays of the Sun.

Finally the old man shrugged and beckoned to Alec, then turned and headed into the village. Alec followed him, staggering, down cold deserted lanes where the snow had been pounded flat and solid by the passage of many feet.

The old man led him to a hut. "In there," he said, in a ragged, age-roughened voice.

Alec pushed the door open and stumbled into the room. A flood of warmth from the fireplace was the first thing he sensed. It made his face hurt. Then he saw the two men at the table, startled, half out of their chairs, a steaming bowl of food on the table between them.

They were two of Alec's men. That was all he noticed. He fell face down and was unconscious before he reached the hut's bare earthen floor.

They spent a couple of days pumping warm food into him and letting him rest on their pallet. Miraculously, Alec realized, he had not come down with a fever. A touch of frostbite and a lot of raw, chaffed skin. But otherwise no damage that rest and food could not cure.

The men—Zimmerman and Peters—had decided to remain at the village when Alec's force had broken up. Most of the group had joined Will Russo's band, once they learned that Alec was Douglas's prisoner. Jameson had taken the rest south. No one knew what had become of Ferret; he had disappeared. Gradually, Alec realized that Zimmerman and Peters were living together as lovers. He was startled at first, although homosexuality was not rare in the lunar community. After a few days, Alec was more embarrassed than anything else. He wished he had another hut to live in.

"You say Jameson headed south?" he asked Peters over breakfast on the third day. Zimmerman had already left to help the other village men who were shovelling newly-fallen snow out of the village lanes.

Peters shook his head solemnly. He had grown a luxuriant dark beard since Alec had last seen him. Now it was speckled with crumbs of bread and beads of honey.

"He said he would try to link up with Kobol," Peters explained, between bites.

"How did he know Kobol had landed?"

"Russo told us. Jameson let us make up our own minds about what we wanted to do. That's when Zim and I . . . well, we decided we'd done enough soldiering. We helped the people here take in their harvest and they invited us to stay. They've been very kind and understanding."

Alec thought, And they probably think everybody on the Moon is homosexual. Aloud, he asked, "How many of the men went with Jameson?"

"Four, I think. No, it was five."

Alec sank back in his chair. There's no one left to join you, he told himself. You're completely on your own.

After a week the elders of the village came to Alec. They were polite, even deferential. But they were also firm. They had no desire to be caught in whatever high politics was taking place between The Douglas and his son. And they had only so much food, which had to last the winter. So would Alec please leave as soon as he was strong enough? They would give him food and ammunition and even a good horse. But he must leave the village, and tomorrow would be an excellent day for his departure.

Alec smiled and agreed with them. The next morning they solemnly led a big, gentle-looking chestnut mare from their communal barn and loaded it with a bedroll, packs of food, and boxes of ammunition. Peters gave Alec an ancient single-shot rifle, good for hunting small game. Zimmerman gave him his own pistol, holster, and cartridge belt.

The elders watched without a word as Alec said goodbye to his two former comrades and swung up into the saddle. With a nod to the older men he kicked the horse into motion and trotted through the gate and out of the village.

To where? he wondered. South to join Kobol? Instinctively he shook his head, vetoing the idea.

He puzzled over his situation for the whole day, and when the Sun dipped low on the brow of the western hills he found a cave in a little snow-covered ridge and decided to spend the night there.

Kobol will come here in the spring, he thought as he unsaddled the horse. Let *him* come to *me*. But another part of his mind answered ironically, You have to get through the winter, first.

He pulled enough deadwood from the bare trees outside the cave to make a small fire. He tethered the horse near the cave's entrance. The smoke from the fire wasn't bad, once he got used to the stinging of his eyes. It was better than the horse's smell. Briefly he debated trying Peters' rifle on some small game, but it was already getting too dark. He ate from the stores the villagers had given him: a bit of salted meat and some dried grains.

The horse was standing as still as a rock. The fire had burned down to a few barely glowing ashes. Alec was stretched out in the bedroll, trying to sleep, trying not to think of Angela. But there was nothing else to fill his thoughts. The night outside the cave was dark and silent, with only an occasional sigh of wind breaking the frigid hush.

Would she have come with me? he asked himself. Good thing she didn't; I damned near killed myself. Wouldn't want her to . . .

A crunching sound. Alec's eyes snapped open but there was nothing to see in the darkness. The cave was black, its entrance only slightly lighter. The sound had been faint, but—he heard it again.

Footsteps squeaking on the packed snow.

Alec slid his hand down to the pistol inside his bedroll. The automatic rifle was within arm's reach. He silently rolled over onto his stomach and turned enough to face the entrance to the cave, thinking, It must be the villagers coming to take their gifts back. If The Douglas' son just happens to die in some cave, it's not their fault. And why should they lose a valuable horse?

Listening carefully, Alec thought he heard two horses slowly advancing toward the cave.

"Mr. Morgan?" a young voice called out.

He did not answer.

"Mr. Morgan." A silhouette appeared at the cave's mouth. Then another. "We'd like to join with you, if you'll have us."

They were young, barely into their teens. Bored with life in the village. They saw in Alec a chance to find adventure, an opportunity to see the great wondrous world. Alec tried to dissuade them, told them all he had to offer was danger and an early grave. They grinned and insisted that they weren't afraid and they would follow wherever he led.

So he led them.

First into the nearly abandoned cities, where there were still supplies to be had. Alec avoided the feral gangs that huddled in the burned-out city buildings, and fought only when he was forced to. The two youngsters got sick over the first killings, but soon hardened themselves. Alec traded some ammunition and Peters' rifle for fresh food and an extra horse in a village on the eastern edge of Douglas's territory. They left the village with another recruit, an older man who had lost his wife and child to sickness and wanted no more memories of them.

As they rode from that village, Alec's plan took shape. Let Kobol work his way up here by spring. By then I'll have defenses completely mapped out. I'll be waiting for Kobol, and I'll take command of the force that he brings here.

But he needed a radio. And he knew where to get one.

Alec waited. With newfound patience he bided his time, waited out the blizzards in caves and forest shelters, recruited more men—youngsters, mostly—from the village elders would be wise to treat him fairly because the days of The Douglas' reign were numbered.

He learned the territory, mapped its folds and hills, its forests and streams, the roads, the abandoned cities, the villages. And Douglas's defenses. A new perimeter of wire fencing was going up, he saw; teams of men digging through the snow and frozen ground on the outermost edges of his territory. They also erected wooden watchtowers every kilometer or so, despite the bitter weather. Douglas was not waiting for spring.

Alec located the firebases on hilltops inside the new perimeter fence. He saw scouting parties and larger armed patrols riding across the snowy countryside, but he kept a few jumps away from them. He wanted no serious fighting. Not yet. Once he thought he recognized Will Russo at the head of a column of men on snowshoes. Alec stayed especially far from them.

The days were becoming noticeably longer when he attacked the firebase. He had to lead his men around the long way through a gap in the still-uncompleted fence and watchtower ring. It was still bitterly cold, and the sky seemed to be a constant blank of gray as Alec marched his two dozen men toward the firebase. But toward evening the Sun broke through the western clouds and Alec noticed a tiny blue flower poking its head out of the snow along a hillside brook.

He smiled to himself. Not at the flower's beauty or the promise of the sunset, but at the correctness of his timing for the attack.

They waited until well after midnight and climbed the hill to the firebase stealthily. It was laid out almost exactly like the base Alec had been in. The men clambered over the snow-packed earthen ramparts and used knives and crossbows on the defenders. Alec got to the radio before the base commander could switch it on. He shot the man twice through the chest as he clawed wildly at the console controls. Only when the commander lay twitching and bleeding to death on the floor of the radio room did Alec notice that the man was still gripping his unbelted trousers with one hand and his feet were bare.

They took no prisoners. They carefully disassembled the radio and its generator and packed them onto the firebase's own truck. They used the explosives they found there to blow up the underground dugouts and artillery pieces, leaving no evidence that they had stolen the radio.

He'd suspect, Alec knew. But they'd stay far enough from his other radio equipment so that he wouldn't be able to monitor their calls.

The truck slipped and groaned through the night, bearing the radio equipment and all of Alec's men. They got back safely outside Douglas' perimeter and then pushed on for another whole day before Alec tried to call the satellite station. When he finally made contact, the voice that crackled in his earphones was totally incredulous.

"We thought you were dead or . . ."

"Or gone over to Douglas's side?"

"Well . . ."

"Never mind," Alec said. "Get word to Kobol that I want to see him or his representative as soon as he can get someone up here. There's much planning to do. I'll stay in touch with you at least every other day and relay instructions on where to find me."

"Yessir. I suppose you want to be patched through to the settlement, and speak to your mother?"

Without an eyeblink's hesitation, Alec answered, "No. I can't afford to keep broadcasting that long. My transmission might get picked up. Relay this message to her: Tell her that I'm fine and we'll soon have accomplished our mission."

"That's all?"

"That's everything."

CHAPTER 25

Kobol sent Jameson. He arrived within two weeks of Alec's first radio call.

"How did you get here so quickly?" Alec wondered.

Jameson smiled in his eagle-fierce way. "There are lots of boats down in Florida. And plenty of fuel for them, too. They make the fuel from sea-water—electrolyze the hydrogen and then freeze it down to a liquid."

"I didn't know that level of technology still existed on Earth," Alec said.

"The old civilian spaceport is still there," Jameson explained. "Nobody bothered to bomb it."

"So there are scientists there."

"A few. Some engineers. They needed our help, though, otherwise they would've been overrun by barbarians."

"And you came by boat all this way?"

Jameson nodded tightly. "Up the old inland waterway to Delaware Bay, then up the Delaware River. Scooted past Philadelphia as fast as we could—it's still pretty radioactive. When we ran out of river we trekked overland, and here we are."

Alec and Jameson were standing on the brow of a small hill, sheltered from the wind by a stand of white-barked birches. Their limbs were still gaunt and snow still covered most of the ground. But the Sun was shining out of a perfectly blue sky and warmth was returning to the land. Alec could hear trickles of melting water running beneath the snow. Soon the streams would be rushing noisily again.

"What's Kobol doing down there?" Alec asked.

"He's putting together an army. A real army." Jameson spread his hands outward for emphasis. "Thousands of men. He's recruiting them from the locals. They've got four shuttles landing supplies and weapons almost every day now: lasers, trucks, heavy stuff.

"Thousands of men? Four shuttles?"

With a grim nod, Jameson answered, "The Council's decided that the only way to get the fissionables is to smash Douglas once and for all. So they're giving Kobol everything he wants. There must be more able-bodied lunar men in Florida now than there are left in the settlement."

"Everything *he* wants?" Alec echoed. "Kobol's not in command; I am!"

"You might find that point a little difficult to get across. The official verdict was that you were killed or captured. The *rumor* was that you'd joined Douglas."

"They're both wrong," Alec insisted. "I was named commander of this mission and I've never been relieved of command, no matter what Kobol says or thinks."

"He's not going to be pleasant about that," Jameson warned.

Alec looked at him, thought a moment, then said, "All right, there's no sense arguing about it here and now. We'll have to settle it between us when he gets here."

Jameson looked unconvinced, even slightly amused.

"I assume Kobol has some plan worked out for getting his thousands of troops here?"

"Indeed he does," Jameson said. "He's been studying terrestrial meteorology and he's come up with the irrefutable observation that it's warmer in the southern areas—where he is—than it is up here in the north."

"So?"

"So his plan is to follow the advance of springtime right up the countryside. He's already started to move northward, out of Florida and into some lovely swamplands the natives call Georgia. As the warm weather advances northward, Kobol plans to advance his men along with it, adding new recruits along the way."

"More men?"

"That's right," Jameson said. "He says that nothing succeeds like excess."

"He stole that. It's a quotation from history."

Jameson's stern face showed surprise. "Really? He's been strutting around like he thought of it himself. But no matter who said it first, I think he's right. The more men we have, the more raiders and barbarians will want to join us. And the bigger the army we have to face Douglas, the easier it'll be to beat him."

Alec scuffed a toe on the snowbank where they stood. "It won't be easy to keep an army like that together. Those people aren't going to march more than a thousand klicks and maintain discipline. Why should they?"

"Some of them will. Maybe a lot of them will. Kobol's promised them all the loot and women they can carry, once they've beaten Douglas."

Alec finally understood. And thought of Angela.

"So we can expect Kobol's army to reach here just about the time the spring mud's dried and it's easy to move across country," Alec summarized.

"That's his plan."

"The timing's going to be important. He's got to arrive here just as the travelling turns good again. We've been able to survive so far because it's been more trouble for Douglas to hunt us down than we're worth to him. But when the travelling gets easy again, I don't think we can last very long. If Kobol waits a week or so too long, we could be dead when he gets here."

"I know."

Alec asked, "But does he?"

For a moment Jameson did not answer. His bird-of-prey expression was as emotionless as he could make it. Finally he said, slowly, "He understands your situation, and he'll get here in time. He wants to marry your mother and gain full control of the Council through her. He won't let you get killed. Not that way, at least."

Strangely, his words neither surprised Alec nor upset him. He hasn't told me anything I didn't already suspect.

"All right," Alec said quietly. "It's vital that Kobol and I meet face to face before his troops get here. I've got a nearly complete picture of Douglas's defenses. In another two weeks I'll fill in the few gaps in the information. Even with a big army, he'll need that intelligence."

"I know," Jameson said, a bit stiffly. "He sent me to get that information from you."

Alec shook his head. "No. I'll talk to Kobol and no one else."

Jameson said nothing, gave no hint of what he felt.

"It's more than relaying information on the defenses," Alec tried to explain. "There's the entire question of strategy . . . how we're going to attack Douglas. If you carry back the data I've amassed, Kobol will set up his battle plan before he gets here. That could be disastrous."

"Should I tell him that?"

Alec grinned. "Tell him whatever you like. But I must see him before his army reaches this far north. I'll leave it to you to arrange a time and place."

Jameson looked away from Alec, out across the snowy landscape, the bare patches of ground, the brilliant blue sky. "He won't try to kill you," he said softly, almost to himself. "But he might try to keep you under his eye . . . a prisoner."

"You mean that a meeting with him might be a trap?"

Jameson said, "It could be."

"Can I depend on you to prevent that from happening?"

Swinging around to fix his hawk-like gaze on Alec, Jameson replied, "I'm only one man. He'll have plenty of others with him."

"I know," Alec said. "But if it comes to trouble, will you stand with me?"

For almost a minute, Jameson did not reply. At last he said, "You're still the officially-appointed commander of this expedition, and he's your deputy—by order of the Council." Then he relaxed enough to smile tightly. "I've served under him and I've served under you. If it comes to trouble—I'll stand with you."

Alec breathed out a sigh of relief and put his hand out to the bigger man. Jameson took it in his grip and let his smile broaden. It was like a glacier melting.

"We're both insane, you know," he said.

"I know," Alec answered. "I know."

The meeting was arranged, after several tedious discussions by radio. They agreed to meet on a boat in the upper Delaware River at a spot identified on the map as the Delaware Water Gap. The term puzzled Alec until he saw the place.

The snow was melting fast under the early spring Sun and the ground was muddy and slow for travelling. Alec and four picked men made their way on horseback southward, following the maps. It took a week of hard travel.

On the fifth day, as they picked up the uppermost stream of the Delaware, they were joined by a fifth rider: Ferret. He trotted up alongside Alec's horse, an enormous gap-toothed grin on his pinched, wizened face. He was mud-spattered and filthy, but across the rump of his stringy mount were laid out a brace of game birds.

"Ferret!" Alec called to him, genuinely pleased to see him again. "Where have you been all winter?"

The scrawny young man shrugged. "Around. Huntin'. Mountains, mostly." He waved vaguely south-southwesterly.

"And how did you find us?"

Ferret scratched his jaw, grinned some more, mumbled something unintelligible. Alec didn't care. The strange character had ways of his own, and Alec felt better with him by his side. Ferret carried no gun; as far as Alec could tell he would be useless in a fight. But he could somehow snare game. They would eat better with him along.

The tiny group of horsemen made their way down the valley of the river, where the going was much easier. And once they reached the Water Gap, Alec saw at a glance what the name meant. The Delaware cut between two high-shouldered mountains, slicing through layers of striated rock that had been laid bare by millions of years of the river's erosion.

There was a passable road along the base of the mountains, by the river's bank, the remains of an old paved highway. The cement was broken and covered with rubble, but the horses stepped over the litter easily enough and clopped along, making good time. It was an enormous relief after the rough going of the muddy countryside. Alec and his men kept wary eyes on the slopes rising above them and across the river. Good spots for ambush. The trees and brush had not leafed out yet, however, so the ground was bare and difficult to hide in.

Ferret would disappear for most of the day, and then come back grinning happily with enough game to keep their stomachs full.

At the Gap's narrowest point they found a surprise: the graceful arch of a bridge that still stood, spanning the river with steel and concrete that did not even look particularly begrimed or weathered until they got quite close to it. Anchored at the base of one of the bridge's supporting pillars was a small power boat.

There can't be more than four or five men aboard a boat that size, Alec thought to himself as they nosed their horses down a trail that led to the water's edge. We won't be badly outnumbered—unless Kobol has other boats hidden further down the river.

The boat was close enough to the shore for Alec and two of his men to wade to its boarding ladder. The rest of Alec's men, and two of Kobol's crew, stayed on the shore with the horses.

"Good to see you," Kobol said tonelessly as Alec climbed aboard. He looked thinner than the last time Alec had seen him: harder and leaner, with more lines in his face. He shifted a wooden cane to his left hand and put out his right. The hand felt leathery when Alec shook it. Kobol's eyes were still hooded, masked.

"The outdoor life seems to agree with you," he said, smiling toothily. "You've lost your baby fat."

Alec grunted a noncommittal reply as he glanced around the boat. The forward deck and the top of the cabin were covered with solar cells. No guns were in sight, but something squat and bulky was covered by a tarpaulin at the boat's stern. A laser? he wondered.

With two of his own men preceding him, Kobol led Alec down into the cabin. Alec's two men took up the rear. He saw that Kobol leaned on the cane when he walked. They stepped down into a tight little compartment with foldup bunks locked against the bulkheads and an oversized table jammed between narrow padded benches. Atop the table was pinned a photomap of Douglas' base.

"We pieced this together from satellite photos," Kobol said, sitting down with an audible sigh between his two aides. He put the walking stick carefully by his side. "I think you'll find this map extremely accurate."

Alec slid into the bench on the opposite side of the table, flanked by his two men. He studied the map. The photos were very detailed; he could even make out Angela's house. What were we doing when this picture was taken? he wondered idly.

Another of Kobol's men appeared at the hatchway, bearing a tray of sandwiches and brown bottles of beer.

"It's quite good," he told Alec, proferring a bottle. "Only slightly alcoholic. One of the first things the natives got running again in the Miami area was their brewery. They use half the wood in the region to keep the place supplied with power."

Alec sipped at it. It tasted sour and awful. The homebrew at Douglas's base was far better. He frowned, and Kobol said, with an air of superiority, "You have to develop a taste for it."

"I'd rather not."

"We have fresh milk," said a low voice.

Alec looked up and saw Jameson standing in the compartment's narrow hatchway. Suppressing a smile, Alec answered, "Fine. I'll take milk."

They spent several hours poring over the map. Alec fitted in all the details he knew about Douglas's defenses until the map fairly bristled with inked-in lines representing fences, circles and squares that pinpointed watchtowers and firebases.

Kobol looked impressed. "We'll have to concentrate everything on one massive onslaught—straight up this major road." He swept his bony hand along the map.

"That's just what Douglas would expect," Alec countered. "He'll stop you here . . ." he pointed to a spot where the road snaked between firebase-topped hills, " . . . or here, where the streams and lakes will force you into a narrow line of march."

Kobol tugged at his mustache. "He doesn't have the strength to stop us. We'll have nearly five thousand men by the time we get there."

"The defense always has at least a two-to-one edge," Alec quoted at him. "With someone as clever as Douglas you'll need every man you can get. Remember, he's been preparing these defenses for years. Why throw the men right into his guns?"

"And what would your military genius suggest?" When Kobol became angry or upset his voice ascended from its normal irritable nasal tone into a positively adenoidal whine.

Alec glanced up at him. "We have an advantage in numbers. Let's use it! We'll attack over a broad front, spread Douglas's troops thin trying to defend such a large area. Bypass the firebases and strongpoints . . ."

"And have them chop us to shreds?" Kobol flared.

"They can't. I've seen what they've got there. No more than ten rounds apiece for most of the heavy guns. They'll shell us until they're out of ammunition, then they'll either have to come out and engage us in small groups or sit on their hilltops and wait until we come after them."

Kobol said nothing, but his head was rocking back and forth in an unspoken negative.

"The firebases can discourage small attacks," Alec went on, "or attacks that are so concentrated that a few high-explosive shells can tear the attackers apart. But a broad, thin screen of attackers, moving quickly and staying as far away from the firebases as they can, will make the firebases almost useless."

"Makes sense," muttered one of Kobol's men, sitting on the bench beside him.

"If he's right about the ammunition they have

for their guns."

"I'm right," Alec snapped. "If it'll make you feel any better, we can grab a couple of the closest firebases the night before the attack. But the others, deeper inside Douglas's territory, we should bypass."

Kobol shook his head more negatively. "I don't like leaving pockets of enemy troops in our rear. They'll be fully armed and able to . . ."

Alec slammed a fist on the table. "Dammit, what's our objective? Capturing hilltops or Douglas's headquarters? *Here's* what we're after!" He jabbed a finger at the base. "If we inch along one hill at a time, he can bleed us white and spend all summer delaying us while he gathers strength from the farther countryside. By next autumn we'll be surrounded and starving. We've got to strike hard and fast. Here." He touched the base area again.

"And those men in the strongpoints will just sit where they are and let us walk in?"

"That's right," Alec insisted. "There's only ten or so men in each post. No more than twenty apiece. But they're heavily armed. If we try to attack them, they can hold us up until Douglas brings his reserves onto the scene. But if we bypass them, what can a dozen or two men do to a whole column of troops? If they come down from their hilltops to attack us, they'll be cut to pieces."

"They still have that artillery."

"After the first half hour of fighting, the artillery will be out of ammo."

"They could still knock off a lot of trucks and men."

"Not if we move fast and stay spread out."

"I don't know . . ." Kobol hesitated.

More quietly, Alec said, "I *do* know. We're going to do it this way. We can win quickly and with low casualties." The back of his mind was whispering, And I can get to Angela before anyone else does.

Kobol was staring at him, eyes glittering. "It's not your decision to make."

"Yes it is."

His hands spread flat on the map, as if to ensure ownership, Kobol said, "You can't possibly assume that you're still . . ."

"I'm in command," Alec said evenly. "No one has relieved me of command. You'll take orders from me, Martin."

Kobol tried to laugh, but it froze in his throat. His mouth twitched. He glanced at the men sitting on either side of him, facing Alec.

Alec said nothing. For a long wordless minute they sat glaring at each other; Alec with his two youngsters and Kobol with his men flanking him.

"I think Alec's plan will work," Jameson said. He was still leaning against the hatchway. The gun at his hip loomed enormous. He was slightly turned, facing Kobol, gunhand free and resting easily at his side.

"The men I've assembled don't know you," Kobol said to Alec. "They won't take orders from you."

"They know me," Jameson said flatly. "They'll follow where I lead them."

Kobol glowered at Jameson and let his breath out in a hiss of frustrated rage. "So that's the way it's going to be."

"That's the way it is," Jameson answered, calm as a hawk circling its prey.

Alec said, "To prevent any misunderstandings, Martin, I think you'd better stay with me until the army gets here. Ron, you take this boat back and assume command of the troops."

A smile flickered across Jameson's face. "You're giving them a lot more dignity than they deserve. They're not troops, they're just a big gang. Hardly any discipline. They're coming up here for the spoils. They'll fight your way, Alec. But they'd never stand up in a toe-to-toe battle."

"Whatever you want to call them, then," Alec said. "Get back to them and move them up here. As soon as the ground's dry enough to maneuver, we attack."

"And when you get back to the settlement," Kobol spat, "I'll have you executed. I'll make your mother sign your death warrant!"

Alec smiled at him. "That's assuming that *you* make it back to the settlement, Martin."

CHAPTER 26

The rain was steady, heavy, and driven by a numbingly cold wind. The ground beneath the horse's hooves was unending mud that made obscene sucking noises with each laborious step. The horse was big, powerful, uncomplaining, but it could not go much farther without rest, Alec knew.

Still he pressed on, urging the horse forward with his boots. He was heavily muffled inside a leather coat and hood but the wetness had seeped into him until he felt that icewater was trickling through his veins.

Squinting through the rain and mist, Alec saw that the little stream he had reached had turned into a churning, brown foaming channel that carried tree branches and other debris madly onward.

Won't be able to ford that, he knew.

"Ho-ho!" a familiar voice called. "There you are."

Turning slightly in the rain-slicked saddle, Alec saw Will Russo's bulky form pacing slowly out of the mist, leading a droopy-headed horse step by sloshing step through the mud.

"How did you cross the stream?" Alec blurted.

"Oh, further up. It's not so bad up there."

Alec slid off his horse and walked, with an effort, toward the advancing man. "Is your wound all healed up?" he asked.

Will nodded and a thatch of red hair, glistening with dampness, flopped down from under his hood. "Oh sure, been fine for months now. I got back to Utica and, by golly, the rest of the whisky was still there. You?"

"I'm okay."

Will grinned at him. "For a fish. Look, there's a little cave a bit further upstream. Let's get out of this weather."

They led the horses through the mud and rain for a few minutes and found the cave. It was more of a purposely dug shelter in the hillside than a natural cleft. The inner walls were smooth and even, Alec noticed, as he made a mental note of its location and size.

"I was glad to get the message your scout gave our scout," Will said once they had pulled the horses inside the narrow shelter. "I was worried about you, you know."

Alec was unbuttoning his coat. "Nothing in here for a fire . . ."

"That's okay." Will rummaged through the pockets of his voluminous coat. "Brought a little . . . aha! Here it is." He produced a small dark green bottle. "Saved you some of the whisky."

They both took long pulls from the bottle. Alec could feel the liquor burning out the dampness inside him.

"Well," Will said, as pleasantly as if they were lounging together on the Moon, "what did you want to talk about? Not the weather, I suppose?"

Alec laughed. "No, not that." Then, more seriously, "You know what's going to happen when the ground hardens, don't you?"

Will tried to erase the smile on his face, but he was only partially successful. "Yep. Kobol's bringing a whole raft of raiders and swamp-runners up here to attack us. It's been tried before."

"You don't have to look so damned cheerful about it!" Alec snapped.

"Should I run away and hide? Look, we've been through this kind of thing before. Why, the first winter Douglas and I . . ."

"You've never seen an army this big," Alec interrupted. "And they'll be better armed than any gang that's been put together since the sky burned."

"H'mm. Well. Is that what you came to tell me?"

"I want you to get out before the fighting starts. Take Angela with you. I don't want either of you hurt."

"Leave Douglas? She'd never do that. Neither would I."

"You've got to!" Alec insisted. "There's no way for you to help him now. He's the reason for the fighting, he's the one they're going to be after. If we can get him without risking your lives . . ."

But Will was shaking his head. "You don't understand, Alec. I can't leave Douglas. I'd sooner chop off my arm. My *drinking* arm! We're friends, closer than brothers, really."

Alec said nothing.

"It's really Angela you're worried about, isn't it?"

"Yes."

"She's worried about you, too. She was damned sore when you left without even telling her you were going. I think she would have gone with you, I really do."

"That's why I didn't tell her," Alec said.

"Well, all that's in the past. She surely won't go anywhere now. She'd never leave Douglas, not with all this trouble brewing up . . ." A thought seemed to strike him. "Unless . . ."

"Unless what?"

Will grinned as he answered, "Well, maybe if you were there at the base, helping us to fight off these riff-raff of Kobol's, then if things got really bad you could get her out and get to someplace safe."

Alec stared at him. He's not putting me on. He really believes what he just said.

"Will," Alec said softly, "don't you realize that I can't fight on Douglas's side?"

"Oh, I don't know. There are a lot of things you don't realize, even yet. He tried damned hard for a lot of years to get them to listen to reason back at the settlement. He didn't just decide to go off and make a kingdom for himself here on Earth. He was pushed. By Kobol and the others."

"The others?"

"Other members of the Council. Douglas was pushed out of power by those he trusted most. Those he loved most, too."

"Meaning my mother."

Completely serious now, Will nodded. "Alec, you probably won't believe me, and you may end up hating me for even saying it, but . . . well, by golly, your mother helped to push Douglas into doing what he did. She knew he had no choice. She gave him nothing to return to, and they both knew it when he left for Earth. She didn't want him back."

The coldness congealed over Alec again. "You're right," he said, deadly soft. "I don't believe you."

The big redhead made a helpless gesture with his hands. "It's the truth."

"I'm sure it's what he told you. But it's not the truth. I'll never believe it. Never."

"That's a . . . shame."

"There's something you ought to know, Will," Alec said. "I'm not just joining with Kobol's forces. I'm leading them. I'm in command."

"I was afraid of that."

"Why?"

"Because we're going to have to try to kill each other. And we're friends."

"That's why I want you to get away. And take her with you."

"No, I can't do that. He's my friend too. And your father."

"I'm coming after him. Don't stand in my way. Don't try to protect him."

Sadly, in a voice so low that Alec barely heard it, Will said, "Don't make me choose between you and him, Alec. You'll lose."

"We've already made our choices," Alec said. "They were made twenty years ago."

CHAPTER 27

Even though they assembled as quickly as possible it still took weeks for Kobol's army to straggle all its various units together in a valley on the edge of Douglas's territory.

Alec had never seen so many human beings before. He stood on the crest of the highest hill in the area, under a maple tree that was just breaking out in young fresh leaves and watched the awesome sprawl of trucks, jeeps, horses, wagons, and men.

Ron Jameson stood beside him. "That ought to be enough men to conquer the whole world," he said.

"I don't like having them all bunched together like this," Alec said. "If Douglas's people spot them, and if he's got nuclear weapons or airplanes . . ."

"We've intercepted all his patrols," Jameson said calmly. "And I doubt if there are any nukes or airplanes left in the world."

"It would only take one."

With a slight shrug, Jameson answered, "We can be ready to move in two days. I think we can keep Douglas's patrols from finding us for that long."

"Two days?"

Nodding, "Check. The men have moved a lot harder and faster than they wanted to, just to get here. They need time to catch their breaths, get their weapons ready, and absorb your battle orders."

That leaves me two days to deal with Kobol, Alec thought.

"On the other hand, if we all sit still here for more than two days," Jameson added drily, "the different packs in this glorious conglomeration will start fighting each other. There's not an overabundance of friendship down in that valley."

Alec nodded. "Let's get to work."

It was fully night, after the evening meal, before Alec was able to get to Kobol. The older man was being held under virtual arrest in one of the caves that honey-combed the valley's hillsides.

His quarters were a small cavern whose sloping walls and roof were laced with stalactites of a thousand different hues. The only entrance was a narrow passage, barely wide enough for a man to squeeze through sideways. Alec had posted an armed guard at the outer end of the passage.

Kobol was sitting on an ancient, creaking bunk, his good leg folded under him and his head bent down as he intently wrote in rapid script on a paper he held in his lap. Alec saw that the bunk was covered with sheets of paper, all filled with his writing.

"Good evening," Alec said.

Kobol hardly looked up. A slightly raised eyebrow was his only greeting. Then he returned to his writing. It was damp in the cave, Alec realized. It probably makes his bad leg feel like hell, he thought.

Aloud he said, "There's something I haven't told you."

"Oh?" Still not looking up.

"I know where the fissionables are stored."

The pen stopped in mid-stroke.

"I want you to head a special force to seize them before Douglas has a chance to destroy them."

That straightened Kobol's back. He pushed the paper off his lap and unfolded his long legs. Somehow it reminded Alec of a snake uncoiling. "You think he might sabotage them?" Kobol asked.

"It's a possibility. He might even have them booby-trapped, or set to go off in a nuclear explosion that will take everything with it."

Kobol frowned thoughtfully and ran a finger through his mustache.

Pulling the only chair in the enclosure next to the bunk, Alec straddled it and went on, "You know more about the fissionables than any of us. It's a risky job, but a necessary one. Will you do it?"

Almost smiling, Kobol said, "If I do, I'll only be in charge of a small suicide squad, while you're leading the grand army. If I succeed, it's under your command. If I fail, you get rid of an enemy."

"If you fail," Alec said, "we get rid of each other. And everyone else."

"And the settlement dies for lack of fissionables."

"Yes."

"When I get back to the settlement I'll still accuse you of treason."

Alec let himself smile. "Won't that be a bit difficult to prove, if you have the fissionables?"

"I'll prove it."

"Go ahead and try it, then."

Kobol swayed back a little, and then seemed to tense, as if poised to strike. "If I accept this job and get the fissionables, do you promise me safe conduct back to the settlement?"

"You mean, will I have you shot after we win the battle?"

"That's one way to phrase it."

"You'll be safe. We can settle our differences back at the settlement."

"My safety for the fissionables," Kobol mused. "It's a deal."

Alec nodded. Neither man offered his hand. Alec rose from the chair and started toward the passageway entrance. Halfway there he paused and turned back to Kobol.

"I haven't asked you for a similar guarantee—that you won't try to kill me before we get back to the settlement."

Kobol started to reply, but Alec went on, "I don't need your promise. I wouldn't trust it, anyway. Just keep this in mind. If you try to kill me, I'll kill you. Even if you're successful, there are a dozen men who'll chop you into bite-sized pieces afterward. Just pray that I'm not killed in battle, Martin."

He left Kobol sitting on the bunk, looking angry.

On the morning of the third day the attack began.

It had been a hectic two days, getting the men and equipment ready, keeping Douglas's increasingly heavier patrols from penetrating to the valley, briefing Kobol and putting together his special unit of trucks and protective garments and equipment, keeping in touch with the satellite for constant updates on the weather.

It rained the night before the attack. The troops moved out of the valley and spread to their positions, arcing across nearly half of Douglas's defensive perimeter. They moved swiftly despite the rain, most of them on horseback, but the shock wave all on trucks and jeeps. Each unit was completely mobile, no foot soldiers. The armored trucks mounted lasers, the jeeps bore machine guns and rocket launchers. The cavalry carried everything from automatic rifles to crossbows.

The rain's keeping Douglas' patrols down and screening our deployment, Alec told himself, then added, I hope.

He stood on the laser mount platform of an armored truck. The rain had slackened off to a fine drizzle, and the Sun was starting to edge above the eastern hills, breaking through the clouds, turning them pink and mauve. The ground was wet but not soaked, not impassibly muddy.

Alec wore a battle helmet, and could hear the crosstalk of a hundred different unit commanders by switching frequencies on the dial set into one of the earphones. They had chosen the frequencies carefully to be out of the range of Douglas's antiquated radio equipment. Each sector commander checked in as the drizzle died away. Finally Alec asked Jameson, "Ron, how's it look on your end?"

Jameson's voice was crisp and calm in his earphones. "Everything set here. All unit and sector commanders are ready and eager to go."

Alec glanced at his wristwatch. Five-fifty. The attack was planned to start at six, when Douglas's men would be starting their breakfasts, looking to their cookfires rather than watching for an attack.

As he waited for the minute hand to crawl along, Alec's mind filled with the images of all the things he had been through: the storms, the cold, the mud. And the nights with Angela, the warmth of the fire, the heat of their passion. And the towering gray old man who had driven him away.

With a shake of his head, he focused his thoughts on the reality before him. The morning was clearing rapidly, the clouds breaking up and scuttling away on a fresh, clean breeze. The Sun was bright and already starting to feel warm on his shoulders and neck.

"Minus ten seconds," he muttered to himself.

Turning the dial on his earphone to the general frequency, Alec heard the chime tone that confirmed that the frequency was tuned in and open.

"All sector and unit commanders . . . commence attack. *Now.*"

The truck he was standing on lurched forward, then gained speed smoothly as it climbed toward the top of the hill it had been hiding behind. Trailing it, three other trucks and a pair of jeeps trundled along. The jeeps passed Alec's truck, speeding toward the crest of the hill.

They reached the top and started downslope. Putting the binoculars to his eyes, Alec could see the thin strand of fence wire winding across the rolling countryside, half a kilometer ahead. Two watchtowers were in view and a hill crowned with a firebase stood off on the horizon.

They've seen us now, he knew, watching the figures atop one of the watchtowers moving rapidly and gesticulating. Are they surprised? Or have they been waiting for us? Are they as scared as I am? And Alec realized that his heart was racing; he could feel it pounding in his throat, hear it in his ears, amplified by the 'phones clamped to the sides of his head.

They sped toward the fence and off to his right Alec could see a band of cavalry troops riding hard to keep pace with them. The jeeps were up ahead. Flickers of fire danced at the tops of the watchtowers but Alec could hear nothing except the rush of the wind as his truck tore forward.

The lead jeep fired a missile at the nearest watchtower and Alec followed its smoky exhaust as it passed within a few meters of the tower's top, then arced into the empty ground inside the fence and exploded.

"We're in range of the fence!" shouted the gunner, sitting strapped into the plastic jumpseat that jutted out to one side of the massive laser mount.

Alec turned to him. "Burn it down."

The laser's special power generator hummed into life and then its vibration was drowned out by the high-pitched whine of the laser itself. The beam was invisible, but where it touched the fence the wire mesh flashed into incandescence and charred and curled like the wick of a candle.

The jeeps swerved toward the opening and the laser gunner swung his attention to the watchtowers. The nearest one was still firing when the energy beam touched it. The tower top burst into flame.

And then they were inside the fence, racing across the bumpy countryside. The wind tore at Alec's face. The jeeps were both intact and pulling even further ahead of them, swinging left to put as much distance as possible between themselves and the firebase's artillery. Glancing toward the rear, Alec saw the cavalry squad pouring through the gap in the fence. The watchtower was burned and silent.

He saw a flash from the hilltop and an instant later the ground erupted far off to his right. The dull heavy roar of the explosion reached him as the black cloud hurled tumbling chunks of earth high into the air.

Get past the firebases and engage Douglas's mobile reserve. That was his mission. Leave the firebases isolated and concentrate your forces on his reserves. Smash them before they can organize a counterattack.

Two more artillery shells hit in front of them. The shock and noise hit simultaneously and the driver veered the truck hard to the left as debris pelted down on them. Alec saw a pair of smoking craters where the shells had hit; they looked raw and painful in the gentle earth.

More shellbursts, but falling further behind now. Then one struck close enough to knock one of the jeeps over. It rolled crazily, scattering broken pieces of men and machinery across the grass, and finally came to rest on its side. As the truck swept past it, the jeep burst into flames. No time to stop for the wounded. Not now.

A gently sloping ridge rose ahead of them. Alec knew this countryside by heart. If there was going to be trouble anywhere, it would be this ridge line. Douglas had been turning it into a natural defense line, adding man-made earthworks where the ridge itself flattened out, so that the line completely covered the flank of his base, twenty klicks from the innermost fences. Between the ridge line and those fences was nothing but flat open country.

They charged up the ridge, Alec hanging grimly to the rail of the laser mount, expecting land mines, more artillery fire, small arms fire from troops dug into trenches at the crest.

Nothing. The ridge was bare of defenders. The flat meadowlands stretched out ahead and Alec could see other units of trucks, jeeps and cavalry dashing across the grassland, too.

This is too easy, he told himself. Douglas couldn't possibly be taken so easily.

But they plunged on, bouncing at breakneck speed down the ridge's reverse slope and slewing out onto the flatland. Occasional shellbursts reminded them that the firebases were still active, but the artillery fire was desultory and did nothing to slow them. If anything, the drivers urged extra speed from their electric motors whenever a shell landed near them.

Tense with a mixture of exhilaration and fear, Alec clicked his radio dial for Jameson's frequency. "Ron, where are you now?" he spoke into the helmet's mike.

A heartbeat's delay, then, "We've just crested an artificial ramp of earth, about twenty klicks from the edge of the main base area. Not much opposition yet. Lost a truck that fell into a shell crater and a squad of cavalry that took a direct hit. Everybody else is moving forward at top speed. No sign of any real resistance."

"All right. Keep moving and stay alert." He dialed the general frequency. "All unit commanders, report any delays or ground resistance other than artillery fire."

No response at all. The radio buzzed to itself.

Alec said, "All unit commanders, sound off in order."

"Sector one. No delays, no resistance."

Jameson's voice.

"Sector two. No problems."

"Sector three. Goin' like hell, nobody in our way."

"Sector four . . ."

Alec's attention was pulled away by a tug on his sleeve. The gunner was leaning forward in his seat, gesturing to the rear of the speeding truck. A trio of squat, heavy-looking gray shapes was topping the ridge behind them. With the sector commanders still reporting, Alec turned and raised his binoculars.

They were ugly-looking tracked vehicles, painted dark green and brown. Long cylinders of gun barrels poked from slope-walled turrets. Tanks! Alec recalled seeing them on history tapes.

"Hey, this is sector three," his earphones crackled. "We just picked up some kinda trucks or somethin' following us."

"All units," Alec shouted, "report on the numbers and positions of enemy tanks. They're rolling forts, heavily armored and carrying cannon and machine guns."

As if in answer one of the three tanks in Alec's rear belched flame and a shell whistled over his truck, exploding close enough to jar him.

That's Douglas' plan, Alec realized. He's had the tanks all along, probably spotted them at the firebases last week. Now he's got us caught between the tanks and his reserves.

Strangely, Alec felt almost relieved. Now his father's hand was out in the open, where he could deal with it. Tanks without infantry support, he remembered from his teaching tapes, are vulnerable. Dangerous, but vulnerable. Inadvertently he glanced at the far horizon, in the direction toward which the truck was speeding. Douglas was up there, someplace. You think you can panic us with tanks, Alec said silently to his father. Maybe it will work for you, but we'll see who the military expert is.

"Listen to me," he said urgently into his lip mike. "Engage the tanks at the longest possible ranges with the lasers. Use the jeeps and cavalry to get behind them and destroy them at close range. The lasers should try to immobilize them. Go for their treads, their sensors. Stop them first, then destroy them close-up."

The radio sizzled with confused reports of fighting and losses. Alec tried to sort them out as another shellburst lifted his truck entirely off its wheels and slammed him against the railing. Debris pelted him and stung. He tasted blood in his mouth.

Crouching down near the driver's cab, he shouted, "Zig-zag, dammit! Keep them guessing." He straightened and yelled to the gunner, "The treads, aim for their treads! Their armor's too thick to get through."

Then he realized that the gunner was hanging limply in his seat harness, head lolling, mouth agape and eyes staring sightlessly. Alec reached over and unfastened his harness. The gunner slid out of his seat, rolled over the edge of the mount platform and bounced onto the ground. Another shell rocked the speeding truck as Alec climbed into the seat, suddenly feeling as exposed as a patient stretched naked on a surgical table.

He swung the laser's sighting mirrors around and tried to hold them on the nearest tank. Flicking the fire control to the shortest possible pulse, he rattled off a train of microsecond bursts. The ground near the tank smoked and sputtered but the tank itself rumbled forward unharmed. The truck lurched violently as he fired again.

Where the hell is everybody else?

Alec fired three more times as shellfire racked the truck. He heard shrapnel clanging against the truck's sides, then caught a glance of another truck as they zipped past it. It was gutted, wheels splayed, front end smashed in.

One of the tanks was turning in a tight circle. Got its left tread! Alec rejoiced. A half-dozen mounted men were pulling up alongside it, unlimbering the rocket launchers and grenades they carried. He turned his attention to the second tank and saw, beyond it, that the third one was crawling with men clambering over it, like ants swarming over an invading scorpion. Crumpled bodies lay broken and smashed in the tank's wake.

If we can knock off the tanks before Douglas' reserves get here . . . Alec dialed the frequency for the second truck in his unit. "Get on the left side of that tank that's still fighting. I'll swing to the right. Spray him!"

They swung to the tank's flanks. The gun turret swung toward Alec's side and he fanned the laser beam to maximum width and sprayed the entire turret area. Blind the bastards, he raged to himself, hoping that the infrared energy would at least damage the periscopes poking from the turret. Then the tank bloomed into a roaring fireball. The other truck's laser had found the engine ducts. The tank shuddered, then burst open like an overripe melon, its fuel and ammunition exploding inside it. The turret blew high into the air. With smoke and steam hissing from every joint and port in the heavy armor, the tank died like a dragon consumed by its own internal juices, hissing and rumbling as it disappeared in smoke.

It seemed like hours, but it actually took less than forty minutes to clean up the tank counterattack. Alec's units helped each other as much as they could, but most of them had to fight their own battles, individual jousts of two or three tanks pitted against a handful of trucks and jeeps. The cavalry made the real difference. The horsemen scattered at the sight of the tanks, then while the armored behomeths were engaging the laser trucks and darting jeeps, the cavalry reformed in the rear and attacked with rocket missiles and grenades. Men leaped from horseback onto the tanks and stuffed grenades into the engine ducts or cracked the periscopes and rangefinders that sprouted vulnerably out from the armor. Blinded or immobile, the tanks became more deathtraps than weapons.

Douglas' reserves arrived to join the battle before the last of the tanks were destroyed, but they were either on horseback or riding lightly armored trucks. And they were spread thin. The breadth of Alec's attack had foiled Douglas' defense plan before the battle began, though neither side realized this while the fighting raged.

As the battle eddied away from his sector, Alec ordered his truck back up to the top of the ridge that had masked the tanks' advance. From this higher ground he could see much of the swirling, dust-clouded fight, and he had time to check his commanders by radio and direct their actions. The tanks were a good idea, he thought. If we had come in a massive single thrust they would have converged on us and clobbered us. But Alec's broad, fluid advance offered no heavy concentrations of troops to center on, no massed targets for the tanks' cannon.

As he watched the field peppered with burning pyres and saw his laser trucks slicing through Douglas' lightly-armored reserves, Alec calmly spoke orders into his helmet microphone. Douglas' men were beginning to retreat; in some places they seemed to be panicking blindly and racing away, especially where the laser trucks were burning everything they could reach.

It was not pretty. Alec knew his own casualties were mounting. The stench of death reached him, even up on the ridge; burned flesh and the bitter fumes of explosives and burning oil. The noise was incessant, even through his heavy earphones: explosions punctuating the constant chatter of automatic weapons; roars and groans that might have been the voices of men, but so distorted and tortured that they were unrecognizable.

He climbed down from the gunner's seat and stood on the laser mount platform. His knees were shaking, his vision blurred.

This is what you came for, he told himself as he watched thousands of men trying to kill each other. This is what your entire life has been aimed at. He clutched the binoculars that still hung at his chest and started to put them to his eyes. But he hesitated. What if I see Will's body out there?

Jameson's flat unemotional voice in his earphones snapped him back to reality. "They're breaking up on this end. All the fight's out of them."

"All right," Alec heard himself say. "Don't bother with the stragglers. Let them go. Make a dash for the base and try to take it before they can set up a last-ditch defense. I'll join you from this end of the line."

"Check. What about Kobol and his special unit?"

"He'll follow my squad."

"Right. I presume you'll give the necessary orders in your usual crisp, military fashion."

Alec almost smiled. Jameson had detected his depression, obviously. "Yes, yes. Move out in five minutes, no more."

"We're moving."

Alec quickly checked with the other sector commanders. The battle was disintegrating into a series of separate little skirmishes. Douglas' troops were struggling for their lives now, trying to escape or simply survive. Alec ordered all commanders to ignore the retreating enemy troops and offer surrender to the pockets of men still fighting. Half of each unit he ordered to race for Douglas's headquarters.

As his own truck started bumpily down the ridge to take the lead of one column that was forming up, Alec relayed his orders to Kobol, who had been waiting back at their takeoff point.

"Now?" Kobol sounded shocked. "You're heading for the base already?"

"That's right," Alec said as his truck lurched past a clattering collection of other trucks and jeeps. "We've broken up Douglas' main force. It's nothing more than a mop-up operation now." He silently added, Unless Douglas has more surprises up his sleeve.

Kobol mumbled something vaguely sounding like congratulations and promised he would be on his way immediately.

"Steer clear of the firebases," Alec warned. "They're still in enemy hands. Those people might be in the mood to spend the rest of their ammunition on you."

Before Kobol could respond, Alec clicked the radio off, grinning to himself.

It can't be this easy, he thought as his truck rushed on toward Douglas's base. But what else could he have? He's used more men than I ever saw at the base. He can't have much more.

As they sped over the battlefield, past burned-out tanks and trucks, past twisted bodies and moaning, maimed men, past gaping shell holes and grass made slippery with blood, Alec began to realize that it had not been so easy, after all. Quick, but not easy.

He directed his truck to a road, and the column fell in behind him. It was one of the earth-packed trails that he and Will Russo had ridden. It turned around the shoulders of the last few hillocks, darted under a copse of newly leafed maples and birches, and then the first buildings came into view.

The column of trucks and jeeps fanned out

across the hummocky grass as they approached. The lasers burned down the fence quickly. The watchtowers here seemed to be empty, abandoned. Alec scanned the base area with his binoculars as they raced past the still-smoking remains of the innermost fence. A few people were dashing about in the streets, running for the shelter of the buildings.

Jameson reported, "We're less than a kilometer from the western end of the base. No resistance. Hardly any sign of life."

"Slow down," Alec commanded. "Proceed with caution, but keep advancing. I don't want any civilians hurt, especially the women." He pulled a hand-drawn map of the base from his jacket and told Jameson which buildings his troops should seize. "Get the defenders out of the buildings and into the open. Herd them onto the runways of the old airfield."

"Check," Jameson said.

Alec gave similar orders to all his unit commanders, worrying about how long he could expect the raider packs to maintain any semblance of discipline. He headed his own truck straight for the row of houses where Angela and Will and Douglas had lived. As the truck rolled alone through the streets between three- and four-story barracks buildings, Alec realized what a target he made for snipers standing alone on the back of the truck alongside the gleaming metal bulk of the laser.

So shoot, he silently told his enemies. You'll never get a better chance than now.

But there was no firing anywhere. Not even a sign of life in this part of the base. The houses looked cold and empty as the truck pulled up into the dead-end street. They've gone, Alec told himself, and realized he was a fool for thinking they might still be here.

He made the driver stop in front of Angela's

house. Swinging down off the truck, pistol flapping at his hip, heavy helmet on his head, Alec remembered the night he had left. He had never pictured his return as being quite like this: the conqueror striding into the deserted enemy camp.

The house was empty. The fireplace cold. It looked dusty, abandoned, as though no one had lived there for weeks. Perhaps months.

Grimly, Alec marched down the street toward Douglas' house. He knew it was foolish, but still . . .

He glanced over his shoulder at the truck. The driver sat alone in the armored cab. He had lowered the front armor panel so that he could have more than just a slit to allow fresh air inside. But he still wore his helmet and his hands were gripping the steering wheel. Ready to leave at an instant's notice, Alec saw. Constructive cowardice. The man who wants to save his skin is the man who's got a chance to live through the day.

Fifteen paces from Douglas's front door, Alec froze. A mechanical whirring sound, faint but real, stopped him. Like the sound of a gun mount tracking. He edged off the walkway and stepped close to the shrubbery that was just beginning to turn green, close to the house. One hand on his pistol butt, Alec carefully scanned the empty-looking street.

Nothing.

Then the sound came again, from behind him. He whirled and crouched as he drew the gun from its holster. Still nothing in sight. But there was *something*. Something about the house was different, something that had not been there before.

A glint in the corner of his eyes. A metal pole, strapped hastily against the side of the house with an antenna jury-rigged at the top of it. New, still bright in the late-afternoon sunlight that lanced through the smokey gray sky. A cable led down from the antenna to a second-floor window.

The antenna turned, making a mechanical whirring sound as its little electrical motor moved it.

Alec relaxed his grip on the pistol and commanded himself to stop trembling. Looking back at the truck, he saw that the driver had buttoned up his front panel. Alec called to him on his helmet radio. Whispering, he ordered, "Get Jameson and tell him to bring a squad of men here. On the double."

"Yessir."

Slowly, as quietly as he could, Alec moved along the side of the house and around to the back door. It was unlocked. He pushed it inward gently, almost smiling at Douglas' insistence on good maintenance: the hinges did not squeak.

Once inside he could hear a muffled voice from upstairs. It sounded like Douglas. Alone? Why would he be here and not out in the field with his men?

Alec took the steps two at a time, but very slowly, crouching low and keeping the gun ready for any surprises. With all the stealth he could manage he got to the top of the stairs and moved to the door of the bedroom from which Douglas' voice was coming.

He checked the other rooms with his eyes. The doors were all open; they appeared empty. Then, after pulling in a deep breath and letting it go, he opened the bedroom door and leaped into the room.

The door banged against the wall as Alec landed on the balls of his feet, crouched, balanced, gun rock-steady in his outstretched hand.

Half the room was filled with radio gear, gray and black boxes jumbled together, dials glowing. A wild tangle of wires linked the seeming chaos to a thick cable that wormed its way out through the window that was jammed shut over it.

Douglas sat in the bed, an old-fashioned microphone in one huge fist. His left leg was poking out straight from the hip, encased in a white plastic cast. His trousers had been cut away at the hip. His face looked thinner than before, his hair and beard grayer. His clothes and the bedsheets were rumpled and sweaty-looking. A carbine lay on the bed beside him, with several boxes of ammunition stacked on the table next to the bed.

For an instant Alec crouched there, unmoving.

Then Douglas said, "Well, it's about time you got here. What kept you?"

CHAPTER 28

Alec blinked at his father. "What happened to your leg?"

Glowering, Douglas grumbled, "Thrown from a goddamned horse, would you believe it? Four days ago. Have to sit out the whole goddamned battle here and try to run things by radio." He tossed the microphone down on the bed. It bounced and clattered to the floor.

"You could save a lot of lives by telling . . ."

"I've already ordered my people to stop fighting," Douglas said. He looked weary, even though his voice was as strong in defeat as ever. "That's what I was doing while you were trying to sneak up the stairs. And you can put that popgun away, I'm not going to try to shoot you." Glancing at the carbine beside him, "This thing isn't even loaded."

Alec went to the bed and took the gun. He leaned it against the doorjamb, then holstered his pistol.

"You fought a smart fight," Douglas said grudgingly. "I didn't expect you to spread out that way."

Pulling up the room's only chair, Alec responded, "I didn't expect you to have tanks."

"Think I showed you everything?" Douglas laughed.

"Where is she?"

"Angela? I packed her off to one of the villages a week ago, with the rest of the women. They're all scattered around the valley. She'll be back, now that the fighting's over."

"And Will?"

Douglas shook his head. "Last I heard, his horse had been shot out from under him. Don't worry about Will, he leads a charmed life."

Suddenly there was nothing left to talk about. Everything to be said, but nothing to talk about.

Douglas broke the silence. "So you've won."

"Yes, I've won."

"What are your plans?"

Alec glanced out the window, then returned his gaze to his father's haggard face. "I came for the fissionables. I'll take them back to the settlement."

"You know where they're stored?"

"You showed me, remember?"

"Oh . . . oh yes, that's right. I . . ."

"Kobol's got a trained crew to take care of them."

"Kobol. H'mm."

Alec blurted, "They'll want to execute you. You're a traitor."

"It figures," Douglas said easily. "If it weren't for this damned leg, though, I wouldn't have been so easy to catch."

"He's going to marry mother." As the words came out of him, Alec realized it was true. He had known it all along, but had never allowed the knowledge to reach conscious realization.

"Kobol? Good! Serves him right. She'll have him sliced and neatly served on a platter inside of a year. They deserve each other."

Alec felt his insides tightening.

"Now don't go stupid on me, son," Douglas said. "Kobol's been after her since *I* was there. And she's been letting him chase her. It's one of the reasons why I left. It became obvious, even to me."

"You expect me to believe that?"

Grinning wickedly, Douglas answered, "I don't give a damn what you believe. I've accomplished what I set out to do. My work's just about finished now. Yours is just starting."

"What? What do you mean?"

Before Douglas could reply, a trio of trucks pulled up noisily in front of the house and the voices of two dozen men filled the air. Doors slammed. Boots clumped on stairs.

Jameson stepped into the bedroom, poking the muzzle of an automatic rifle ahead of him. "You okay?" he asked Alec.

Nodding, Alec got up from the chair. "This is Douglas Morgan," he said. "Keep this house guarded. No one goes in or out unless I personally grant permission. I'll set up my headquarters in the first house on this street, where my truck is parked."

"Right," Jameson said.

Douglas spoke up. "I presume the condemned man will get a meal sometime this evening?"

Alec could not look him in the face anymore. To Jameson he said, "See to it."

Then he left his father sitting on the bed, surrounded by the armed strangers.

Alec ate his dinner alone in Angela's house, the first hot meal he'd had in many days. He was almost finished when Kobol burst into the tiny kitchen.

"We've got it!" he crowed, pushing past the protesting guard stationed outside the kitchen door.

Alec looked up tiredly. Kobol was jubilant, practically dancing, bad hip and all.

"We've got the fissionables!" Kobol repeated. "Enough to last fifty years, at least!"

"And then what?"

Kobol stopped in mid-prance. He stood uncertainly before the rough wooden table at which Alec sat. His smile of triumph began to crumble. "What do you mean?"

Alec began to understand part of what Douglas had been telling him. "What then? What happens to the settlement after fifty years?"

Kobol shook his head, a short snap to either side, like a horse shaking off a gadfly. "They'll find more, of course. Fifty years is a long time; we won't be around to worry about it."

"No," Alec said. "I suppose not."

"I'm ordering a pair of shuttles down to start loading the fissionables at first light tomorrow. They can land at the airfield right here."

"All right."

"And I want Douglas packed aboard too. They'll be waiting for him back at the settlement."

Alec pushed his unfinished plate away from him and got to his feet. "No."

"Eh? What do you mean?"

"I mean *no*. You're not taking Douglas back to the settlement. We'll handle him right here. I'll take care of it."

"No you won't." Kobol's tone hardened. "You've been riding pretty high, but it's time you realized that I'm a Council member and I have the final say in . . ."

Alec pulled his gun from its holster. "Martin, you can take the fissionables and yourself back to the settlement tomorrow. I'll follow you there shortly. But Douglas stays here. He chose to live on Earth, he might as well be buried on Earth. If you want to be buried here too, just say one more word." Alec's voice was as soft as the purr of a leopard. "One more word, that's all."

Kobol's mouth opened, but no sound came from it. He snapped it shut with an audible click of his horsy teeth. His face went white with anger and fear.

"Good," Alec said. He pointed to the door with the gun. "Now get out of here and go about your work. Leave Douglas to me. And keep your hands off my mother until I return to the settlement. You can be killed there as easily as here. Remember that."

Seething, Kobol turned and limped out of the house.

Alec holstered his gun and sat down to finish his meal. But he was no longer hungry. Suddenly he felt old, grayer than his father, weary and miserable and completely alone.

The guard peered around the door jamb. "Sir?"

"What is it?"

"We have a prisoner here . . . someone you said you wanted to see."

"Will Russo?"

"That's who he says he is, sir."

"Send him in!" Alec rose again and came around the table.

Will strode in. He was caked with grime and his clothing was torn in several places, but when he stepped into the kitchen and saw Alec his big puppydog grin spread across his face.

"You weren't fooling about a big army, were you?" he said.

Alec put his hand out and Will grabbed it.

"Are you all right?" Alec asked. "Have you eaten? Are you hurt?"

"I'm starving, but otherwise okay. Your boys had us pinned down for six hours. Never saw so many guns and lasers in my life."

Alec sat him down at the table and ordered the guard to bring more food. He watched as Will wolfed down everything in sight and washed it down with a liter of fresh cow's milk.

"Which village did Angela go to?" Alec asked as Will ate.

"Dunno," Will said, his mouth bulging. "But she'll be here. She'll want to see Douglas, tend to him."

Tend to him, Alec thought jealously.

"You took a lot of casualties?" he changed the subject.

Will nodded. "It was pretty heavy out there. You had us outgunned and outsmarted."

"I'm glad you weren't hurt."

"So'm I!" Will said, with a laugh. But almost immediately, the laughter died away. "A lot of good men died out there today. A lot of good men."

Alec agreed with a nod. "But at least it's over now."

"Over? Oh no! By golly, it's really just beginning."

"Begin . . . what do you mean?"

"Ask Douglas about it," Will replied. "I'm surprised he hasn't told you about it already."

"Told me what?"

But all Will would say was, "Ask Douglas."

"Dammit!" Alec snapped. "You know he's under arrest for treason. Kobol wants to bring him back to the settlement and make a public exhibit out of him."

"You won't let them?"

"No, I won't. But I can't let him live, either."

Will shrugged.

"Technically, you're as guilty as he is," Alec added. "You refused to return to the settlement, too. But it's Douglas they want to punish. You won't have to . . ."

"No," Will said. There was iron in it.

Alec stared at him.

"I'm Douglas's man. What happens to him happens to me. I'm as guilty as he is. We planned this thing together. Kill him and you've got to kill me, too. Or else."

"Or else what?"

"Or else I'll hunt you down and kill you."

"Hell's fire, Will! You're talking like a medieval barbarian."

"Maybe that's what I am. Maybe that's what we all are. I love you like my own son, Alec. I owe my life to you. But if you kill that man I won't be able to rest until I've avenged him."

"Jesus Christ."

"Exactly," said Will Russo.

It was late when Alec walked down the lonely street to Douglas's house. Late and dark. The spring night had turned cold; the stars glittered with winter hardness. The street was deserted except for the two guards lounging near the truck parked at the cul-de-sac end of the street. All of Douglas's troops had been disarmed and penned into a few of the big barracks buildings. No women at all had been found in the base. Tomorrow, Alec knew, the women would start returning from the outlying villages.

The guards straightened up when they recognized Alec. He saw that they had a small electric grill plugged into the truck's generator, and they were warming themselves with it.

"Chilly night," Alec said to them.

"Sure is."

Inside Douglas' house two more men were drowsing in the living room. They snapped to their feet when Alec let the front door bang shut.

"Everything quiet in here?" he asked.

"Yessir." They were both embarrassed, even a touch fearful.

Without another word, Alec tiptoed up the steps and pushed at the door to Douglas' room. The old man was sitting on the bed in almost exactly the same position that Alec had left him earlier. He was wearing glasses now, and reading a battered, well-thumbed book. Alec squinted at the cover but it was too worn to make out the title.

"Come on in," Douglas said softly, barely looking up from the book. "I've been waiting for you."

Alec stepped into the room and took the chair, feeling oddly nervous, edgy. As he sat down, he realized that Douglas' voice was no longer the booming, demanding, self-assured roar it had once been. He was quieter, his voice subdued. From defeat? Alec found that hard to believe.

Douglas waggled the book. "Found this in a city library, years ago. Hemingway. *The Fifth Column and the First Forty-Nine.* Forty-nine short stories, that is. Magnificent. You ought to read them."

Alec shrugged.

"So." Douglas put the book down on the table beside his bed. The radio equipment had been cleared away; nothing was left except the torn end of the cable still hanging from the room's one window. "You've come to see if I'm comfortable and enjoyed my meal?"

"No."

"Come to read me my death sentence?" He actually looked amused.

"Not that either," Alec said. "I've come to find out what you meant when you said that your work's nearly finished, but mine is just beginning. Will said something very much like it a couple of hours ago . . ."

"You've seen Will?" Douglas asked, suddenly eager. "He's all right?"

"He's fine. Hungry as a bear . . ."

"And thirsty, I'll bet."

Alec felt a grin bend his lips. "Yes, that too."

"But you've finally started to tumble to the fact that there's more to life than beating your old man, eh?"

Alec hunched forward in the chair. "I want to know what all these mysterious hints are about."

"It's not too complicated," Douglas said. "Everything's worked out pretty much as I had planned it. I admit that I expected to beat you today, rather than the other way around. But the plan can work either way."

"What plan?" Alec demanded, suddenly irritated.

Douglas smiled at him. A genuinely benign, paternal smile in that grizzled, lined face. "The plan to reunite the human race. The plan to rebuild civilization."

"That!"

"Yes, that. It happens to be the reason behind everything I've done over the past twenty years and more. But now it's going to be up to you to put the plan into action."

Alec shook his head.

"Listen to me!" Douglas snapped, with some of the old fire. Jabbing a thick finger at him, he said, "It's finally been accomplished. Don't you understand that? Look around you, what do you see? And I don't mean just this room. What's happened out there today?"

"We beat you."

"Who beat me?"

"We did—the army that Kobol put together and I led."

"And who's in that army?"

Puzzled, Alec answered, "Who's in it? Men from all over: as far south as Florida, as close as some of the villages just over the hills from here."

"And who else?" Douglas' eyes were gleaming.

Alec thought a moment. "Us," he finally realized. "Men from the settlement."

Douglas leaned back on the pillows, satisfied. "Excellent. You got the right answer with only a few prods. You might make a real leader yet. An army made up of bands of men who've been fighting each other for the past twenty-some years—raiders and farmers, city barbarians and fishermen from the warm country—plus you lunar people with your high technology. For the first time since the sky burned and organization of Earth and Moon people has worked together."

Alec blinked at him. "What's so marvelous about that?"

"I'll tell you." Douglas was obviously enjoying this; his voice had regained some of its former strength. "When the sky burned civilization on Earth ended. But on the Moon we were all right—for the time being. Then the leaders in the settlement got the notion that there was nothing they could do to help what was left of Earth's people."

"They were right," Alec said. "They were barely able to survive themselves, those first years."

"They were right, *at that time,*" Douglas

corrected. "But that doesn't mean the decision was right for all time. From that first decision, it was a short step to decide that the settlement could survive on its own, and all they needed from Earth was an occasional re-supply of the things that couldn't be produced on the Moon."

"The fissionables."

"And medicinal plants, a few other things. So while the lunar people were looking down their noses at the so-called barbarians of Earth, it was *they* who were really behaving like barbarians—raiding Earth for what they wanted but could not or would not produce for themselves. *That's* barbarism!"

"Now wait . . ."

But Douglas plowed on. "The truth is, the settlement cannot survive on its own and never could. Genetically it's a dead end. Already the cancer rate and birth defects are skyrocketing."

Alec said, "We've been through all this before."

"Indeed we have. But now we have the opportunity to set things straight. You're in command of a joint Earth-Moon army. You're sitting on the fissionables that the settlement wants. You can *force* them to start working with the people here on Earth, to start rebuilding civilization in earnest. What I've done is to set the stage. Now you can make it actually happen."

Alec felt the strength leach out of him. His jaw fell open. When he realized he was gaping, he straightened up in the chair and asked, "Me? You want me . . ." He ran out of words.

"Yes, you," Douglas said gently. "I've been waiting for you for twenty years, son."

"But you tried to kill me!"

"No, I didn't. I tried to see what you were made of. I set up conditions that would test you, so we could *both* find out what you were made of. You came through in fine shape. You survived. What's more, you learned. You understand now exactly what I'm saying, and you know that I'm right. I can see it."

"No . . ."

"Yes!" Douglas was beaming now. "*You're* the leader of this entire ramshackle alliance. *You're* the one man with the power to force those hothouse lovelies up there to rejoin their brothers and sisters here on Earth. Alone, separated from the knowledge and technology of the Moon, Earth's civilization will need another five centuries to be rekindled. Nobody knows that better than I do! I've spent twenty years bringing a miniscule number of people back from absolute barbarism as far as a feudal society."

Douglas's fists clenched. "But the lunar settlement—alone, separated from Earth, cut off from the lifeblood of the human race, the genetic pool—the settlement will die. There's no other word for it. They'll be dead within another two generations. Three, at most."

Alec heard Kobol's voice in his mind, his response to the question about what would happen when the fissionables ran out. *"Fifty years is a long time, we won't be around to worry about it."*

"You're worrying about my children," Alec said to his father.

"Your grandchildren."

"But why did you set up this battle? Why couldn't we have done this peacefully?"

Douglas's smile turned into a sardonic grimace. "Would you have believed me? I tried to tell you. And do you think those barbarians out there would have kindly consented to work together in sweet brotherhood for the furtherance of an ideal they can't even imagine? They have no conception of what civilization means, you know. Not even the best of them. Oh, they'll follow a leader they can trust or someone who brings them victories and loot. But all they really understand is survival, and survival means fighting." He paused, but only for an instant. "What brought all those fine fighting men here? A yearning for culture or the chance for loot?"

"Loot, of course," Alec answered.

"Damned right. And you'd better keep them happy, too, until you can halfway civilize them. Get them up at least to the standard of loyalty the old Mongol hordes had. You can build a civilization with warriors like that, even though they themselves are barbarians."

But a new thought was burning through Alec's awareness. "You . . ." he said. "What am I supposed to do with you?"

Douglas snorted. "Kill me, of course! I'm superfluous now. I'm a problem for you. My men will stay loyal to me as long as I'm alive, and the people in the settlement won't trust you if you let me live."

"But your men won't follow me if I have you executed." It's insane! You don't sit in a bedroom and talk with your father about killing him!

"They'll follow Will, and Will is fully aware of the plan. If he's loyal to you, the rest of my people will be, too. That's why it was important for both of you to survive the battle."

"It's crazy," Alec muttered.

"No," Douglas corrected. "It's politics. A little rougher than the polite debating orgies you've seen in the settlement, but basically the same thing. To make yourself leader of the whole coalition, you've got to get rid of me."

"I came to Earth to kill you."

"I know," Douglas said, softly, kindly. "Now you can get the job done."

Alec jumped up from the chair, knocking it over backwards behind him. "No, I can't do it! I can't!"

"Don't be an idiot," Douglas snapped. "You've got to."

But Alec bolted from the room and ran down the stairs and out into the night.

CHAPTER 29

Ferret had spent the day hiding in the woods, terrified by the horrendous sounds of explosions and gunfire that rocked the world and made the very air taste of burning, acrid fumes. He knew that Alec was there in the midst of the fighting, and all the others. But he clung to the safe, living earth, deep in the brush that grew among the younger trees along the edge of the forest. Instinct told him to run away, to go deeper into the mottled shadows of the woods, to hide so far away that the guns and explosions would never reach him.

Yet he stayed at the edge of the trees, despite his terror, held in an agonizing balance between his fear and the dim, wordless loyalty he felt for Alec.

The Sun was halfway down the western sky when the fighting stopped. Curled up behind a sturdy oak, half buried in the brush at its base, Ferret waited for the better part of an hour after he realized that the gunfire and explosions had ended. He listened intently, heard nothing but the renewed chirp of birds, the buzz of insects. A squirrel popped out of the bushes a few feet in front of him, stood on its hind legs and sniffed the air, nose twitching. It looked around hesitantly, then scampered up the tree that Ferret hid behind.

The world had gone back to normal. It was safe to come out. Ferret took a few hesitant steps out into the slanting light of light afternoon. The sky over toward the valley was gray with smoke. That was where Alec would be. He started walking toward the smoke, toward Alec. Maybe he would find a rabbit or squirrel along the way and bring it to Alec. It would be good to eat.

A truckload of jubilant troops rattled by on the road leading into the valley, slowed down, and he clambered aboard. They were strangers to him, but they were all laughing and whooping with relieved excitement. Ferret laughed with them, feeling relieved too.

By the time they reached the base it was full night. The truck squealed to a halt in front of one of the big warehouses, near the airfield. Troops were milling everywhere, still full of energy, still adrenalin-high.

"Where's th' fuckin' women?" one man yelled.

"There was supposed t'be gold in the streets here," someone else bellowed. "I don't see no gold."

"Hey, never mind that!" said an excited, high-pitched voice. "They found booze over in that warehouse! Real stuff! Wine and liquor and all! C'mon!"

With a ragged roar, the soldiers of the victorious army surged toward the warehouse, carrying Ferret along with them the way a tidal wave carries a bit of flotsam.

Jameson was waiting outside Douglas's house when Alec came running blindly from his meeting with his father. He pointed wordlessly to the sullen red glow lighting up the night sky.

"They're torching the warehouses," Jameson said. "Kobol's barbarians."

Alec stared at the glowering light. Sparks shot up. He said nothing, desperately trying to focus his concentration on what was happening. But his mind was still filled with the image of his father calmly discussing his own execution.

"We've locked up all the weapons, ammo, and vehicles," Jameson was telling Alec. "And the prisoners are under guard by our own men. But those warehouses . . ." Jameson shook his head. "We just don't have enough reliable troops to keep the barbarians away from everything."

With an effort, Alec made himself ask, "What's in those warehouses?"

"Machinery, spare parts . . . one of them has several hundred crates of wine and grain alcohol, from what Will tells me."

"They won't burn that," Alec said.

Jameson turned his bird-of-prey visage toward the glowing flames. "Might be a good idea to let them have their fun tonight."

"And let them destroy everything they can get their hands on?" Alec shook his head. "Get fifty men and four laser trucks. Find Will and ask him to join us, with as many reliable men as he can muster."

An instant of skepticism flashed across Jameson's face.

Alec said, "If we let them dissolve into rabble they'll be killing each other before sunrise."

"There is that," Jameson admitted.

Within half an hour they met at the motor pool, an ancient garage where voices boomed hollowly off the metal walls and silent trucks. Alec laid out a battle plan for the men who assembled there.

"They're rampaging through the warehouses, burning whatever they can't drink or carry. We'll converge on the warehouse area from three different directions," he traced lines with his finger on the street map spread across the oil-smeared table before him, "and get them under control."

Jameson looked doubtful. "If they decide to fight us . . ."

"They won't if we work things properly," Alec said.

Will Russo agreed with a nod. "Especially if we pack them in pretty tight here, where the streets converge. They won't be in a fighting mood."

His hand sliding to the pistol strapped to his hip, Alec added, "And if we grab the ringleaders and make examples out of them, the rest will calm down fast enough."

Three columns of heavily armed troops converged on the burning warehouses and the drunken, rampaging men. In the guttering light of the fires that crackled through the warehouse windows and roofs, the looters slowly realized that they were being hemmed in, herded toward the open area where the streets came together. And waiting for them there, in front of the only warehouse that had not yet been torched, were a quartet of laser trucks, their firing mirrors pointed at street level.

Alec stood on the back of one of the trucks with an electrically-powered megaphone in his hand.

"Listen to me," he commanded, his voice magnified to the dimensions of godhood. "Listen to me, because the men who don't will be dead before the Sun rises."

They stood in a befuddled, drunken, sullen mass draped with blankets and sacks of flour and wine bottles and new boots and less identifiable plunder. The fires groaned at their backs. A wall collapsed, showering sparks into the night sky.

"Who started this?" Alec demanded. "I want the ringleaders, and I want them now."

The men muttered and shifted on their suddenly-tired feet. They stared at the ground or glanced at each other. Alec saw that many of them had left their rifles and automatic weapons behind, once they started looting. But there were still plenty of pistols and carbines among them.

"If you think that your discipline has ended just because you won a battle today, then think again," Alec boomed at them. "Now, who started this looting? Bring them up front, where I can deal with them the way they deserve." He pulled the pistol from its holster.

No one moved, except for the nervous shuffling of little boys caught being naughty.

"All right," Alec said, his voice as cold as sharpened steel, "then we'll do it the way the Roman legions did it. Jameson—pick out ten men at random. Now."

With a dozen fully armed troops beside him, Jameson began grabbing men by their arms and shoving them toward the truck where Alec stood. He did not go deeply into the sullen crowd; he picked the men from the front few rows.

Suddenly there was a movement from deep in the crowd. A single figure was worming its way toward the front.

"Alec, Alec . . . me. Me. Me!"

The looters backed away from him, and Alec recognized Ferret making his way up to the front, to join the men that were going to be executed.

"Me, Alec!" Ferret said, his pinched face smiling innocently in the glow of the smoldering fires. "Pick me!"

The pistol suddenly felt unbearably heavy in Alec's hand. The weight of the world had somehow been absorbed by the square-snouted shining black gun.

He looked down at the faces of the men standing at his feet. The looters whom Jamesom had shoved to the front looked up at him, sullen, afraid, drunk. Ferret was smiling, a child's hopeful, expectant smile. The crowd had melted back, away from the men who were doomed.

Alec let his arm drop to his side. The gun was too heavy to hold up. Jameson stood frozen at the edge of the crowd, his strong hand locked onto the shoulder of one of the looters.

"I was bad, Alec," Ferret said. "I'm sorry."

It was the longest sentence Alec had ever heard out of him.

He raised the bullhorn to his lips once more and

said slowly, "You've been saved. All of you—you've been saved by this one man."

An audible sigh went through the crowd.

Holstering the gun, Alec said, "You've had all the fun you're going to. From here on, there will be no more looting. You are part of an army—a victorious army. You have a right to be proud of your victory. But you are going to follow orders and maintain discipline. Anyone who can't follow orders, from this moment on, will be shot. You've been reprieved tonight, but from now on there will be no second chances for any of you."

They muttered sullenly, but did no more than that.

Alec realized that they needed more than the threat of discipline. The stick by itself was useless, unless there was a carrot attached to it.

"You are going to become the richest men on Earth," he said, and waited for a moment for their response. They stirred, they murmured. "Not from looting. That's over and done with. You're going to become rich from your fair share of the riches that this land can provide.

"You've spent your lives as raiders, as rat packs, and your lives have been short and painful. But now you are going to live safer, more comfortable lives. You will never have to worry about a meal or a bed again. You will live longer and better than you ever dreamed would be possible. And we—all of us, together—will rule this entire land."

There were more than a thousand men standing there. The crowd surged, edged closer toward Alec.

"Your days of looting and stealing are finished," he told them, "because you will no longer have to loot and steal. You'll get everything you've ever wanted, and more of it than you ever saw in your lives."

"What about women?" a voice from the rear shouted.

"When you're a raider, a looter, the women run away and hide," Alec answered into the bullhorn. "When you're a member of the army that rules the Earth, the women will chase after you!"

They laughed. Alec could feel the tension, the sullenness, easing out of them.

"All right, then," Alec said firmly. "From this moment on you are members of the army that will rule the world. You will follow orders. And when tomorrow dawns, this world will see something it hasn't seen since the sky burned: a new force that will conquer everything that stands in its way!"

They cheered. They actually cheered. Alec watched them, wondering, Will I always be able to control them? It was like riding atop a wild animal. Grimly, he realized, It will always be a battle to stay in control.

He spent the rest of the night touring the base, riding atop the battle-dented truck and checking every street and building in the area. Quiet prevailed. The men were exhausted from the battle, drunk with the wine they had found and the exhilaration of being alive when so many others had died. Now the wine and the exhaustion and the emotional fatigue had caught up with them. A taste of discipline was the only excuse most of them needed to fold up into the oblivion of sleep.

With the sunrise came Angela.

She arrived in a horse-drawn wagon, protected by six village youths armed with ancient rifles and shotguns. The posted guards stopped her at the edge of the base. She asked to see Douglas. The guards radioed for Jameson, who in turn informed Alec.

He had her driven to his quarters, the house they had shared to many months earlier. Alec was waiting for her in the still-unfurnished living room when her wagon creaked to a stop. She jumped down and walked straight to the front door.

Without hesitating, she entered. She looked tense, worried, thinner, tauter, just as beautiful as ever.

"Where's Douglas? Why can't I see him?"

Alec had to struggle to control his voice. "He's perfectly all right. You'll see . . ."

"No, he's not all right. You don't understand." She seemed genuinely frightened, her eyes wide with fear.

"It's all right," Alec insisted, crossing the tiny room to reach her. "No one's going to hurt him. Don't be afraid."

He took her in his arms, in front of the dead ashes of the dark fireplace. Angela was trembling.

"Alec, please, you've got to let me see him. I don't know how much he's told you . . ." Abruptly she pushed away from him. "Alec, I don't even know if I can believe what you're telling me! You *want* him dead, don't you?"

"No," he said. "That's over now."

"But it would help if he conveniently died, wouldn't it?"

"That's what he said last night."

"You still don't understand what he's doing, all the plans he's made."

"Yes I do . . ." But suddenly Alec realized that there was still more for him to learn.

"Alec, pleased take me to him," Angela urged. "Please, right now, before it's too late."

He hesitated only a moment. "All right. Come on. He's still in his own bedroom. We didn't move him because of his leg."

"What about his leg?"

"He broke it in an accident a few days ago . . . fell off his horse."

"No!" she screamed. "He's been in that room for the past month! He's been sick, deathly sick!" She dashed for the door.

Alec raced after her. They tore down the street, past a startled guard at his front door, heading for Douglas's house. With the perfect clarity of adrenalin-sharpened vision, Alec saw the two guards loafing sleepily in front of Douglas's front door. Heard the shots. Saw the guards jerk to attention and burst into the house.

"No!" Angela was screaming. "No . . . don't . . . he can't . . ."

More shots. Then no sounds except Alec's own gasping breath and the pulse hammering in his ears. He outdistanced Angela and ran into the house, pushed through the open door and skidded to a halt.

His father lay sprawled at the foot of the steps, his legs resting on the bottommost stairs. A machine pistol was in his hand, its wire stock grotesquely bent under his heavy forearm. Douglas' chest and gut were covered with bright red blood. The room smelled of gunsmoke. The two outside guards were standing frozen, guns still hot in their hands. Upstairs, the third guard was kneeling against the railing, babbling:

"He came at me, he came at me. Shooting. He was shooting."

None of the guards were scratched. The cast was gone from Douglas's leg. His eyes were open; his chest heaving in rapid painful gasps.

Angela clattered into the house and broke into a racking sob. Pushing past Alec, she sank to her knees next to Douglas.

"Nooo," she moaned, "Noooo . . ."

"It's all right," Douglas said, his voice a throaty groan. "Better this way . . ."

"He was shooting," said one of the guards next to Alec. "You can see the bullet holes all over the walls. He was trying to bust out."

The bullet holes were all up near the ceiling, over the windows, well above head level. Ignoring the guard, Alec bent down on one knee beside Angela, next to his father.

"Why?" he asked. "I would have saved you. I wouldn't let them take you."

Douglas managed to grin at his son. "How do you . . ." a gasp of pain, " . . . how do you think I found out about the cancer rate in the settlement?"

Alec's head drooped.

"Only had . . . a few months left," Douglas panted. "Sorry to scare your boys . . . tried not to hurt them . . ."

He closed his eyes.

Angela collapsed over the dead body. Tears won't help him, Alec said silently. Then he realized that the tears are always for the living, not the dead. All right then. Cry for both of us. Alec couldn't cry. Not now. Perhaps not ever. But surely not now. There was too much to be done. Too much unfinished work hung in the balance.

He straightened up and turned to the guards. None of them had moved a millimeter. They were staring at Alec, their own lives showing in their eyes.

"It's all right," he told them softly. "You saved us all a lot of trouble."

They did not relax, but that did not matter.

"You," he pointed to the one nearest the door. "Get Jameson and Will Russo here. There's work to do."

Then he glanced down at Angela's sobbing form. To the other two guards he said, "Get outside and don't let anyone in here until I tell you to."

They hurried out of the house. The guard who had been upstairs had to step, shakily, over Douglas' body. Then he ran to the door and left.

Alec knelt down beside Angela again and took her tear-streaked face in his hands. "It's time," he said, as gently as he knew how.

She gazed at him searchingly. "Time for what?"

"To begin."